A BORROWED HELL

L. D. Colter

DIGITAL FICTION

P U B L I S H I N G   C O R P

Copyright © 2017 Liz Colter [L. D. Colter]
Published 2017 Digital Fiction Publishing Corp.
All rights reserved. 2nd Edition
ISBN-13 (paperback): 978-1-988863-50-4
ISBN-13 (e-book): 978-1-988863-51-1

DEDICATION
To my mother for always supporting my
dreams, and to my husband for sharing
them.

ACKNOWLEDGMENT
Many thanks to Cory Skerry and Barbara Jo
Fleming for their input and feedback over
this lengthy process, and to my many
talented friends in GSWG for their support
and help.

Part One

"What's gone and what's past help…"
Wm. Shakespeare, The Winter's Tale

Chapter 1

"Julie Davish," the banker called into the nearly empty lobby, mispronouncing July's first name.

The air flowed back into the vinyl covered chair seat as July got to his feet. He glanced at the clock in the lobby. Ten minutes till five. "July. Like the month," he said as he crossed the short space and shook hands with the banker.

The banker double-checked the note the teller had handed him. "Sorry about that. Robert Vegas, nice to meet you."

"We've met before, actually," July said. "You brokered my mortgage when I bought my house three years ago."

Vegas must be around thirty now, same as July, but otherwise had changed little. His suit jacket jutted out beyond the edges of his narrow shoulders, and his long, thin face, polka-dotted with vestiges of acne, still reminded July of a scarred and underfed coyote. Vegas indicated the chairs in front of his desk and July took a seat.

The banker looked at his watch as he sat. "How can I help

you today, Mr. Davish?"

He could have helped by seeing July this morning at nine o'clock if he hadn't been in a meeting. He could have helped at three o'clock if he hadn't been with a client when July swung by again on his way back from a job interview. He could have helped him at four twenty-five, when July returned for the third time, if he hadn't been on a conference call. July tried to tell himself it hadn't been the man's fault.

"I received this in the mail yesterday." He pulled the letter from his back pocket and handed it across the desk.

Vegas scanned it. "I'm sorry, Mr. Davish, our mortgage center in Illinois dictates foreclosure proceedings." He didn't look sorry at all. "There's an 800 number here at the bottom if you'd like to speak to them about the matter." He set the letter on the desk in front of July and tapped the number with a finger. His hand looked too large for his frame, like it might be glued on just above the cuff of his blue shirt.

"When I got laid-off from my second job in a row, back in May, I called here and you told me to talk to them, so I did. I'd never been late on a payment and they agreed to a short-term forbearance. They said I could have up to six months, and I'd owe the accrued interest over three payments. My first payment isn't due for another six weeks. Now they've sent me an eviction notice, saying I'm in default all the way back to May. I was hoping you could help me straighten this out with them."

Vegas glanced at his watch again before typing an account number from the letter into his computer. "I'm sorry," he said. "I don't see any record of an adjusted payment plan in your account."

"That's the problem. Either the person I set this up with didn't document it or the record of the arrangement got lost.

Now that person doesn't work there anymore. It took the notice a few days to reach me and I spent over a week seeing if I could get a loan somewhere else. The eviction notice was for thirty days, and I'm down now to only a couple of weeks left."

"There's been a lot of transition over the past few months with the bank merger going on," Vegas said. "The mortgage department has been a bit overwhelmed. Really, the best thing would be to call them again. I'm afraid they're the only ones who can help you with this." He held the letter out, but July made no move to take it. He didn't want the notice back, he wanted the problem resolved. Vegas set the paper down in front of him.

"Well can you at least put a hold on the foreclosure? Make a note in my file or something until I can get this straightened out?"

"I'm sorry, Mr. Davish, I really don't have any authority in this. The best thing would be to just call the 800 number and let them know what you told me."

"Look. You're telling me to go through the people that already screwed this up." July leaned forward, trying to get through to the man. "My home is on the line here. Can't you just make a call for me? Get the ball rolling the right direction? I work construction. The last couple of jobs I've had didn't last long enough to qualify me for unemployment, so I've got nothing to fall back on. I'm looking for work every day, doing any pick-up work I can find. I had an interview today that I think is going to come through. All I'm asking is that they honor the deal they already promised me. Those extra six weeks could make all the difference."

"I'm sorry Mr. Davish, I'm really not able to help you with this. The mortgage center is the place you have to call to make

special arrangements or appeal an action. I really am sorry."

Vegas stood and held out his hand, ending the conversation. July stood, ignored his outstretched hand, and picked up the letter. He looked square into the man's eyes. There was so much to say that he said nothing at all.

Walk away, he told himself. He turned and strode out of the bank.

He pushed through the double set of doors into hazy, San Diego sunshine. Shoving at his frustration, he tried to stuff it into a corner of his mind. The space felt too cramped to accept any more disappointments. He told himself he'd done the right thing by not venting at the mortgage broker. He'd been through worse in his life; he'd get through this.

His old Chevy truck, faded more to gray primer than the maroon it had once been, stood alone in the corner of the half-empty parking lot near the busy intersection. Traffic on Garnet was always bad this time of day, and now he'd be driving home in that mess. His anger wasn't compartmentalizing well. Like soft putty, pushing on one side of it only made it billow somewhere else.

Catching a flash of movement to his right, July turned to Vegas, hurrying down the sidewalk nearly parallel with him. *Keep walking,* he told himself. Control was the mantra of his life, the glue that held all the rest together.

He angled toward the banker anyway. It was different now that they were outside; an even playing field with two equal people, the way it should have been inside. It was a second opportunity to say the things boiling inside him. Getting off work right at five shouldn't have been more important than a customer about to get evicted due to a bank error.

"Hey, Vegas."

The man turned with a startled expression then looked away, as if he only thought he'd heard something. He walked faster, but traffic forced him to halt at the corner. His thin face went tight with apprehension as July bore down.

July wasn't much more than average height, but he was toned from a dozen years of construction work and definitely more solid than the slender banker. Not that he needed to assess the man's physical prowess. He was just going to give him a piece of his mind. Maybe Vegas didn't understand what it felt like to lose your job, your savings, your girlfriend; to have a mortgage company promise leniency and then send an eviction notice.

Within arm's length, July felt a flash-burn of adrenaline surge into his hands, thighs, and jaw like a brush fire. It receded just as quickly, leaving him jangly and tense, his anger less controlled. A part of him wished he'd kept walking to his truck, and a bigger part felt his emotions building like a rising pressure gauge with no release valve. He stopped in front of Vegas and leaned into the banker's personal space. July's ever-present control dissipated into the San Diego haze.

A cacophony of shattering glass and metal bodies slamming together deafened July. He flinched and turned to see two cars skimming over the blacktop like overweight ice-dancers in a clumsy glide. Momentarily released from their routine responses to friction and gravity, they slid sideways toward the sidewalk where he and Vegas stood.

The accident shouldn't have allowed time for the thoughts that marched through his mind. A theory of what had caused the accident. An analysis of the velocity and vectors of the cars. Knowing that it would be the blue Prius on the left that would hit him. The wide-eyed shock on the driver's face. An image of

Mia from when they still lived together, trying on her new red dress for him and shaking the ruffles like a salsa dancer. His father, aging faster than his years, with no one to take care of him if July died. The thoughts ticked through his head, frame-by-frame, though only a second or two passed.

The two cars continued to spin, front bumpers gliding together for a kiss, forming a single, long vehicle. July was closer to the rear of the left-hand car. He thought he might be able to dive clear, but Vegas didn't stand a chance.

The smell of rubber grinding across the road filled the air and the squeal of tires eclipsed all other sound. There was no time to consider options. July bent his knees for extra power and leaned into Vegas. His hands molded to the banker's ribs, prominent under the man's dress shirt, and July shoved with all his adrenaline-enhanced strength. Robert Vegas flew backward through the air, a third performer joining the routine. The car in front of July hit the curb with both passenger tires, launching it into an ungainly, rolling jump.

July threw himself to the side as far as he could, knowing he was a second too late.

Chapter 2

"He's here," a woman said.

July opened his eyes.

The first thing he saw were buildings jutting high into the foggy sky, forming a tall, jagged skyline that matched nothing on the San Diego coastline. He sat with his back against a rough, brick wall. Across the street rose the unmistakable pyramid shape of the Transamerica building in San Francisco's financial district. July's mind struggled with the incongruity. He should be five hundred miles to the south, squashed like a bug under a three-thousand-pound Prius. The last thing he'd seen before opening his eyes here had been a close-up of the car in mid-roll.

Maybe he was dead. The thought was too uncomfortable to contemplate.

A man squatted next to him. Smudges of dirt stood out in grey-brown streaks against his dark skin. He wore faded green fatigues—the jungle kind that had preceded the desert kind—

and an olive-green T-shirt covered with dirt and holes. His hair lay flat against his head in small, tight plaits, and a single, bone-colored bead decorated the end of each braid.

"Hey there," he said. His smile was genuine, wide, and natural. It was the smile of someone at ease with himself and his surroundings. July found it reassuring in this place where nothing else was.

"How did I get here?"

The man shrugged. July looked to the woman standing behind the man. She shrugged.

Woman may have been a stretch; she looked more a girl, ultra-thin and waifish. Her worn blue jeans sported gaudy sequins at the frayed hems, and her long T-shirt emphasized her skinny legs. Dish-water blonde hair hung lank on either side of her face. Her eyes held a hunted look.

"I don't understand," July said.

"Then best to just move on," the man said, standing and stretching. "Come on."

He and the young woman turned from July and began walking. July pushed to his feet, still finding no pain or injuries. He looked the other direction, down the length of the empty business district. Empty. The wrongness he had been feeling crystallized. Not only was he in the wrong city, but the city itself was wrong. Other than the two people walking away from him, there was not a car or a person in sight.

The pair receded at a steady pace. Panic prodded July to jog after them. He wanted to believe this was a dream but couldn't, everything here felt too visceral. The man and the young woman walked side-by-side taking up the center of the sidewalk; July caught up to them and walked behind.

The silence of the city hung heavy around him, the slap of

shoes on concrete loud in the unnatural quiet. It brought to mind old *Twilight Zone* episodes of people thrown into muted, artificial environments, but everything around him confirmed the reality of his surroundings. He could feel the breeze ebb and gust against his skin, heard the rustle of a candy wrapper crunch underfoot. He saw low clouds drifting above, and smelled warm brick, paved road, and the odor of the two unwashed people in front of him.

"Where is everybody?"

The young woman looked back at him without answering. The man answered without looking back. "They're around."

A dozen questions formed in July's mind but none of them made sense. He let the silence take him. Chinatown lay empty and quiet only a couple of blocks to his left and Telegraph Hill just ahead. The Embarcadero must be to the right. They were walking through perhaps the most quintessential square mile in the city; places that would normally be some of his favorite to visit. They climbed steadily for twenty minutes or so until they reached Pioneer Park, where a tall, whitewashed cylinder dominated the grassy knoll. A sign near the parking lot announced it was Coit Tower. It looked like a lighthouse had gotten lost and wandered into the park for a rest. He found it as eerie as the rest of the deserted city.

The door to the tower stood open and July followed the man and young woman inside, stepping into a circular hallway that looked to run full circle around the base of the tower. Enormous murals covered the walls of the hallway. Directly ahead stood a door to what appeared to be a small round foyer leading to a gift shop, an elevator that he could see and, according to a placard posted near the elevator, a staircase that he couldn't. A solitary mural occupied the header over the door.

It depicted an enormous pair of eyes hooded within a storm cloud. Lightning struck down from the left side of the cloud and the eyes weighed and judged him as he entered their domain.

July looked to the right and left around the curving hallway. The murals along the walls were as disturbing as the one above him. They stretched nearly floor to ceiling, making the characters in them larger than life-sized. Facing him at the far curve of the wall to his left was a butcher. A pig hung by its hind feet and the butcher was gutting it with a metal hook as blood ran down the belly of the pig. A morose woman in the next panel weighed huge hunks of fresh meat.

The characters and their clothing looked dated, depression era he guessed. There were customers sitting at a diner counter; their sad faces spoke more eloquently than words of their difficult lives. An immense cowboy near July stared down at him with a severe expression, as if he didn't approve of his new visitor. A lariat hung from one hand to coil at his booted feet and July thought if the giant man could step out of the painting, the cowboy might bind and brand him like any other animal.

"Make yourself at home."

The words jerked his attention from the murals. The black man gestured to the inner room and disappeared through the arch. July followed. Inside the room, sleeping bags lay scattered around the curved walls. Trash littered the concrete floor and a small camp stove near the gift shop listed on its broken and bandaged leg.

The man settled cross-legged on a sleeping bag and indicated that July should help himself to one of the others. He chose a red one against the opposite wall. The young woman dropped bonelessly to the sleeping bag at his left, her weight too meager to make much impact with the ground.

"Something to eat?" The man leaned back and rummaged one-handed through a small paper sack. He tossed July a Kit-Kat and an energy bar, one after the other. "There's a water fountain over there," he pointed, "and the bathrooms are in the hallway."

"Thanks. My name's July Davish."

The man just nodded.

"What should I call you?" July prompted.

The man thought for a second and shrugged. "How about Pat."

The young woman giggled. July looked at her, but she didn't deign to share the joke.

"And you?" he asked her.

"Pat," she said.

Great. "Patty okay?"

"Sure." She flopped onto her back, crossing one ankle over her bent knee.

Wherever July was, it seemed the season hadn't changed. The evening air bore a fall chill. He'd been here maybe an hour or a little less and the sun balanced on the horizon. If time ran the same here that would make it a little after six, which was about right for sunset in September. He could only guess at the time. The clock in the gift shop pronounced perpetual noon or midnight, and he wasn't in the habit of wearing a watch after cracking the glass on half a dozen of them at work.

Of all the questions July had, only the most morbid had the strength to push its way through the strangeness and silence of this place.

"Am I dead?" he asked Pat.

The tangibility of this place was undeniable. If it wasn't a dream, then death seemed the only explanation.

Pat huffed a quiet laugh. He picked a small cellophane wrapper off the floor and watched it twist and untwist as he rolled the ends between his fingers, smiling that comfortable smile of his. "No, man. You aren't dead."

Pat looked up. The confidence in his dark eyes was too certain to gainsay. July believed him. He clung to the man's calm reassurance like he would to a life-ring in the middle of the ocean.

"What then?" his voice broke on the words. He felt strangely let down to hear that he wasn't dead. At least that he could have understood.

"It just is." Pat said the words slowly, his gaze still locked on July. "When you come here, you got to roll with things. That's how you get through this, okay?"

July didn't reply. Rolling with things was something he knew how to do. It was how he'd weathered the first seventeen years of his life; keeping his head up, his eyes open, his mouth shut.

Dusk morphed into darkness over the small park and more people arrived. Not many, maybe a dozen or so. He could see some still outside in the park, a few drifted into the hallway, some climbed the stairs to the open top of the tower.

Most of them walked past July without noticing him, but he watched them all—the loud woman laughing with her male companion, the hunched shoulders of the lone woman hurrying through the room, the arrogant carriage of the tall, elderly man. All were shabby in appearance but their personalities seemed as varied as the colors in a rainbow. July wondered if these were all the people in the city. Or all the people in the world. He wondered why they lived homeless in a city full of empty homes.

"Why this place?" he finally asked Pat.

Pat was lying on his back reading by candlelight, a book from the gift shop about the history of San Francisco. He dog-eared his page, set his book aside, and propped himself on one elbow. "It seems a good place. The murals represent such a slice of humanity. Did you read the plaque explaining them?"

July shook his head. He'd used the bathroom earlier and walked partway down the corridor, but the empty hallway and grim paintings had kept him from exploring too far. Things felt too surreal and he didn't understand the rules of this place yet.

"Lillie Hitchcock Coit donated money from her estate for projects to beautify San Francisco," Pat said, sitting up. "She was an interesting character, a turn-of-the-century socialite who liked to smoke cigars and wear trousers and gamble. Anyway, the city used her money to build the tower and commission the murals in the 1930s. The goal was to portray the essence of California life."

July looked around the small room at the sleeping bags on the concrete floor of what he found to be a fairly disturbing tourist attraction. He didn't get the appeal Pat felt for this place. "Why not live in a house and just visit here?"

"Is a home really that important?"

July thought of the foreclosure looming over his house. "I guess to me it is."

Pat shook his head, as if July's opinion had been incorrect. "You need to learn to let go, July. You need to let go of a lot of things."

July wondered what made this man think he knew anything about what he did and didn't need to do. Before he could form a retort he heard footsteps. A man entered the tower alone. He had long brown hair and a heavy mustache, and wore a knee-length oiled duster over a tattered T-shirt and jeans. The intensity in his dark eyes and the tension in his posture set off July's inner alarms.

The man's head swiveled toward July when he entered the foyer, as if he sensed him there. A slow frown spread across his face. He turned to glare at Pat. "Playing God again?" His voice rumbled in his chest, coming out in a growl. "Don't you learn from your mistakes? Or do you just not give a damn?"

"We don't initiate this, Bill," Pat said. "You know that. We're trying to go slower this time. I'd appreciate it if you help us with that."

The man in the duster crossed the room and squatted on his heels in front of July. The back of July's neck prickled as goosebumps raised the small hairs there.

"Leave," Bill said. "Leave now, and don't ever come back." It might have been advice, but Bill's expression and gruff voice made it seem like a threat.

July made no answer. Every muscle in his body tensed for a fight. The fellow was stocky and looked unpredictable. It would be a fight July wasn't sure he would win.

"Bill," Pat said with quiet authority, "let's go slow, okay?"

Bill stood and turned to Pat, barking a laugh that had no humor in it. "Slow? Yeah, sure, 'cause we have all the time in the world, right?" He twisted to look back at July. "Want to know what forever feels like Sonny-boy? 'Cause that's how long you could end up being here."

"Bill," Pat said again, with more weight. He said no more.

"You tell him or I will," the man said. He marched to the staircase and took the stairs two at a time.

July looked to Pat. He expected a vague explanation if he got one at all. Pat looked down, weighing some decision. He sighed. "Bill's wrong on one point, right on another," he began. He pulled the book into his lap and thumbed the pages at an unbound corner. Patty watched them both in silence.

"He's wrong that you have the option to leave here and never come back. Things were set in motion the moment you arrived. Before, really." He gave a one-shouldered shrug. "You won't be staying this time, but you will come back." He paused long enough that July began to wonder if that was all he'd say. "He's right, though, that being here comes with a risk. I hope this all works out well for you, July. I truly do. And I think it can," Pat looked him in the eye with that convincing sincerity. "But if it doesn't, Bill's right. You'd stay here with us. Forever."

"If *what* works out?" Frustration and apprehension made him speak louder than he'd intended.

"Nothing you need to know this time." Pat said. He stood, his book still in his hand. "Don't worry about it for now. We'll have a chance to talk later." He walked out into the hallway.

July wanted to laugh, but couldn't muster the nonchalance. Pat had assured him he wasn't dead. That left nothing this could be but a dream, regardless of how real it felt. He tried willing himself to wake up, but nothing changed.

A movement caught the corner of his eye. Something lingered at the main entrance. Something not human. July leaned forward to get a better look. A coyote stood head and shoulders inside the door. He watched in amazement as the animal danced a little dance of uncertainty, shifting one front paw and then the other, unwilling to commit fully to entering the building. It spotted July and bowed its chest to the doorjamb, head resting on its forelegs. The animal's tail wagged, then the coyote sprang away and vanished into the night.

He turned to Patty. She was watching him with hazel eyes as cautious as the coyote's. From her angle, she wouldn't have been able to see the front door. She took his look to be one of invitation and stood, stepping from her bag onto July's. She plopped down next to him cross-legged, one knee touching his thigh.

Something in her reminded him of Mia and, in a way, of most girls he'd dated, all the way back to junior high. Not a physical attribute; it was a look in her eye, a casual unconcern that veiled her vulnerability. A capable woman with a fear of things that go bump in the night. That was why Mia had left him. The fear. Fear that after he lost a second job things would fall apart. He wouldn't have enough money. Things might go badly. She had run before those things had even had a chance to happen.

"Can I stay with you tonight?" Patty asked, not meeting his eyes. Her tone was almost harsh, daring him to say no, showing her indifference to his possible denial before he answered.

July looked at her sleeping bag lying toe-to-toe with his. "I think you already are."

Her lips puckered into a wounded pout. Reaching out, she stroked the inside of his forearm in a gesture at odds with her expression. "You know what I mean."

Women like her had always intrigued him. Their hard exteriors usually hid deep pain. It made him want to take care of them, to tease that shell open and reveal the person inside. This one was rougher than the women he dated, though, and his father's endless pursuits of women had long ago turned July off to casual sex. Anyway, she looked barely twenty, maybe not even that. He was only thirty-one, and trying to believe that none of this was real; still, he wouldn't encourage her. All he wanted was to go to sleep and wake up in his own bed.

"Not a good idea today," he said, trying to be gentle.

"Yeah, whatever." She stood, blew out the candle, and flounced back to her bag.

July unzipped his own bag and got in. Despite the events of the day, despite the concrete floor, he escaped into sleep like a man running for sanctuary.

He woke in the deep of the night to a wriggling against his chest and legs. He hadn't zipped his bag and Patty was squirming in, her slight form pushing against him. Her back molded to his chest, her lank hair spread across his forearm where it bent to pillow his head. She felt damp, as if she had just bathed. The street-smell still clung to her clothing, but the strong, pink odor of the liquid soap in the bathroom dispensers overpowered it.

Her proximity didn't change his lack of physical attraction to her, but whatever insecurity drove her to him sent out its own siren call, one he'd never been able to deny. July slid his free arm around her waist and fell back into a sound sleep.

Chapter 3

The crowd mumbled and rustled. The evening was a perfect Oregon summer evening, still light, warm but not hot, with no hint of rain. July opened his program. "Troilus and Cressida" was rarely produced and he was looking forward to the play.

"Hey," he nudged Mia's shoulder with his own, "Isn't he the guy who played Rosencrantz last year?" He pointed to an actor in the playlist. "Or was he Guildenstern?" He smiled at his own joke, pleased to know Hamlet well enough to joke with her about it.

When she had taken him to his first Shakespeare play, three years ago, he'd expected to hate it, and for the first quarter hour he had. He might as well have gone to a foreign film where they forgot to put in the subtitles. But fifteen minutes into it, something unexpected happened. It was like a translator materialized in his head; the words began to make sense and the gestures and intonations made them clearer still. The jokes were funny, the actors were excellent, and by the time he took Mia to the snack bar at intermission he talked about the first half with genuine interest.

Mia had been wise to start him with a comedy, but since then they had gone to histories and tragedies and more comedies, and July had loved them all. Coming up to Ashland and packing in two or three plays in a weekend had become an annual summer tradition.

The Elizabethan theatre, where they sat tonight, was his favorite of the multiple venues. He looked up, past the circle of the theatre. The vast sky had darkened to steel blue and the first evening star glowed above the rim of the theatre. A blare of recorded trumpets brought his eyes back to the stage as the lights came up. The crowd hushed. July reached over and took Mia's hand.

"Mr. Davish?"

July heard the voice as though cocooned in thick insulation. He heard it from the bottom of a deep well. A distant, insistent, persistent buzzing of a voice.

"Mr. Davish? July?" the voice said loudly. "Is that right?" the woman's voice said more quietly. "July? That's different." She spoke loudly again. "Can you hear me?"

He cracked his eyes open to slits. Light burned, bright as a welding arc, and he shut them again.

"He's waking up. Page Dr. Malhotra." A louder voice again. "Mr. Davish, can you open your eyes?"

He tried, but the light ignited pain in his head. It was like staring at the brightness of a burning fuse on a stick of dynamite. He blinked and forced his eyes to remain half open, waiting for the detonation in his skull. He was in bed. A woman in baby blue scrubs was taking his blood pressure with a digital cuff that remained attached to his right arm after she finished. His left collarbone ached and his left hand felt trapped under the sheet by something heavy and uncomfortable. A cast he thought.

"You've been in an accident," she said. "You're in the hospital."

The head of the bed at a thirty-degree angle, the white gown with the little blue diamond pattern that had decorated hospital gowns for decades, the wall-mounted TV, the curtained divider, the IV. Yes, it was unmistakably a hospital.

"How long?" he tried to ask. His throat was raw. The words came out in a whisper.

"Two days," she said. "Do you remember what happened?"

He shook his head. It hurt and he stopped.

"You were in an accident. You were hit by a car. Do you remember that?"

He wished she would stop asking him questions. His brain hurt too much to try and remember.

"Can you tell me your name?"

She'd already given him the answer. "July Davish."

"Good. Do you know what city this is?"

That was trickier considering he'd just been in San Francisco and Ashland, though he was pretty sure Ashland had been a dream. "San Diego," he guessed.

"Good. Do you know the date today?"

He gently shook his head 'no' and closed his eyes again, too tired and hurt to play anymore.

Another nurse came into the room and hung a second IV bag on the pole. The one attached to him was running low. "He's oriented times two," the first nurse said. "Did you get hold of Malhotra?"

"I paged him but he hasn't called back yet."

July dreamed again of Mia.

Dr. Malhotra turned out to be a neurologist; a serious man with a thick accent and little in the way of bedside manner. If Mr. Potato Head came in a dark umber shade he could have been based on the doctor: broad nose, large ears, thick eyebrows, oval body. He had everything but the mustache, though July could imagine him sporting one in the past.

The doctor ordered July transferred from the ICU to a room with a phlegmy, elderly man who was in the process of being discharged. When a nurse came by in the afternoon to pick up his dinner selections, she handed him a card and a wrapped gift that fit in his palm. "The ICU said you'd been sleeping before your transfer and they hadn't had the chance to give this to you."

He tore off the wrapping and opened the small box, unable to guess who might have sent it. His brows lifted in surprise at the gold Krugerrand coin inside. The get-well card was dominated by a large cross in the middle draped with flowers painted in pastel colors. He wondered if his dad had met some born-again woman and converted, or whatever it was they did, but couldn't imagine him getting the coin, much less giving it away. Instead, July had found a short note from Robert Vegas.

I don't know how to begin to thank you. It's due to you that I lived to hug my daughter when I got home and to celebrate my fifth anniversary with my wife that night.

The coin is a small token compared to your gift to me, but I hope it may be of some help to you now or in the future.

I'm praying for your full and speedy recovery.

God bless and keep you,
Robert Vegas
P.S. I called the mortgage center on your behalf. I am very sorry to tell
you that it did no good. They asked that you call them personally as soon
as you are able. I did inform them of your current situation.
Robert

The next few days consisted of a steady flow of tests, doctors, and physical therapists. On his fifth day in hospital he tried his father's home phone again. This time he reached him.

"Hey there, July," his father said. His voice was less booming than in July's youth, but just as jovial. "I got your message. I've been meaning to call you back but haven't had the chance." July didn't doubt that his father genuinely had intended to call, but intentions were often as far as things went.

"Were you on the road?"

"No. Well not working anyway. I had some days off between runs, so Louise and me headed for Las Vegas. I only just got your message when we got back."

July wondered how long ago that had been. "Las Vegas, huh?" He didn't ask who Louise was.

"Yeah. How about that? I was over at The Brick House last week and I met this gorgeous woman and, well, off we went." His dad chuckled.

July's dad was a sixty-year-old long-haul trucker, potbellied, and on oxygen. He could imagine the gorgeous Louise.

"So how you doing?" his dad asked, when July still didn't take the bait. "Are you home now?"

"They're still keeping me for observation, but they're talking about letting me go tomorrow."

"Oh, well good. Good. That must have been some accident

to land you in hospital. That old truck of yours still on all four tires?"

"Yeah, the truck's fine." There was no point in correcting the details now.

"I worry about you, you know. I keep hoping they'll send me on a run out to the west coast soon, so we can have a visit." His dad had said that for all of the three years that July had lived in San Diego.

"That'd be nice. I'd like to see you too. How's *your* health doing?"

"I'm getting by pretty good. Nothing's managed to kill me yet, and there's plenty that should have."

"You aren't smoking are you?"

"Oh, once in a while. I gave up on them patches. They didn't do a damn bit of good."

"Dad, you can't smoke now that you're on oxygen."

"I just take it off for a little while if I need a smoke. It don't hurt a thing. Besides, we've all gotta die of something. I might as well enjoy the trip. Oh hey, I talked to your Uncle Eddie while we were in Las Vegas" he said, deftly changing the subject. "Sounds like he has some business he needs to see to out your way."

"You didn't give him my address did you?"

"Well, of course I did, July. He's my brother. You put him up for a day or two if he needs it, okay? He was real good to us all back when you and Alice were kids and I was between jobs."

July squeezed his eyes shut. His head hurt again.

A pouty voice in the background said something. His dad answered that he was coming. "I gotta go, July, but you take care. You call me if you need anything. Oh, and I sent you a little something from Las Vegas. Figured it might cheer you up about the accident and being out of work and all. You should be getting it any day now. It's kind of special, so watch out for it."

His dad seldom picked things up for him on the road anymore. It made July smile to think of what he might have sent. "Okay, I will. Stay in touch, Dad. I love you." He stayed on the line until he heard the dial tone.

The things his father picked up for him on the road had been truck-stop junk, but they'd meant the world to July and his little sister, Alice, when they were young. A hundred trinkets had covered the desk and dresser and shelves in July's room when he was a child: tiny plastic horses and paperweights with bugs or cityscapes inside. Playing cards with scenes of Chicago, a child-sized mug from Wall Drug in South Dakota, a keychain from Daytona with a picture of Dale Earnhardt's racecar in an acrylic square.

The surprise of what their dad would bring was only part of the excitement for July and Alice; the real gift was the tangible proof that he had returned. It reassured them that he'd thought of them while he was gone and gave them something to remember him by when he left again.

Even now, when July unexpectedly received some piece of touristy junk in the mail, it brought back that childhood reassurance that his father had been thinking of him. The step-moms and girlfriends had come and gone when he was growing up. His dad had never been good at being alone and July understood that, but for July there had just been his dad. The one anchor in the storm of his childhood.

A repeat CAT scan later that day showed the blood clot in July's head had gotten no larger. According to his doctor, he had a subdural hematoma—a collection of blood above his right ear, sandwiched between the membranes covering his brain. As long as it didn't start bleeding again, he wouldn't need an operation to cauterize the vessels. Whether the clot reabsorbed or would need to be removed remained to be seen.

Television held little appeal, and in the few quiet stretches between sleep and treatments, medications and doctors, memories of the strange, vivid dream of Coit Tower haunted July. It continued to feel real, and the details hadn't faded the way his dream of Ashland and other dreams had done. He'd never been to Coit Tower that he could remember, and asked a couple of his nurses if they'd ever seen it. One printed off information from the internet for him. Goosebumps raised on his arms when he saw that the pictures of the murals were identical to the images in his dream. He rationalized that he must have seen photos of them at some time in his life and forgotten. Perhaps the pressure of the blood clot had stimulated some part of his brain holding remote memories.

The following day, doctor Malhotra confirmed he was releasing July. Once the attending internist signed his discharge papers, he'd be free to go. July called a couple of friends from past jobs to see if he could get a ride home but, being a weekday, wasn't surprised when he didn't reach either of them. The couple of neighbors he knew well enough to call would be at work as well. His nurse offered to arrange a cab for him. He wondered how much it would cost and tried to remember how much cash he'd had on him at the time of the accident.

His phone rang and he assumed a callback number had shown on one of his friends' phones. His IV had already been removed, allowing him to roll and reach the phone with his good arm.

"Hello?"

"Well howdy, July," his uncle's smoke-roughened voice replied. "Walter called me this morning about the time I hit Temecula and told me you were in the hospital."

"Uh. Yeah. Where are you?"

"Well, sitting outside your place, actually. I know your dad told you I was coming by. Since you weren't here, I figured I'd see if you had a spare key."

He did, but in the backyard and well hidden. He considered telling his uncle he'd be in hospital a while in hopes he'd move on, but they were sending him home soon and he'd probably get there to find his uncle had found the key or had discovered the broken latch on the bedroom window and climbed inside. He told him where to find the key.

"They're getting ready to release me now. I could use a ride home if you've got the time. My truck is still in the parking lot where I had the accident." He hoped it was, anyway.

"Sure, July. Glad to help."

"Could you grab a set of clothes for me? They cut all mine off in the ambulance. I got a bunch of rags handed to me when I woke up."

Eddie showed up half an hour later and handed him a grocery bag containing underwear, socks, jeans, and a T-shirt. He'd bet his uncle had rummaged more than warranted to find them. July didn't do drugs and certainly had no spare cash hidden anywhere, but he wondered which way the scales might have tipped if Uncle Eddie had run across either.

He pulled the fresh clothes out of the bag while they waited on the last of the paperwork to be finished.

"What's with that cast?" Eddie asked.

July glanced down at the garishly bright fiberglass on his

arm. "I guess they had a run on casts that day. Hot pink was all they had left. At least that's what they told me when I came to. Maybe it's just how they have fun around here." He pulled on the underwear and jeans one-handed, then slipped out of his sling and slid the gown off. A wave of nausea hit him and he waited for it to settle before pulling on his shirt.

Eddie stared at the gauze bandage around his head, his split lip, the red and purple blotches running down his chest, the bandage over the surgical incision where they'd repaired his collarbone, and his broken wrist. At least July was in the habit of keeping his hair cropped short. The bald patch around his stapled scalp laceration should grow out quickly.

"You look like something the cat drug in, boy," Eddie said.

He felt like it, too. "At least I'll heal," July said. "You're stuck with what you've got." He wasn't kidding but his uncle laughed.

The sallow skin and dark circles under Eddie's eyes had been there as long as July could remember. His teeth were small and stained. His hair was artificially black. It was thinning, and combed back with enough gel that it separated into long strands running from his forehead out of sight over the curve of his skull. It made July think of the braids of the black man in his dream.

"So what happened to you?" Eddie said. "Your dad told me you were in a wreck but he was a bit sketchy on the details."

"He's half right. I was standing too close to one." He sat to slip on his shoes, grateful that his expensive work boots had been the one bit of clothing that had survived the accident intact. "Bystanders said the car near me flipped while I tried to jump out of the way. The rear of the car whacked me in the head while we were both still airborne." He stood, looking around to see if he'd left anything unpacked. "If I'd been anchored to the ground when I was hit, I'd have probably gotten a bed in the morgue instead of this one. I went down with my left arm out," he flapped his blue-slinged wing and pink-casted wrist. "The car landed on two tires just past me, so I wasn't crushed, and instead of coming down on me, it rolled over onto the roof."

Eddie shook his head. "You are one lucky bastard."

"Lucky would have been not getting hit." If he'd left Robert Vegas alone and kept walking to his truck, that's exactly what would have happened.

He picked up the large, white plastic bag the nurse had given him earlier. It held his keys, wallet, hospital brochures, discharge instructions, a pair of socks with tread on the bottom, an emesis basin, and a large plastic cup with the hospital logo stamped on it and a straw attached to the lid. July walked around the bed to his nightstand. Keeping his back to his uncle, he tossed Robert Vegas' card and present in with the other items.

July pulled the plastic ribbon to close the bag and glanced once more around the room, knowing he hadn't forgotten anything. What else could there be? His life was composed of a father who spent most of his time on the road, a dead mother, five ex-stepmothers, and an ex-girlfriend.

A volunteer made July sit in a wheelchair and wheeled him outside while Eddie brought his car around, a faded gold 1992 Buick Century. She opened the passenger door and Eddie moved a 12-pack of beer from the front seat to the back.

"Would you drop me off at my truck?" July asked, once they were on the road. If they went in from the Pacific Beach side, the route from Mercy Hospital to July's Mission Beach home would take them right past his bank.

"Are you okay to drive?" Eddie asked.

High on Percocet, with blurry vision and nausea, July wasn't sure at all. "Yeah. I'll be fine. So how long are you in town for?"

"Just two or three days. Walter said you'd be okay with me staying with you."

"Sure," July said, turning to look out the side window. Even healthy he wouldn't welcome his uncle's company. At least with Mia gone, she wouldn't be around for Eddie to ogle.

A few miles later they turned into the parking lot of the bank. Thankfully, the Silverado was still there. July climbed out and hauled himself into the old truck. After sitting for most of a week it took two tries and a few pumps of the accelerator before it roared to life and he pulled out onto the road. He felt strange driving again, part of the moving world, taking action instead of being acted upon. Maybe it was just the Percocet.

Less than two miles later, he pulled into the narrow carport at the side of his bungalow and pushed open the picket gate to a tiny front lawn covered more by beach sand than grass. July had been on the move, state to state, for most of his life. He'd never considered settling in one place until he met Mia. When he came across a deal too good to pass up on the tiny, circa WWII bungalow, he'd taken the plunge. It was the first place he had ever owned, the first place he had ever wanted to own, and the thought of losing it hurt more than he could have imagined.

Eddie parked in the driveway behind him. He collected the beer from the back seat and a battered, hard-sided suitcase from the trunk. July held the front door open and led him into the kitchen where Eddie set the beer on the ancient Formica table

that July had found at a second-hand store near the dump. He'd
gotten it with the original chairs, vinyl seats decorated with the
same pastel pink and silver speckles as the top of the table. The
fifties furniture looked right at home in the old bungalow.

Eddie took a chair, reached into the opened case of beer,
and held a can out. July shook his head and fished in the fridge
for a Coke. "Still not drinking?" Eddie said. "You've been on
that kick for a coon's age."

"Yeah, I guess so," July said.

"So how'd someone like you score a place at the beach?"

July held the Coke in his good hand and used his foot to
pull out a chair opposite Eddie. It was a relief to sit, though he'd
only been on his feet a few minutes.

"A buddy I worked with had a side job here, doing some
work on the place. The old couple that owned it had to go into
a nursing home and the family told him they'd rather have a
quick sell than fix everything that needed fixing." He popped
the tab on the soda can with a loud click-hiss. "I made an offer
before it hit the market. Nobody outside California believes
something this small and old might be worth what it appraised
for."

Eddie ran a thumb along the aluminum trim on the table.
His nail was yellow and flaking. July had seen it before in meth-
heads he'd worked with. "Good for you." He looked out the
small kitchen window over the sink, but his thoughts seemed
further away than Mission Beach. "I guess I should have settled
down at some point."

"Why didn't you?"

His uncle never heard the question. He stared out the
window, lost in some reflection or regret. It was just as well,
July thought. Any answer he was willing to give would have

probably been a lie.

"Look, I'm beat," July said. "This is the longest I've been up in days."

"Sure, sure," Eddie said. "Go hit the sack. I can see to myself. I've got some things I need to do while I'm in town anyway."

July didn't ask what. The less he knew about Eddie's business, the better. "You can have the couch or the recliner. There are blankets and pillows in the hall closet."

He headed for his bedroom, found places to hide the gold coin and pain pills, and dropped into bed fully dressed.

Chapter 4

The strident ring of the phone woke July. Morning light filled the bedroom. His head pounded, and it took him a moment to orient. Once he did, he hauled himself up, hoping to get to the phone before his uncle could.

"Joe's Bar and Grill," he heard Eddie say. July found Eddie standing in the living room in his boxers and held out a hand for the phone. "No, wait," Eddie grumbled. "Don't hang up. He's here." He passed the phone to July. "Fuckers shouldn't call this early," Eddie muttered, lying down on the couch and pulling the blanket back over himself. Four beer cans littered the coffee table. July felt certain that hadn't been the total casualty count.

"This is July."

"July, George Kostos." July recognized the name of the construction foreman he'd interviewed with the day he'd been hospitalized. "I wanted to let you know you have the job if you'd like it. Work starts Monday morning at 8:00. You'd need to be there about an hour early for paperwork, some HR stuff, and a safety briefing."

It was the first offer July had received in four months.

"I appreciate it, George." He winced in frustration, trying to find the best way to say the next part. A hard hat would cover the staples in his scalp, and he could cut the cast off himself by Monday, but there'd be no covering for his fractured collarbone.

"I had an accident last week and have to keep my left arm still for a while. It should only be for a couple of weeks. I'd be happy to start with any light duty job you've got. You've seen my work history. I've got experience in a lot of different areas."

His doctors would probably disagree wholeheartedly with a return to full duty in two weeks. They might even disagree with light duty starting Monday, but he'd figure out a way to make it work.

"Sorry to hear about the accident," George said. "A lot of guys don't have the high-rise experience I need, but we've got deadlines right from the first week. I've got to have a full crew. Give me a call when you get medical clearance and I'll see where I'm at." His tone of voice said he was calling the next guy on his list.

The foreman hung up. July threw the handset at the recliner.

A few hours later, Eddie woke, dressed, and went out to do whatever he was there to do. July spent the day arguing with the mortgage center and the creditors, scanning the want ads, and calling personal injury lawyers. He found a lawyer, Alex Schiff, willing to meet with him later that day. At their appointment, Schiff seemed optimistic about getting a good settlement and

July retained him. When July asked about the possibility of an advance the lawyer sounded doubtful, but said if he'd be willing to settle for an initial offer, things shouldn't take long.

That night, Eddie started on the Jim Beam. He returned from the store with the steaks he'd promised, and the bottle that he hadn't.

"It feels good to beat the heat of Las Vegas for a bit," he said, taking a stout drink from his glass as July grilled the steaks on his Hibachi propped on the back steps.

The stench of bourbon drifted to July with the words. It smelled to him of rotting orchids and rubbing alcohol, and brought with it, as always, memories of his mother. Eddie tipped his glass toward July. "Sure?"

July, again, declined the offer. He'd quit drinking as a teenager, when it became obvious he was headed down the same path as the rest of the family. With alcoholics and drug addicts on both sides, he'd figured out pretty quickly that it wouldn't take much for him to join them.

Eddie got louder the more he drank over the course of the evening, and became increasingly offensive before finally passing out on the couch. July thought about covering him with a blanket but didn't. He reached down and moved the bottle from the floor to the coffee table. He stared down at his uncle a long minute.

The corruption of first New York and then Las Vegas had seeped into his uncle's bones over the years, deforming him in some indefinable way. Eddie had lived his life trying to weasel his way next to powerful and dangerous people, always striving to be one of them, always with a scheme that was just about to make him rich. It was evident to everyone but Eddie that he was nothing but a court jester who fancied himself a prince. He had inherited the lion's share of the bony Italian features in the family, and they looked prominent now against the drunk-relaxed muscles. They pushed against his skin, making shadows under the heavy brow, and thinning his lips under the strong, bowed arch of his nose. July wondered if the man's thin lips or dry hands had ever touched Alice.

Alice in Wonderland had been his sister's namesake, though *his* Alice's life had held too little wonder. If July had any proof that Eddie had hurt her, he would gladly smother his uncle where he lay. All he had were his memories of his sister, angry and sullen whenever Eddie visited, though she would never say why. It was too late now to ask her. The answer had died with her years ago.

His uncle was an uncomfortable guest over the next few days, alternately gregarious and abusive depending on the amount of alcohol he consumed and, possibly, the drugs he did when he went out. Fortunately, July saw little of him. Eddie was gone from afternoon until late at night, and July's days were filled with appointments. He saw an orthopedist for his shoulder, and started physical therapy, got the staples removed from his head laceration and the incision over his collarbone, and had a follow-up CT. The CAT scan showed the subdural hematoma was stable. Dr. Malhotra thought the clot small enough that it might reabsorb on its own. They wouldn't know for another week or so, but for now it was good news that he might not need a burr hole drilled into his skull to drain the blood.

He thought things might be looking up until he received a seven-day eviction reminder the following afternoon. July looked at it spread out on the table in front of him; four days left, as the note was dated the day it had been generated. The time counter on the phone said he'd been on hold for his lawyer for thirteen minutes. The recorded message saying someone would be with him shortly cut off with a click.

"Mr. Davish, sorry to keep you waiting."

"Mr. Schiff, I was calling to find out where things are at with the settlement." July heard the front door open and cursed his uncle's timing. "As far as my mortgage company is concerned, I owe them five months mortgage before that eviction date comes up. I'm down to just a few days left."

Eddie came to the edge of the kitchen and leaned in the archway, listening unselfconsciously. He cradled a new bottle of bourbon and 12-pack of beer in his arms.

"We won't get this settled as soon as we'd hoped, I'm afraid," Schiff said. "We've hit a small snag."

"What kind of a snag?" July felt a tug at the pit of his stomach.

"The insurance company for the Prius is blaming the accident on the uninsured driver in the other car. It'll work out eventually. It just means we won't be able to get a number as soon as you'd hoped."

"What about putting my foreclosure on hold? Any progress there?" July had explained the situation when he'd retained the lawyer. Schiff had told him that bankruptcy and foreclosures weren't his area, but in the end had agreed to send a letter for July.

"I'm sorry, Mr. Davish. I requested documentation of your arrangement with them and they told me the same as they told you, that there isn't any arrangement. I did request a delay in the foreclosure as we discussed, but without proof, we have no legal right to demand one. I haven't heard back from them and, to be honest, I don't know that I will. Maybe you could get a loan to tide you over?"

"I tried that already. I tried borrowing against the accident settlement too, but nobody will touch it until there's an agreement in place." He'd even looked up the value of the coin Robert Vegas had given him and found that the Krugerrand was equal to one ounce of gold, far short of what the mortgage company was trying to get out of him.

"I'm sorry, Mr. Davish. It's Thursday afternoon and if you have to be out by the 26th, that means midnight Sunday. If I don't hear from them tomorrow, there's nothing I can do. I'll make a call today, but the chances of them taking action in the next twenty-four hours are slim. Especially since your verbal arrangement with the service representative last May can't be proven."

"I see."

"I'll be in court most of the day tomorrow, but I'll be sure to call you if I get any news."

July hung up.

Eddie set the bourbon and beer on the table. He peeled open the cardboard end of the beer case and held one out. July felt tempted for the first time in years. He shook his head.

"Go on, kid," Eddie said. "No need to be so stiff-necked. It'll make you feel better, relax you a bit. You always were wound too tight." Eddie popped the beer open and set it in front of July.

A little bit of oblivion in arm's reach. And what good had all his fucking control ever done him, anyway? He pushed it back across the table to Eddie.

"Five months mortgage, eh?" Eddie said. "I don't have that kind of cash on hand or I'd loan it to you, but I know people who carry more than that around as pocket change. I could ask around if you want. I wouldn't borrow it in my name, you understand. You'd have to be the one to work out a deal."

July weighed his home against his soul. With the kind of people his uncle was talking about, that's what it came down to. Who knew what they'd want in return, or if they'd come back someday wanting a favor of their own. And if the settlement didn't work out... Luck had never been on his side; he'd be a fool to count on it now.

"I'll think about it," he said.

"Sure. Whatever you want," Eddie said. He took an unopened beer out to the living room and turned on the TV.

July felt an overwhelming need to get out of the house. He kicked his shoes off under the table and headed out of the kitchen. Pausing in the archway, he looked back at the open beer. Maybe Eddie was right; maybe he should give himself a break for once. One beer to relax a little. He grabbed it off the table and walked out to the beach.

Chapter 5

Hazy clouds muted the sky and shadowed the ocean to a steel gray. The summer tourists were gone, like some flock of noisy, featherless birds that had migrated away the day after Labor Day, leaving a gaping silence in their wake. Mission Beach was never empty though, and July melded with the joggers, locals, and late-season visitors as he walked to the edge of the surf.

He let the cool water wash over his feet and soak the hem of his jeans. The sounds of the ocean soothed him with its primal ebb and flow of waves, the greedy cries of the gulls. It felt good to be out of the house. After three happy years there, his home had become a symbol for his job losses and failures of the past few months.

He looked out at the water, wishing he'd taken more advantage of the ocean while he was here. When he first bought the house he'd wanted to get a catamaran and learn how to sail, but Mia had never liked boats and the idea fell by the wayside.

He tipped the beer can to his mouth and tasted the bitter hops and yeast. Despite his hell-with-it attitude, he felt a twisting in his gut. Self-control was all that had kept him from turning out like the rest of his family. If he only did it sometimes, it wasn't control at all. He took another sip anyway. Turning north, he walked toward the Pacific Beach pier, nursing his beer and thinking about Eddie's offer. He tossed the empty can in a trash barrel on the way back, still unsure what to do. He was angling up the beach toward his house when someone called his name.

"July!"

Looking to his left, he saw Melissa waving a big, full-armed wave at him. He hadn't seen much of her lately, even though she lived in the condos just behind him. She'd hit on him a few times after Mia left, when they saw each other around the neighborhood or at the beach. When he never showed up at any of the half-dozen parties at her place that she'd invited him to, she'd quit trying.

"Come join us," she hollered, waving again.

There were a dozen or so people bunched near her, some he recognized, though no one he really knew. July made his way through the deep sand, heading for the knot of people. His customary solitude didn't hold much appeal at the moment and he was in no rush to go home to Eddie and the eviction notice.

Mel sat on a beach towel near a fire-pit. Her ever-changing hair was black today, and hung around her face in a not-quite-goth cut. "Have a seat," she said. She scooted over, but he took a seat in the sand. A few of the people nearby introduced themselves.

"Matt," one fellow offered, lifting a hand in greeting. He had a surfer's build and peroxide blond hair.

"July," he replied.

Another blond man squatting behind Matt looked up from unpacking a volleyball net. He resembled Matt enough to be a brother. "Oh yeah?" he said. "I was born in July. Missed July 4th by twelve minutes. How about you?"

"January," July replied.

Even his dad didn't know why his mom had picked his name. "She just fancied it," was all his father would ever say on the subject. July counted himself lucky; he could have been named Walter after his dad. Or Orville, in memory of his granddad.

"So what happened to you?" Mel indicated the sling and cast. Her voice was uncomfortably loud at this close range. She laughed, though he couldn't guess why.

"Car accident."

"Bummer. I was in one three years ago. I went right into a light post. I don't remember any of it, but I fractured some ribs. Gaawd," she drew the word out, the volume increasing a notch, "I hope you didn't break any ribs 'cause that hurts like a mother." She gave another high-pitched giggle, as much a part of her speech as punctuation to writing. "Good thing I wasn't feeling any pain that night but, oh my gawd, the next morning…" She put one hand to the ribs that must have broken, and laughed again, louder. "Love the color you picked for your cast, though." She pointed to her chest. Her neon pink swimsuit top emphasized the soft flesh between the top and her tight, denim shorts.

"Yeah, well, dare to be different, that's me."

The guy he thought of as 3rd of July squatted in front of a cooler near them and pulled two beers out. He held one out to him. Melted ice water dripped down the brown bottle. The first beer had done nothing worse than unwind him a bit and if there was ever a day to cut loose a little, it was today. "Sure," he said, taking it before the moment grew awkward.

"Mel, you want to play?" 3rd of July asked, indicating the volleyball net others had carried off to set up away from the fire. She said no and he jogged off as teams formed up.

"So, you ever hear from Mia?" Mel asked, reaching across and opening his bottle when his cast and sling made him struggle with the twist cap.

"Uh, no. Not really." Mel had come to his back fence one day when he was working outside and dragged the information out of him. "Not into volleyball?" he asked her, changing the subject.

She rolled her eyes. "Yeah, right. I grew up in North Dakota."

Despite the fact he didn't usually hang out with the party crowd, it felt good to be outside. He wished he'd spent more time on the beach these past few months, but he'd been busy looking for work and trying to hang on to Mia, then dealing with her leaving.

Those who weren't playing volleyball ebbed and flowed like the ocean waves, hauling firewood to the fire pit, surfing, or sitting awhile near July and Mel to talk and drink. More coolers appeared; more drinks were passed around. Dusk brought everyone to the fire. Small groups merged into one. By the time the nearly-full moon was cresting in the east, hot dogs were roasting, the coolers were mostly empty of beer, and bottles of schnapps were being passed around; peach first, then peppermint. The dare went up to do flaming shots and a twig from the fire was used to light them. July downed one regular shot and two flaming shots along with another beer.

He laughed more than he'd laughed in years, but the uncontrolled quality to it wound a rancid thread through his stomach. Distant memories of his mother's parties, raucous with artificial joviality, flitted in and out of his fogged mind. Parties where it had frightened him as a child to hear the laughter begin.

Matt pulled a bong out of a backpack. He filled it from a water bottle and packed the little metal cup with pot. He took a hit and passed it to Mel. Smoke and vapor drifted free when she came up for air. It reminded July of an illustration from his mother's copy of Alice in Wonderland, of the caterpillar and its hookah. He tried on a mental image of the blue caterpillar sporting her facial piercings.

She handed the bong to him and he passed it on before it could tempt him to break another rule.

"Wow, that ocean breeze gets chilly at night," Mel said. She scrunched closer and leaned into his side.

His chest and shins were warm from the fire, but the skin on his back and arms prickled with every gust. He turned and looked at the ocean as if he could see the offensive draft, but saw only the white tips of the surf and the reflection of the moon skipping across the tops of the waves. Turning back to Mel, his brain seemed to keep spinning after his head had stopped moving. He found the sensation fun.

"Yeah, it does," he said. He looked up the beach toward his house. "I could grab a sweatshirt for you if you want."

"I'd rather you kept me warm instead," she said, then surprised him by stretching up to kiss him. He kissed her back.

"You want to go over to my place?" she said.

He started to decline. "Sure," he said, instead. He hadn't had sex since Mia left. Why the hell *should* he say no? He enjoyed the impulsiveness of his answer as much as he was enjoying his buzz.

Mel stood and pulled July to his feet by his good hand. They both swayed. She led him to the two-story condo on the block behind his house. He careened off a fence in the alley and had to grab the metal hand-rail as he climbed the stairs. He distantly wondered how easily the vessel in his head would re-injure or the screws in his collarbone might pop loose if he fell. She fumbled with the key and opened the door to a two-bedroom apartment. It was slightly bigger than his bungalow, furnished with mismatched furniture, and sported cheaply framed movie and band posters on the walls.

"Where's your roommate?"

"She and her boyfriend went to Joshua Tree for the weekend."

July had never been inside Mel's apartment before. The curtains were open and he walked to the front window. Between the full moon and the streetlamps, he could see the back of his little house clearly. *Three days until it's the bank's house,* he thought

It disturbed him to see just how clear the view was of his bedroom. He tried to remember if he always dropped the shades at night and wondered if the slats in his cheap metal blinds had ever shown a zebra'd version of him making love to Mia in the afternoons or at night by candlelight. He pictured how they would have looked from this distance as he moved over her in their rhythmic horizontal dance or with him lying naked on the bed, Mia straddling his hips. He wondered how everything could have gone so all to hell in such a short time. A few months ago he had been happier than ever before in his life. Now he had nearly nothing to his name.

Mel stepped up behind him in the dark and slipped her arms around his waist. One hand dropped to massage his crotch. Beer and schnapps breath drifted to him as she nuzzled his neck. His body responded to the touch, but he couldn't pull his gaze from the little bungalow where the best of his life had been lived. He'd had something real there, not this; not the sort of thing his father chased all his life like a Greyhound chases a lure. July stepped forward, out of her embrace. He swayed.

"I should get going," he said.

"You don't have to go, you know" she said, as if she hadn't made the offer clear enough. She took his hand and tugged gently toward the bedroom.

"I better make sure my uncle isn't setting the place on fire with a cigarette. Maybe I'll see you over at Mike's." Or maybe the blond-haired guy's name had been Matt. Somebody tonight had said he was having the next party. July didn't care; he wouldn't be here anyway.

Taking a shortcut through the neighbor's yard to his back gate, he was glad he'd left the back door unlocked. He couldn't remember if he was supposed to have his keys with him and Eddie still had the spare. Already aware of the hangover to come, he drank some water and crawled into bed.

He felt like hell in the morning. The bathroom mirror told him that he looked as bad as he felt. He scrubbed his good hand through his hair as if it could rub away the headache and muzziness. Next, he found the pain pills he'd hidden and took one, pretty sure there were fewer even though he hadn't been taking any. Pulling on a pair of shorts one-handed, he shambled barefoot and shirtless into the kitchen to make coffee. He found a note on the kitchen table.

Got a call this morning. Heading back to Vegas. Call me about that loan. If you need a job, I could get you lined up with something. I know a lot of people who could use a smart kid like you. Eddie

July turned the TV on low for some background noise and lay on the couch while the coffee brewed. When it was ready, he poured a cup as thick as mud into the reindeer mug that his father had sent one Christmas long ago. Under the cartoonish Rudolph pulling a sleigh full of toys, Huntsville, Alabama was printed in large lettering around the base.

July pulled a chair out at the kitchen table. The scrape of the metal legs scratched at his headache like claws. He sat heavily and raised the cup to his lips, only then noticing the eviction notice at the far end of the table. He set the coffee down untouched and stared at the paper. Pulling it to him, he re-read the sterile and emotionless language of lawyer-speak. He paused over the most brutal sections, reading the passages slowly, rubbing the words into his wounds like salt. *Reversion of ownership to the bank. Eviction date. Forcible eviction in the case of non compliance.*

Injured, no job, no prospect of a job, and fucked—that was him. It must be an inherent quality to foreclosures that they always came at the worst possible time, but knowing that helped nothing. He checked his voicemail but his lawyer hadn't called. He wondered if Eddie had still been here if he would have taken him up on his offer of introducing him to someone for a loan, but it was nearly noon on Friday now and Eddie was on the road. He tried to tell himself it was for the best.

Eddie had left the remains of his Jim Beam on the kitchen table. A splash of that in his coffee might take away the headache and dull some of the worry, at least for a while. *What the hell*, he thought. He'd already broken all his drinking rules last night. He'd cope better with things this afternoon when he didn't feel like shit.

Unscrewing the top, he splashed a large shot into his mug. The smell of bourbon wafted up, memories of his childhood drifting to him with the fumes. He ignored the revulsion and took a sip, grimacing at the taste. The bourbon cooled the coffee and he purposefully took a longer drink. The alcohol burned his throat and belly. He leaned against the sink and took another drink, finishing half the mug.

The Jim Beam smelled of New Mexico and Eddie and a dozen other things July despised. Anger welled up from a source deeper than just the job losses and the foreclosure. He felt sick to his stomach at dealing with hardship like the rest of his family; numbing the pain like his mom, chasing one-night stands like his dad, and losing everything, like they all had.

"God damn it!" July yelled at the world in general. He heaved the mug into the arch of the wall. The cup smashed against the edge, spraying the laced coffee across the vinyl kitchen floor and the short, tan weave of the living room carpet. He dropped back into the kitchen chair and laid his forehead on the table. It rested on the eviction notice. The paper felt sticky against his skin, and when he opened his eyes the words telling him he was losing his home were large and blurred.

He pushed away from the table and went back to bed.

It was mid-afternoon when July woke again. The pain pill and bourbon combo left him groggy, but the hangover had mostly lifted and he felt hungry. He mulled over his options while he heated and ate sausage and eggs.

He'd sunk a lifetime of savings into the down payment on this place, and after months of unemployment he didn't even have enough reserves for first, last, and deposit on a cheap rental. What did that leave? Shack up with Mel? Ask one of his work buddies if he could stay with them? Wait for the police to come and drag him from his home for non-compliance of his eviction? As far as July could see, he had only one choice. It was time to say goodbye to yet another thing he loved.

He crossed the living room, stepping over the shards of the reindeer mug on the floor, and hunted in the bedroom until he found his nylon gym bag. Tossing it onto the bed, he threw in as many clothes as would fit. He dumped rags out of a cardboard box and piled in boots and tennis shoes. The small box Robert Vegas had given him tumbled out from where he'd hidden it among the rags, and he packed that in a side pocket. The remaining pain meds went into the toilet, the antibiotics went into his bag.

He took his mother's old green hardback of "Alice's Adventures in Wonderland" down from a shelf. He'd never asked his father if she'd owned the book as a child or had found the 1950s version in some thrift store, but it was the one thing he would never leave behind. He padded it with clothes to protect it. On the same shelf was the booklet of Pericles that Mia had given him last Christmas. They'd planned to see the play this summer, before everything changed. He'd stopped reading it when she left and didn't know yet if he wanted to finish it. July remembered his dream of Coit Tower, Pat homeless, reading by candlelight. He tossed the booklet in the bag.

He searched his carport until he found his camping gear, then shoved everything into a canvas duffle and threw the bag in the truck bed. Back in the house, he put canned food into a few of the plastic grocery bags that billowed out from the cupboard under his sink. The remainder of the Jim Beam went down the drain.

He hauled the things from the house to the truck, then double-checked for anything else he might need. Remembering his mail, he went out front and opened the mailbox. He found three second-notice bills that he tossed back into the mailbox and a package, a rectangular box wrapped in brown grocery bag paper and postmarked from Iowa, where his father lived. It was about the size of a box of checks; just the right size to hold a stack of dollar bills...or a stack of twenties.

For one heartbeat, July wondered if the special gift was money his father had won in Vegas, maybe enough money to turn his luck around. But that would mean his father's luck had changed also. The odds of that were too long to imagine.

He couldn't entirely banish that old feeling of anticipation as he unwrapped the package. Lifting off the top of the box, he removed the tissue paper. A plastic statue of Elvis lay on a bed of more tissue paper. A flimsy plaque at the bottom stated that it was a collector's edition, series twenty-four. It wasn't going to save him from eviction. Somehow, though, it improved his day just a little.

He set the white-caped figure on his old behemoth of a TV to greet the bank's agents when they came. When he walked out, he left the front door standing open. The less the bank got, the better.

He backed out of the carport and pointed the truck east.

July reached the little town of Alpine just before dusk and pulled off to buy a soda and find a bathroom. The tiny, Mayberry town in the pine forest didn't seem like it belonged in San Diego County. There were Mr. Greenjeans' and Mr.

Rodgers' and Aunt Beas everywhere, working in their yards, getting ready for fall. July parked downtown and found what he needed in a quaint, touristy drugstore. It sold a bit of everything, from food and pharmaceuticals and pots and pans, to toys and hardware and trinkets. He got back in the truck and popped his soda open as he drove down the main street looking for a side road that would take him out of town and into the woods.

He bumped along a dirt road east of town and followed it deep into the trees until he found a good place to pull off that didn't look like private land. The act of unpacking his sleeping bag and camp stove hammered home the reality that he'd left his home for good. Pat had told him in his dream that he needed to learn to let go, and maybe he'd been right. The man had seemed more real than most real people July knew. Even if it had been a dream—and it must have been—Pat's confidence still oddly comforted him.

July dumped a can of Dinty Moore stew into a pan and fired up the stove. He could go anywhere and all he wanted was to go back home. While he ate, he thought about all the places he'd been, the cities he didn't want to go back to and the ones he'd never seen. Flagstaff wasn't far and it was somewhere he'd thought about in the past. It was small, but University towns sometimes offered more opportunity than big cities, where competition for jobs could be fiercer. He collected firewood for a campfire and watched the flames flutter yellow and red in the light breeze, like a Tibetan monk's robes. He wasn't used to so much quiet and space, but it felt good. Life had been coming at him too fast lately.

He finished eating and got up to piss against a tree. There was a buzz in both ears when he stood and a moment of unsteadiness. He froze, focused inward, analyzing the sensations. A wave of dizziness and nausea smothered him. His ears buzzed louder and his vision tunneled. July dropped to his knees and braced himself on his good hand, trying to stave off the encroaching unconsciousness. The tunnel vision narrowed to total blackness. He tried to draw a full breath and couldn't. Sweat sprang out on his face and neck. His head pounded.

He fell face-first into the dirt.

Chapter 6

July opened his eyes to a polished, granite floor. It stretched away to the horizon of a long room. The walls above his head were covered with elegantly framed and lit paintings, hung in a neat, long row.

He pushed himself to his hands and knees and waited. No vertigo. No headache. His sling was missing but the dirty pink cast still covered his left wrist. He got to his feet, careful not to put pressure on his collarbone, though he felt no pain in his shoulder.

The large, empty floor space contained nothing but three benches of polished dark wood. A man sat on the middle bench with his back to July. Directly in front of the man was a maritime painting, which he seemed to be studying.

July skirted the bench, wary. The man had a compact but fit body and a mop of thick blonde hair, but when he turned to face July, it was the smile that sparked the connection—an easy grin and a confident, knowing glint in the eyes.

"Pat?" July said uncertainly.

"How you doing, July?"

He didn't know if he should bother to respond. If this was all something he dreamt while unconscious, what did it matter? He tried to convince himself a dream was all this could be, but the hardness of the granite beneath his feet and the cool air in the museum felt too crisp and real. His peripheral vision was too detailed, and the minute sounds and perceptions that his brain processed were the myriad inputs of real life.

"Been better," he said.

Pat nodded knowingly. He tipped his head toward the bench and July sat next to him.

"So what is this place?"

"The Metropolitan Museum of Art."

"Yeah, not that." July had been to the museum two decades ago on a school trip when his family lived briefly in the Bronx. "What is *this* place?" July waved a hand at the deserted room and the empty hall beyond."

Pat shrugged. "It's still the museum. A version of it, anyway."

If there was no getting a straight answer, he'd try the long way around. "So, you got a thing for art?"

Pat scanned the classics before him. "I guess I do. Art is such a powerful way to portray life."

The painting directly in front of Pat was from the Dutch Masters series according to a sign on the wall. It depicted a boat struggling through a storm-tossed sea, masts tilting dangerously toward the waves, sails flapping in the erratic winds. The painter had captured the angry sea so well that July could almost taste the salt spray of the gray waves and feel the water-laden blasts of wind as the boat listed crazily, traversing the edge of doom.

The painting was uncomfortably fierce, depressingly real. The sailors in the grip of that storm would be fighting a despair and fear so huge that it could drown them as surely as the ocean. The artist hadn't depicted their certain doom, but if the boat foundered and sank, as it seemed it surely would, their suffering wouldn't end there. Even with no hope of survival, instinct would force them to fight on to exhaustion, until the ocean finally beat them to death, shoving a watery fist down their throats.

July turned away from the scene and scanned some of the other works, trying to shake the emotions stirred by the painting.

"Life can feel like that kind of struggle sometimes, can't it?" Pat asked, still looking at the foundering boat.

"I wouldn't know," July lied. "For some people I guess."

Pat turned to him. "I think for you too."

This dream-world was disturbing enough without it deteriorating into psychoanalysis. He stood, angry that Pat was right. "You don't know the first thing about my life."

Pat showed not the slightest remorse. He looked like a parent, patient with a wayward child.

July couldn't care less about Pat's philosophies on either art or life right now, and certainly not the man's opinions on *his* life. He looked around for the sleeping bags. The last time he had been in this strange world, he'd gone to sleep here and woken up in his own reality. Even if he was unconscious at his campsite, maybe he could dream that he slept and when he regained consciousness, things would be normal again. And at least he wouldn't have to deal with Pat's bullshit in the meantime.

He walked to the archway leading out of the gallery.

"I want to help you prepare for what's coming." Pat said.

July turned. "Fine. Give me some answers then. What's coming? Who are you? Is anything here real?"

"Your physical body is still in your own world, but everything here is, in its own way, as real as your life there. Something difficult is coming. It's why I want to talk to you about your life. Your struggles. Things from your past."

"Yeah, right." He shouldn't have bothered asking. No matter how real this felt, it was nothing more than a product of his head injury and his subconscious. All he was getting was dream-shit rhetoric. And he didn't talk about his past with anyone. Not even himself. July walked through the archway.

Pat's voice followed him. "Running away won't help, July. You ought to know that by now."

He didn't look back.

Much as he wanted to deny this place, July couldn't help entering the galleries. He wandered past works from ancient sculptures to modern paintings. He studied pieces he vaguely recognized like the man in a bowler with his face covered by an apple, learning that the painting was named "Son of Man." He walked around a Greek statue of Aphrodite, examining it in intricate detail. He went into rooms with not a single work of art that he recognized and wondered how his imagination could conjure so many images down to the smallest detail on any given canvas or sculpture. He wondered at it long enough that he stopped going into the galleries.

At Coit Tower, the camp had been near the gift shop. It was as good a place to look as any. If he didn't find the sleeping bags, maybe he'd go outside. On the heels of that thought he remembered the coyote from the last dream. Maybe he'd better stay inside. Things might be stranger out there than they were in here.

July followed the exit signs to the stairs leading down to the Great Hall and the front doors. At the top of the stairs he heard the click of heels on the polished floor and turned to see a woman following him.

"July, wait," she said.

Her dark hair was bobbed at her shoulders, like Mia used to wear hers, but instead of brown eyes and a soft, round face, this woman had eyes as green and piercing as a cat's. In profile, her face was all shadows and angles created by high cheekbones and narrow jaw.

He paused at the top step.

"It's good to see you again," she said, catching up.

He looked hard at those emerald eyes. "Yeah, you too." He wasn't sure if he meant it. Last time Patty had been petulant and moody. Maybe it was just the manicured look—styled hair, dress pants, and sweater—that made her seem more mature, more stable. But what he saw in the green depths still showed need and uncertainty. So like Mia.

They went down the stairs side by side. The staircase was wide enough for five people, yet she walked close to him, her shoulder brushing his. Her flat heels clacked lightly on the stone, lighter than his heavy tread.

"So do you believe yet that you're not dead?"

"Yeah." He smiled. "But I don't believe I'm not dreaming."

"You're not." She smiled back and it transformed her. Her similarities to Mia became suddenly more pronounced and a shard of longing stabbed him in the side, shrapnel left over from the final battle and Mia's subsequent moving out. He'd heard through a friend that Mia had met some rich guy from Big Sur and moved up there. Maybe money would solve her issues. What he'd been able to give her certainly hadn't.

They reached the bottom of the stairs. The Great Hall of the museum stretched before them, all neo-classical columns and arches. A circle of white marble, squat and obstructive in the otherwise open space, defined the information desk. The gift shop lay on his left. True to his instincts, he saw a smattering of colored nylon bags in front of and within the gift shop. With Patty following him, though, his plan to try and sleep himself back to consciousness and his own reality seemed unlikely.

"Why are you so like her?" he asked, as they walked toward the gift shop. He didn't know why he kept asking his dream characters questions that he could probably answer better himself.

"I'm not like her, she's like me."

"What?" July stopped and turned to Patty.

"She's like me. I'm the original."

"You're the original Mia?"

"No. I'm the original."

"Okay, what's your name then?"

"You can call me Mia if you want to."

He didn't want to. "Patty's fine."

A momentary flash of hurt tightened her eyes and vanished just as quickly. Reaching up, she stroked down the side of his neck and rested her hand on his chest. Her touch on his body felt good and he remembered, as clearly as if it had really happened, falling asleep with his arm around her—around another version of her anyway.

Her green eyes entreated him to accept her, to want her. The expression was so very Mia that it was like seeing Mia change her mind about him. Like she wanted him back. Except this wasn't her. He laid his hand over Patty's, holding it against his heart a moment longer, then gently removed her hand from his chest.

She gasped, looking over his shoulder instead of at his face. He opened his mouth to give her an 'it's not you, it's me' speech.

"Please, don't," she said.

He realized she wasn't speaking to him. July turned partway around to see who she was talking to when a large hand shoved his shoulder, knocking him sideways and causing him to stumble. Patty stepped back, anxiety tightening the lean lines of her body.

The owner of the large hand roared at him, "Why did you come back?"

Unlike Pat and Patty, Bill was unchanged. He had the same stocky build, the same long, dark hair and mustache. Even the clothes were the same: an oiled duster worn over a dirty T-shirt and jeans. "I told you to go home." Bill shoved him again, knocking July into the information stand.

Last time, the man's intense eyes had troubled July. This time Bill looked more insane than intense. Angry didn't work on the insane. July suppressed the urge to fight back and tried for a rational tone. "I don't want to be here. I don't even know how I get here."

"You have to stay vigilant!" the man exploded, volcanically angry. "Don't get in accidents! Don't pass out!" Bill paced away in frustration, muttering to himself. He paced back again. "Get away before it starts and don't *ever* come back."

"Before what starts?" July said calmly, thinking it best to keep him talking.

"Before they send you back!" Bill poked him hard in the

chest with one large finger, emphasizing it every time he said it. "Back. Back."

July had had enough. He slapped the man's hand away before the last poke, and struck Bill on both shoulders with the heels of his hands, shoving him. He turned sideways to the desk, giving himself some fighting room.

It might have been the wrong tactic. Bill's eyes went wide with rage. He launched for July's throat.

Patty ran. Maybe for help.

Maybe not.

July braced to dodge and counter, but Bill's size belied his quickness. He got his hands on July and his weight carried them both to the floor, slamming July's bad shoulder and head onto the granite.

Bill's fingers pressed at July's throat and neck. One thumb squeezed the sensitive flesh over his carotid artery and the other searched for his windpipe as July bucked and thrashed, trying to pull Bill's hands away. Bill's thumb inched toward his windpipe. His hands applied a crushing pressure. July's world started to dim.

Bill's strength and July's cast kept July from breaking the man's grip. He knew if he didn't abandon his instinct to protect his throat he was going to die. He let go of Bill's wrists, allowing the man to squeeze with all his strength, and went for Bill's eyes with his good hand. With his casted arm, he punched at the chin, the Adam's apple and the nose. He tried for the groin with one knee.

The cast connected with Bill's nose and blood gushed over July's hand. Bill pushed away and stood, hand to his nose. One eye watered and blinked. July curled into a ball, gasping.

There was a patter of heels clicking rapidly on the stairs and a more measured tread behind. From the corner of his vision he could see Patty leading Pat down the steps. The world tilted and hazed. July lay helpless on the floor while air returned to his lungs, and blood to his brain.

"Bill," Pat said. His calm, reasonable tone floated through the Great Hall. "Why don't we all sit down and talk about this?" Pat's voice seemed to have an effect on Bill. Enough, at least, that he didn't come after July again.

Bill spoke without looking up. "Are you still going to do it?" he asked Pat.

"You know we don't have a choice." Pat had reached the bottom of the stairs. "Let's sit down and talk," he said again. "I'll tell him as much as I can."

"If I kill him, he won't have to go."

Patty had stopped at the bottom of the stairs, keeping to a safe distance, but Pat continued to approach slowly. July thought he could stand now but he stayed where he was. If he got to his feet, it would probably just incite the crazy fucker to attack again.

"You don't want to kill him," Pat said. "Besides, he deserves this chance."

Bill studied July like a bug, then walked past him. He skirted the information desk until he came to the opening at the back. July heard paper clips, pens and other small items clatter across the desk and floor as Bill tipped the desk supplies out of drawers and containers.

He returned with a black Magic Marker in one hand. Blood still ran from one nostril, down his face and neck, staining the duster and soaking into his T-shirt. Bill grabbed July's cast, smudging blotches of red blood into the pink fiberglass. July tensed to defend himself. Pat watched carefully, but said nothing.

Bill focused only on July's arm. "You need a reminder," he growled. He scrawled on the cast in large, thick letters. When he finished, he let July's arm drop. July read the message upside-down.

Don't come back.

Bill stood over him, calmer now and seemingly satisfied.

"I won't kill him," he said, looking to Pat, "but I'll betcha' I can send him home again."

"No!" Pat said, but it was too late.

A large boot swung into the field of July's vision. The world went black.

Chapter 7

Dirt caked July's lips. His campfire still burned, though not as high. He gauged that he might have been unconscious for ten or twenty minutes. A long time as far as being unconscious went.

His face hurt like hell on the right side where he had fallen against a fist-sized rock. The dream image of the large boot connecting with his jaw, just there, came back vividly as he rolled onto his side and then into a cross-legged sit. The front of his neck was tender. When he'd come to, his sling had been tight across his neck, his left elbow propped up in the air with his fist in the dirt—like a grasshopper's hind leg—splinted into the odd position by the cast and the sling. Feeling around the base of his throat, he thought there would be bruises by tomorrow. He remembered Bill's hands pressing there, squeezing air and life out of him, and had to remind himself it hadn't been real. Maybe the dreams of the unconscious were more vivid than the dreams of the sleeping.

His thoughts drifted, as hard to catch as the smoke of his campfire. Slowly the world of his unconsciousness faded and the night around him became more solid. He knew he was outside Alpine, California and, after a panicky moment, was able to reconstruct the date, September twenty-first. He'd miss his appointment with Dr. Malhotra tomorrow. The one that would have determined if the blood clot was reabsorbing or if they needed to drill a burr-hole in his skull to suction it out.

July cataloged the scarier what-ifs of his head injury. What if new bleeding had started? What if the blood clot had done some kind of permanent damage? What if he passed out and never woke up or passed out while driving? In the end, there was nothing he could do about any of it tonight.

He doused the fire with a water bottle, took off his boots and jeans, and slid into the sleeping bag, using his wadded-up jacket as a pillow. Before lying down, he slipped the sling over his head. It was more comfortable to sleep without it and seemed to do no harm as long as he stayed on his back. He tossed the sling to the side and twisted his casted arm to grab the sleeping bag zipper. There were dark marks at the outer edge of the cast. His stomach lurched as he rotated his arm to see better by the light of the full moon. Thick, dark letters looked back at him. He read them upside-down.

Don't come back.

Chapter 8

July stared at the words, trying desperately for some rational explanation. Perhaps he hadn't been unconscious but had been in some altered state, walking around delirious. Maybe he'd written those words himself. He looked for a black marker on the ground, knowing there wouldn't be one.

He dropped his head back onto his makeshift pillow and stared up through the pine branches at the stars. Fear teased his back, making the muscles pull and twitch as if ants were climbing up his backbone. Rubbing against the hard ground, he tried to dispel the sensation.

He lay awake late into the night trying for any explanation except the one he was avoiding. In the end, no matter how much he wanted to deny it, his cast confirmed what his gut had known from the start. That other world and the people in it were real.

July slept fitfully and woke up tired. There was no way to

confront the events of the previous night, so there was little to do except get up, brush his teeth, make breakfast, and pack the truck. Every time he caught sight of the lettering on his cast it was a constant and uncomfortable reminder of things he didn't understand.

He crossed the Arizona border and passed through Yuma just after ten o'clock. When he stopped for lunch in Casa Grande, a bank signboard flashed an announcement of the time and the temperature, alternating with an upcoming local rodeo they sponsored. 103-degrees Fahrenheit. He took I-17 north out of town, looking forward to the higher altitude and starting to feel solid about his decision to try Flagstaff for a while. There was nothing good about losing his house but at least he had a goal, and being on the road was nothing new for him.

It was mid-afternoon when he entered Phoenix. Traffic on the interstate was already heavy or, more likely, traffic was probably never light. A headache was coming on and he worried it might be an indicator he'd pass out again. He didn't want to think about what would happen if he passed out while driving on the interstate. He saw a sign for Lincoln Hospital, and took the exit.

July checked himself into the ER using the insurance information that his lawyer told him to use for the Mercy Hospital bills, and supplying his old address in San Diego. The emergency room doctor who saw him an hour and a half later was a woman with the healthy-anorexic look of a marathon runner. She was deeply tanned and lined from the Arizona sun, maybe in her early forties, give or take a decade for fitness or sun exposure. He told her about the accident and about passing out the night before.

"Well, for starters we need an updated CAT scan. Let's get

that and some lab work and go from there." She snapped the metal chart closed and set it on the rolling bed table. She examined his neck and pressed on the bruising at his throat and jaw. "Let me have a look at your arm." Removing his sling, she took the dirty cast in her hand, rolling his arm this way and that. She paused at the scrawled warning and bloody fingerprints but said only, "We'll get an x-ray of your wrist and clavicle while we're at it."

A chatty young woman showed up from the lab and drew his blood, after which an aide wheeled him to radiology. She left him in a waiting room full of patients who looked like so many dried prunes fallen from their trees. It seemed that ER took precedence and his name was called almost as soon as the aide left. Thirty minutes later an orderly rolled him back to the ER.

The doctor returned and studied the digital pictures on a viewer mounted on the wall while she spoke. "We don't have your previous images to compare to, but I did get the reports faxed over." Pulling a pen out of her breast pocket she pointed to a blob filling the first square of many that all looked like Rorschach tests to July.

"Your subdural hematoma is here. As you can see, the blood clot is still present."

He tried to make out what she pointed to and, with some imagination, thought he saw a smaller blob within the larger one. Tucking her pen back into her pocket she found a pair of calipers in a jar on a counter and measured the blob, then consulted the chart again.

"It's about three millimeters larger than it was before. Have you had any additional trauma since your accident?"

"Just the fall last night." He didn't mention the impact with the floor of the museum, the strangulation, or the boot to the jaw.

"I think we need to admit you and get a neuro consult for surgery. The pressure that clot is creating is probably what caused your syncopal episode last night, and I don't like the fact that it's gotten larger, even if it's only by a little. I'll write up the admission papers and see who's on call for neurosurgery today." She turned to leave.

"No," July said, stopping her. "I'm on my way to Flagstaff. I'll get it done there."

"You know that you can't drive yourself." Her tone was absolute.

Perhaps he shouldn't put this off, but he'd had too much pressure from too many quarters lately. He wanted a few hours to think about this.

"I have friends in Flagstaff who can come down and get me."

He'd never been one to lie easily or well, and hoped the falsehood didn't show in his face.

"Alright. As long as you don't get behind the wheel until you're seen. If your friends can't come right away, there are hotels and restaurants nearby. You could take a cab to one to wait for them. The receptionist can give you a list."

"Sure. That sounds like a good idea."

"You understand I still recommend admitting you to the hospital for observation and an immediate consult with a neurosurgeon?"

He nodded. "I'll arrange it as soon as I get to Flagstaff."

She closed the CT films and pulled up his other x-rays. He saw nothing on his wrist x-ray except bones, but his clavicle sported an ugly fracture now spanned by a metal strut held in place by four screws running deep into the bone.

"It looks like both of these are healing well," she said. "I think you can go without the sling as long as you don't use that arm for lifting. Make sure you continue with your physical therapy. We'll leave that cast on your wrist for another week or so. When you know where your head surgery's going to be, you can call medical records here and they'll send my notes to your doctor in Flagstaff."

He signed a release at the front desk allowing his records to be shared then went through the charade of asking the receptionist for the phone number of a cab company. Out in the parking lot, he started his truck. Flagstaff was only about two and a half hours north. He could make it that far. He was pretty sure he could, anyway.

July used his credit card to fill the gas tank and found his way back to I-17 North. He pulled onto the ramp and saw a dreadlocked woman standing on the shoulder holding her thumb out. She wore a patchwork skirt, a faded sleeveless top, and sandals. An old, external frame pack indicated she was headed out of town, and a long, black bundle hung over the backpack from one shoulder to the opposite hip.

The woman was jumping up and down, grinning and waving at each driver, leaning down to peer in the passenger windows as they passed. Her small breasts bounced with her antics, and the bundle strap that crossed her chest emphasized the fact that she was braless. He wondered if she knew the effect it produced or if she was just naive. Either way, someone like her was a sure bet to get picked up by the wrong sort of person.

The bright eyes and wide grin met him as he passed her, though she had to bounce on tip-toe to stay on the shoulder and be level with his truck window. He pulled over just in front of her. She ran to the door and pulled it open. The door protested with a loud creak and a pop.

"I'm only going as far as Flagstaff," he said.

"Great, as long as I get out of Phoenix." She lifted the strap over her head and tossed the long bundle into the back seat. When she turned to shrug out of the backpack and heave it into the truck bed, July saw that her top was backless, tied only at the neck and mid-back with thin strings.

She appeared in the door again, and July tipped his head toward the bundle in the back seat. "Mind if I ask what's in that?" It was made of soft fabric, about the length of a rifle case.

"My fire-dance stuff."

He didn't know what that meant, but as long as it wasn't a rifle he didn't much care. "Can I ask a favor?" he asked. She paused, hands on the door frame, one foot on the sideboard. "Would you mind driving? I'd appreciate a break."

She eyed him, weighing the offer, probably analyzing it for some way he could use the arrangement to do her harm. Her dark blonde dreads jutted at all angles from her head, before the weight of the long coils pulled them downward toward her shoulders. It made her look somehow native to Arizona, like she was another variety of the cacti here. Her eyes were an odd shade of blue-green, almost turquoise, and he found himself fascinated by them while he waited for her answer.

"Sure," she said, and dropped back out the door.

She walked around the front of the truck and he slid over. She was tall enough that she didn't bother to adjust the seat. With a glance at the shift pattern, she eased the truck back into traffic and merged competently onto the interstate.

"My name's July," he said to be friendly, though she didn't

look the least bit concerned at being in a truck with a stranger. He waited for the inevitable question about his name.

"Hi, July." She turned to him with a wide smile. "I'm Valerian."

He returned her courtesy of not asking if he had been born in July by not asking if she made people go to sleep or drove cats crazy, though that was everything he knew about the herb that was her namesake. "Where are you headed?" he asked.

"Colorado. I'm going to perform in the ski areas over the winter."

"Oh. Which ones?"

"Whichever. I think there are like a dozen of them. I thought I'd start in Vail, but I'll bet all of them allow street performers."

July wasn't the person to judge poorly defined life plans. When he'd left home as a boy, he'd thrown the few tools he owned into his first truck, not caring where he was headed as long as he left everything he knew in the rear-view mirror. His current situation wasn't much different.

"Are you from Phoenix?" he asked.

"Not hardly. I grew up on a wheat farm in Kansas."

He leaned back against the door and looked at her profile as she drove. Under the dreads and retro-hippy clothes she did look like a farm-girl. There was a healthy, outdoorsy fullness to her face, a 'hey-neighbor' quality to her grin. He pictured her minus the dreads, riding in a tractor with her father, or in the 4-H wagon next to a goat in the town's Fourth of July parade. It fit.

"Where are you from?" she asked.

"A little bit of everywhere. Dad was a long-haul trucker for about a dozen different companies."

As always, suppressing thoughts of the earliest part of his life in New Mexico somehow brought them on more strongly, and he spent a moment shoving them back into their hiding places.

"So what's fire-dancing?" he asked, hoping to distract him from himself.

"You've never seen it?" She looked at him with a questioning smile.

"Not that I know of."

"Well, pretty much it's dancing with fire. Some people just do fire-twirling, but dance is integral to it in a lot of cultures. It really brings it to another level."

"How'd you learn it?"

"My boyfriend here. Ex-boyfriend. He's been doing it for years, but when he wanted to pimp me out to do erotic fire-dance shows I told him to screw himself and I split." Her smile was gone.

"Good for you."

"Thanks."

The silence between them grew large, crowding the cab of the truck, so July shared with her that he'd been through a breakup recently too. He told her he'd just moved from San Diego, and she said she'd never been there. He talked about the beaches in winter and wishing he'd bought a boat and other things more private than he would have guessed he'd share with a stranger. He quit talking when his headache started getting worse.

"I'm going to try and catch a few minutes of shut-eye if you don't mind." He closed his eyes and then opened one. "Be sure to stop in Flagstaff, okay?"

She grinned. "I promise."

July leaned back against the door jamb. Within minutes he felt himself drifting.

He woke again when Valerian drove over a rough patch of road under construction. They were close to Flagstaff and the day was transitioning from late afternoon to early evening. He rubbed his eyes and took a drink of water to repair the dry tongue that probably meant he'd been sleeping with his mouth open.

"Do you know Flagstaff at all?" he asked.

"Sure. We used to come up here from Phoenix to ski and hike and stuff."

"Is there a good place to camp?"

"There's National Forest on the north side of town. I know a road with some good camping spots."

"Great. Anywhere in particular you'd like me to drop you off in town?"

She turned to look at him. "I wasn't really planning on hitchhiking in the dark."

"Oh. Right."

"If it's okay to camp with you, I can hitch from there in the morning."

"Uh, sure, if you want." Unless that really was a rifle in that case, she was altogether too trusting to be hitchhiking.

They stopped at a grocery store and she insisted on buying their food: tortillas, beans, cheese, and instant oatmeal. When they came back out to the truck she got behind the wheel without asking. His headache felt better after sleeping but he was grateful she was still willing to drive. When they passed an RV park, he had her pull in so he could fill the five-gallon water jug he'd brought along before they drove out the north side of town.

A few miles later, Valerian slowed and scanned the right side of the road. Twilight was muting the details of the landscape but she turned off on a dirt road marked only with a number on a brown forest service road marker.

"I'm pretty sure this is it," she said. A hundred feet later they came to a signboard listing trails and indicating that the road went on for some miles. "Yep. This is it."

They agreed on a flat area less than half a mile down the road. The site was primitive—no more than a trampled clearing and a ring of blackened stones filled with old campfire ash. She pulled off and, working together, they had the tent set up and a fire going before full dark.

Valerian looked to be utterly comfortable sitting in the dirt, eating her burrito from the frying pan they'd used to warm the beans and cheese. Mia would have wanted chairs and a picnic table with plates and utensils. Hell, she wouldn't have stayed here even with all that, she would have wanted a hotel and a restaurant. Good thing he was traveling with Valerian instead; he couldn't have afforded either one. He'd taken out most of his remaining cash already in a single withdrawal from an ATM. Thinking of it reminded him he needed to stop somewhere tomorrow and take out the rest before his account could be frozen.

Valerian finished her burrito, wiped out the pan with some toilet paper torn off a roll in her pack, and put the pan back in its box. "So, you ready to learn about fire dancing?" she asked.

"Sure," he said, glad to be distracted from thoughts about his financial situation.

She opened the long, black bag and pulled out a variety of items, explaining the chains and staves of varying lengths as she laid them out. "I'm not going to work too long. The wicking is kind of expensive and I don't have much left."

He wondered what her parents back on the farm thought of their daughter's career ambitions. "You don't have to do this for me, you know."

"Oh, I know. It's all good. I need to practice at least a couple of times a week anyway. More, if I'm working on a new routine."

She had pulled on a wool sweater while they set up camp but took it off now and stood barefoot in her skirt and brief top. Her nipples pushed at the thin fabric, stiffening at the touch of the cool breeze of mountain air. She started with the tools she called poi: wooden handles with forearm-length chains and balls of wicking at the ends. Taking a can of fuel from her backpack, she soaked the wicks and touched them to the campfire. They burst into yellow flame. July felt more intense heat emanating from the small, burning balls than he did from the campfire.

Valerian stepped back. With a quick rotation of her wrists she set the chains spinning. The fist-sized fireballs at the ends blurred into solid patterns of flame drawn against the black night. She changed the movement of her wrists subtly and the balls described fiery circles, figure-eights, and swirls; burning their images on July's retinas. As she twirled the poi, she began to sing with a clear, tonal voice, in a musical language full of vowels; Polynesian perhaps, or Hawaiian. Then she began to move to the rhythm. The fire twirled dangerously behind her back and over her head in increasingly complex patterns. Her body undulated to her song. She moved with serpentine grace, spinning while she twisted and arced in curling shapes and deep backbends. An unwanted image of what erotic fire dancing might entail flashed in his mind.

Her routine lasted nearly ten minutes. When she stopped and blew out the flames, she sported a sheen of sweat on her face and chest. He applauded the performance and she plopped down next to him.

"That was great," he said. "How long did it take you to learn that?"

"I worked at it every day for about three years and most days this past year. All except the days Steve and I were fighting." She reached forward to her sweater lying on the ground and the lower half of her brief top billowed away from her, exposing her belly and showing the expanse of skin on her side and back as she stretched. It hinted at showing more. July turned his head and stared at the fire.

She pulled her sweater over her head. "How's your headache doing?"

"Better."

"Did you get in a fight?" She wrapped her arms around her knees and pointed with one finger to his cast.

He told her about being hit by the car, and hoped she would assume the new bruises on his neck and jaw were from the same accident.

"Oh, wow. You're lucky to be alive."

"Yeah. That's what they say. The last thing I remember is the car coming at me. I don't remember anything else until I came to a couple of days later." That wasn't strictly true, of course, now that he knew Coit Tower hadn't been a dream.

"So were you a pain in the ass at the hospital?"

He smiled uncertainly at her question. "Why do you ask?"

She reached over and turned his cast so the ominous warning showed. It still rocked him every time he saw the writing. He tried not to look flustered.

"Some joker wrote that on there."

She rested one cheek on her knees. "So why Flagstaff?"

He shrugged, glad for the change of subject. "I don't know. I've never been here but I've always heard it was nice. My house just got foreclosed on, so I'm not tied to San Diego anymore." It felt good to tell someone about his house.

"Sorry," she said. "That must suck. I didn't lose a home or anything but it is kind-of weird just leaving everything behind. I left Phoenix with less stuff and less of a plan than I really meant to. But, you know, it's not all bad. Kind of freeing really." She pulled a long twig out of the fire and poked the burning end into the dirt, smothering the flame. "I've got myself and that's all I really need. It's good to experience that once in a while. You know, remind yourself of who you are without all your stuff."

He hoped it was a good thing, considering he was in the same boat.

"So what are you going to do here?" she asked.

"Look for a job when I get released for work. Hopefully they've got enough economy to have some construction work. If not, well, then I'll have seen Flagstaff and I'll move on."

"You ought to come to Colorado. The ski towns have tons of money and I'll bet they're always building new stuff."

He heard the hope in her voice that someone she trusted would travel the rest of the way with her. Colorado sounded tempting. "Thanks, but I need to stay here for a bit. I have to see a doctor about my headaches and I'm not really supposed to be driving right now."

"Oh. Well, I like driving, so the offer's open if you want." She stood. "I'm going to go to bed now. It's been a long day."

July remembered the emotional fallout he'd gone through the day Mia had moved out. It had been exhausting. He offered Valerian the tent. She insisted he take it. He offered to share it, trying not to sound creepy. She agreed without hesitation.

She untied her sleeping bag from the bottom of her backpack and crawled into the tent with it. He gave her the privacy to get settled and saw to putting the rest of the food up and extinguishing the fire. When he climbed in the tent, she was already in her bag, rolled away from him. He saw her skirt and top lying at the foot of her bag. With a mental shrug, he removed his boots and jeans. She stayed turned to the tent wall, though he was pretty sure she wasn't asleep.

He zipped up his bag and lay on his back. She rolled over to face him. The large moon lit the tent enough for him to see her well; head pillowed on her sweater, dreads contained in something that looked like a big, felt tube. Her face was less than two feet from his and her voice was clear, though she spoke quietly. "Do you have some Native American in you? Your bone structure looks like it, but the green eyes don't fit."

"Some. I'm not entirely sure what mom was. Apache I think, or so my dad said, and maybe some new Hispanic and old Spanish, with a bit of white settler thrown in here and there. The eyes are Italian. Dad's definitely Italian, but who knows what else. Pretty much, I'm an all-American mutt."

"Is your last name Italian?"

"Yeah. It's Davish," he told her, adding, "It probably used to be Davi or something until dad's family arrived at Ellis Island." He shifted onto his right side. "Okay, so what's your last name?"

"Smith." She sounded either disgusted or embarrassed. "Can you believe it? Dad swears we're Swedish or Norwegian somewhere way back, but he can't prove it."

"Don't worry, you're anything but ordinary, no matter what your last name is." He paused into the silence that followed and then had to ask, "So what's your first name? I mean, it's hard to imagine Mr. and Mrs. Smith of the Kansas wheat-farming Smiths naming their daughter Valerian."

She chuckled. "It's Valerie. Valerie Smith of Oxford, Kansas, pleased to meet you."

"July Davish. Nowheresville, New Mexico." Even all these years and miles away he had trouble invoking the place by name. "Glad to make your acquaintance, Ms. Smith."

She chuckled again. "Nowheresville, eh?"

"Might as well be. Pretty much a wide spot in the road near the border with West Texas." He shifted his hip off a small rock or tree root. "So why'd you start going by Valerian?"

"Steve suggested it for the shows. Introducing Valerie Smith didn't have quite the oomph he was looking for, I guess. I've been calling myself that for so long that I think of myself that way most of the time."

There was another silence. The quiet between them was as comfortable as the conversation.

"Goodnight, Valerie Valerian Smith. Sleep well."

"Goodnight, July Davish of Nowheresville, New Mexico."

Chapter 9

Breakfast was a quiet affair. Valerian seemed preoccupied with thoughts of Colorado, only speaking occasionally to say that the weather looked good for traveling or that she hoped to make it there in one day. July hated the idea of her hitchhiking, but he had no right to tell her so, and so he said little about anything at all. They broke down the camp in silence, packed the truck, and were at the highway by seven-thirty.

"Are you sure this is okay?" he said when he pulled over. "I can take you back into town if you want, to I-40, so you'd be on the interstate."

"No. This is better. Going north from here is more direct to where I'm headed." Her hand was on the door latch but she didn't open it. "You know, I'm kind-of going to worry about you getting your head drilled open. If I gave you my phone number do you think you could call me when you get it done? Or text me at least?"

"Sure. Someday when I have a phone again."

"No cell phone?"

He shook his head. "It got shut off last month."

"Geez, you *are* a mess."

"Yup."

She got out and pulled her long bag and backpack from the truck bed. Appearing in the open passenger door again, she took a quick look around to make sure she wasn't leaving anything, then gave him a radiant smile.

She really did have amazing eyes.

He leaned his forearms on the wheel, wishing she'd change her mind and get back in the truck. "You sure Flagstaff isn't a good place for a fire dancer?"

"Too close to Phoenix."

"Ah." He nodded. "You know, I can't believe it's me you're worried about when you're getting ready to hitchhike alone across two hundred and fifty miles of desert. You take care, Val. Don't be afraid to turn down a ride if it feels wrong."

"Yes, dad." She grinned again and then she closed the door with a loud clunk.

She gave him a big goodbye wave and started down the shoulder of the highway, turning to walk backward with her thumb out when a car topped the rise and headed her way.

The thin, harem-style pants she wore today were tie-dyed in vibrant colors of turquoise, purple and blue, and her T-shirt, washed and worn to pale pink, was snug against her small breasts. The pull of her backpack and the strap of the black bag running across her chest made it evident, again, that she still wore no bra beneath the T-shirt. He wondered if she even owned one.

With her gaily colored clothes and blonde dreads, she was a strange and beautiful flower in the dry, Arizona landscape, impossible to miss. "See where she comes appareled like the spring…" The line from Pericles came to mind as July watched her walking backward down the shoulder.

She looked far too vulnerable and he didn't want to see who picked her up in case it left him more uneasy than he already felt. He left the truck idling anyway, watching to see if the car stopped for her. It passed her without slowing, rippling her pants with its speed. He continued to let the truck idle while four more cars passed. She grinned and waved at each one.

He couldn't take it anymore. Pulling onto the highway, he drove up beside her. He leaned across the bench seat and rolled down the passenger window. "How about a compromise? You come to Flagstaff with me and make sure I don't die before I get my operation. After I have my surgery, I'll drive you to Colorado."

"When do you think that will be?" She had to shout to be heard over the rumble of the truck's engine.

"It shouldn't be that long." Her expression spoke volumes of doubt. "No, seriously," he said, "my doctor in San Diego said it's a lot simpler than it sounds. I won't be able to work construction or anything for a while, but I could travel in maybe a week." He turned the engine off so they could talk at a normal volume. "Besides, what's your hurry? You do know that it's the off-season at the ski resorts, right? The couple of months between Labor Day and ski season is probably the deadest time of the whole year. This way, I'd have you to chauffer me around until my surgery, and in a few days you get a ride straight through to Vail with someone you already know. It sounds like a win-win to me."

When she paused, he realized how very much he wanted her to say yes. She weighed the options long enough that he tried to come up with more arguments for his case, but she answered him first.

"Deal," she said. "Scoot over."

She came around to his side and restarted the truck. When there was a sufficient break in the traffic, she made a U-turn back toward Flagstaff.

"So why don't you have a car, anyway?" he asked.

"Steve and I were trying to be green. We shared a car. His car. I sold mine a couple of years ago." She rolled her eyes. "With moving and everything, I won't have enough cash to get another car just yet. Student loans at seven percent since I graduated, and all."

Considering her current career plans, he'd assumed she was a drop-out. He felt guilty for the underestimation.

"Would your folks help?"

"Probably, but they got a lot of rain in June and July during first harvest, so I don't want to ask. I'll be okay on my own. I just need to get where I'm going and get set up. It's another reason I decided to go to the ski areas; small towns, easy to get around."

She was so different from Mia. Different from most women he'd known.

"What was your bachelor's in?"

"Applied math. Actually, it's a PhD. I was on a three-year accelerated program, Master's and PhD together. I graduated in June."

He turned and stared at her. "You have a PhD in applied mathematics and you're hitchhiking to Colorado to be a fire dancer? Come on."

She shrugged, and her mouth twisted into a tight, self-conscious smile. "I wanted some time off before I start job hunting, you know? I went straight through: high school to University of Kansas to ASU. I thought I'd take a little while for myself. Especially after the last month or so with Steve."

"Wow." He didn't know what else to say. Farm-girl, hippie fire dancer, and PhD in math. A woman who certainly didn't limit herself to one path. He reassessed her age. He'd guessed her at early twenties, but adjusted it now to mid- or late-twenties.

They reached the outskirts of town and the first traffic signal. Valerian slowed for the red light. "I guess the first order of business is to get your surgery arranged," she said. "Where do we start?"

"Find a neurosurgeon, I guess."

"Here," Valerian said, fishing in her pocket, "use my phone."

July wasn't exactly up on the latest smart-phones and she had to talk him through the search features. He found four clinics that fit the bill and called them all, but available appointments ranged from a week to three weeks out.

"I'm not sure this should wait a week," he said after the last call, fairly sure that it shouldn't.

"Is your headache that bad?"

"The headache comes and goes, but, well, I kind-of passed out night before last."

"You what?"

He told her the story—leaving out what had happened to him while he was unconscious.

Valerian parked at the next corner and took the phone from him. "Mind if I try?" She called again saying her friend had a head injury and had passed out recently. The second clinic had an opening for urgent cases later that afternoon.

There wasn't much to do while they waited, so they drove around learning the town and picked up some lunch at Taco Bell. July suggested eating in a local park, but when they got there, he had a bout of nausea and left his food mostly uneaten. He fished the booklet of Pericles out of his pack and tried to read while Valerian ate, but the words were blurry so he set it down in the grass and closed his eyes.

July woke to the sound of a phone ringing. The sight of blue sky and tree branches above him sent a jolt of panic through his muscles. For a moment he thought that he had gone back to the other world, until he remembered he was in a park in Flagstaff. Valerian was standing with her back to him, a finger plugging one ear, her phone held tightly to the other.

"I'm not ready to talk to you." She sounded upset. There was a pause. "I'm not even in Phoenix anymore. It's too late, Steve. I was serious when I said I was leaving." Another pause. "I haven't decided yet if that's where I'm going. When I'm ready to tell you, I will, but it really doesn't matter anyway. We're not together anymore. No, Steve. Please don't. Steve, please…"

Valerian lowered the phone and turned it off. Turning around, she blushed when she saw July watching her. She glanced at her watch and said, "We'd better get going. It's about time for your appointment."

As they walked back to the truck, a dark mood covered her like an ill-fitting cloak. Melancholy seemed so out of character for Valerian that he searched for a way to cheer her up.

"Well," he said, as she tried to turn the engine over. The starter whined without firing. She grunted in exasperation and tried again. "He may have tried to pimp you out, but it could be worse. He could have been your father, and you could've had an incestuous relationship, and he could have pretended to want to marry you off by holding a contest for men from all over the world to win your hand if they could answer a riddle. And then, when they didn't answer the riddle, which nobody could because it was rigged, they could have all been put to death."

She quit grinding the starter and looked at him. "What?"

He flapped the little booklet of Pericles that he was holding. "King Antiochus. He was doing it with his daughter. He didn't want anybody to find out so he found a way to kill all her suitors. Pericles figured it out, and now the king wants to kill him, so he's running for his life even though he's a king too. Or maybe he's a prince, I'm not sure. That's as far as I've gotten. I'm just saying, it could be worse. Pump the gas pedal three times, then try again."

She pumped the gas pedal, and the truck turned over. She smiled. "You're a nut."

July checked in at the doctor's office using the accident insurance information and his old address again. The receptionist was a large woman with orange-red hair. She was older and less gullible than the receptionist at the hospital.

"Do you still live in San Diego, Mr. Davish?"

"Yes." He tried to tell himself it was more truth than lie. The bank hadn't repossessed the house yet, and he certainly didn't live anywhere else.

She looked skeptical. "And you're planning to have surgery done here?"

"I have a friend here who's going to take care of me after the operation." He glanced at Valerian who smiled and waved at the woman.

July was relieved when the receptionist accepted the

explanation without further questions. At least no one seemed to have any issue with his accident insurance—like work comp, it was probably a more sure pay off than private insurance. He didn't offer up that his claim was currently unresolved. When the nurse called July's name, Valerian gave him an encouraging smile and a little farewell wave. July wondered if everyone in Kansas waved as much as she did.

Sitting alone in the exam room, he thought maybe he should have asked Valerian if she wanted to come back with him, since it looked like she was going to be a part of this whole process. It was foreign to July to have someone looking out for him, and he didn't know what the protocols were. Too late now. If he went back out and asked her, he'd probably miss the doctor and look like he was scared of his surgery rather than just trying to include her.

The door to the exam room suddenly opened and the doctor strode in. He shook hands with July, introduced himself as Dr. Weslyn and took a seat at the computer desk. The doctor's long, black fingers paged quickly through the records his nurse had obtained from Phoenix, which included the copies of Malhoutra's notes and the original radiology reports from Mercy Hospital.

Dr. Weslyn's exam was efficient and thorough, though July thought he looked too elegant to be a surgeon. He was tall and slender, with hazel eyes contrasting his dark skin. His suit jacket was impeccably tailored and his clothes were perfectly color-coordinated.

The doctor leaned close with the ophthalmoscope to examine July's eyes. "How have you been feeling since the night you passed out?" he asked, with their faces only inches apart. His purple-striped silk tie and plum-colored shirt brushed July's arm. The expensive suit made July wonder what his surgery was going to cost. And who would end up paying for it.

"Fine, really. Some headaches, a little nausea."

The doctor tapped July's knees, ankles, and wrists with a rubber hammer. "Well, I agree with the doctor you saw in Phoenix," Dr. Weslyn said, setting the hammer on the counter. "Based on the increase in the size of the hematoma and the syncopal episode you had the other night, I think we need to schedule you for surgery, but with what I see today, I don't think emergency surgery is indicated. I'll have Barbara come back in and we'll get you set up for later this week."

July asked the short list of questions he and Valerian had come up with and Dr. Weslyn confirmed what Malhoutra had said; the surgery was simpler than it sounded. A dime-sized hole would be drilled into the skull, a small incision made in the connective tissue covering the brain, and the clot would be suctioned out. Barring unexpected complications, the brain itself should never be exposed. The hole in his skull would be covered with a permanent metal plate, but the scalp would be sewn over this and his hair would grow back. A quick procedure, complications were rare, and recovery time relatively short.

"Friday at two o'clock," July said, stuffing the pre-op instructions and a little pamphlet on subdural hematomas into the visor as he and Valerian got back in the truck. He'd taken the pamphlet more for Valerian than for himself. He knew she was suspicious that he was oversimplifying the procedure to keep her from worrying. Despite the doctor's reassurances, July was more than a little worried about the procedure himself, though he wasn't about to say so to Valerian.

"How do you feel about staying at our campsite until Friday?" he asked.

"Sure. When you get out of the hospital we can get a motel room. That way you won't have to rent an apartment or whatever until you get back from Colorado. And I want you to promise to stay with me in Colorado until you're a hundred percent to drive back on your own."

He smiled. "Deal."

July had her stop at an ATM so he could withdraw the rest of his cash, then at the local KOA so they could shower. The blood work and CT he'd had in Phoenix were current enough that they didn't need to be repeated, so there was little to do before his surgery except wait. Valerian picked up a local paper to see if there were any festivals where she might be able to perform for a little extra money, but there was nothing until the weekend and it was only Tuesday. At a loss for anything else to do, they headed back to their campsite.

He was unloading the truck when July realized that Taco Bell may not have been the best choice for lunch. "You know the grocery leftovers are burrito stuff. That makes burritos for dinner last night, lunch today and again tonight. I have some canned food from home if you'd rather have...well, I'm not sure what I have."

He returned to the truck and rummaged in the back seat. Digging through a plastic bag, he called out each label. "Spaghetti-O's, stew, corned-beef hash, beef and vegetable soup…"

"What, no Spam?"

He looked back to see Valerian smiling. She was kneeling on the flattened tent, sorting tent poles. "I'm fine with burrito leftovers, but you have whatever you want."

She said something else, but all July heard was a buzzing whine. Her mouth continued to shape words, but the whining noise grew progressively louder, like an old fan belt being pushed to accelerate.

She stopped sorting the poles, and looked at him strangely. His knees buckled.

Chapter 10

"Oh, shit." Valerian said. She ran to July, trying to recall her first aid ABC's. "Oh shit, oh shit, oh shit."

She'd been admiring his backside while he fished around in the truck. When he turned around to talk to her about dinner he'd suddenly stared at her with the sort of puzzled look someone might get if they'd just unexpectedly been stabbed. He'd gone very pale, dropped to his knees, and toppled to his side, unconscious.

It was good that he was on his side, she thought. Or was an unconscious person supposed to be rolled onto their back? She couldn't remember. Placing one hand on his shoulder and one on his hip, she tried to decide whether or not she should move him.

"July!" She shook him. There was no response.

His body felt muscular and healthy under her hands, too strong for him to be unconscious like this. She could see the rise and fall of his chest but she placed her face near his, trying to feel his breath just to be sure. She tried for a pulse at his wrist and couldn't find one, but she guessed she was doing it wrong. Sliding one hand down the front of his shirt and over his heart, she was reassured by the strong, regular beat.

ABC's done, she ran for her phone, praying that she was in cell range. She wasn't sure she could drag July up into the truck without causing more injury.

"911, where is your emergency?"

"Oh, thank God," she blurted in relief at getting through. She gave the dispatcher the location and explained the situation. The dispatcher spoke in a calm and sure tone. He asked if there had been any bodily injury in the fall and she said she didn't think so. He talked her through rolling July onto his back to ensure a better airway. *So it was the back,* she chided herself.

Valerian kneeled at July's head and kept an eye on his airway. The dispatcher had her position July's arms and legs so that he could be rolled onto his side in case he vomited. She was unwilling to set the phone down even for a minute, so she awkwardly held the phone under her chin while she moved him. She knew his collarbone had been fractured on the same side as his broken wrist, so she lifted his uninjured right arm above his head and bent his left knee, ready to roll him to his good side. It felt strange moving his slack and unresisting body, but she took small comforts in his warm skin and steady respirations.

"Yes, I have him positioned." she answered the dispatcher. "Yes, he's still breathing."

July's right hand lay near her knee and she grasped it, more for her own reassurance than for his. Valerian resisted an urge to touch his face. She wanted to trace his high Native American cheekbones, to run a thumb across his long, dark lashes, to brush her fingers against his five o'clock shadow. She wanted to kiss him between his brows. She didn't do any of those things.

This man was so different from Steve. He was dark to Steve's blond, quiet to Steve's brashness, serious to Steve's flippancy. He had been a safe ride and a perfect gentleman to a woman hitchhiking alone. It hurt her in a deeply poignant way to see him unconscious and helpless. She squeezed his hand, willing him to wake up. A streak of red pulled her gaze higher on his arm.

His right forearm split open and began to bleed.

"Oh, my God," she whispered, still holding the phone to her ear. It was like watching one of those religious statues that spontaneously bled tears or that dripped red liquid from the hands and feet. She was certain that his arm hadn't been cut a moment ago.

Valerian stared at the wound, bleeding heavily now, too stunned for the moment to do anything to staunch the flow of blood. The dispatcher's voice brought her back to herself. "Yes," she said, in a whisper. "Yes, I'm still here."

Part Two

"This thing of darkness…"
Wm. Shakespeare, The Tempest

Chapter 11

July woke up face down in the dirt. Again.

The ground beneath his hands was a fine, warm sand, instead of the cool, earthy dirt at the campsite he shared with Valerian. He opened his eyes. The headache and nausea were gone. He rolled to one side and pushed up onto his knees.

A cliff wall loomed above him to his right and a narrow dirt road curved away on his left. Desert landscape stretched before him, broken by rocky spires and dry shrubs. The road and the fire-ring in front of him told him he wasn't far off the beaten path, but a smattering of trash littering the pullout was the only evidence of humanity—until he looked over his shoulder. There, along the base of the cliff, were scattered a few brightly colored sleeping bags.

Shit.

He sat back on the ground. His pink cast was still in place and the warning not to come back glared at him from the side.

Looking up the cliff, he was surprised to see pictographs

maybe fifty feet above his head, about halfway up the cliff. A narrow shelf ran just below them and above them curved a sharp overhang that must have protected the drawings from the centuries of weather and erosion.

He'd never seen pictographs so large. The human figures were bigger than life-sized. They were blocky and featureless, devoid of arms or legs, though one figure clearly held a snake dangling from the triangular shoulder. Next to the triangular people were an assortment of oddly proportioned animals, and far to the left side was a squat figure with stick arms and horns.

"Interesting, aren't they?"

July turned his head. A man stood behind him, Native American, somewhere on the continuum of elderly. A red-checked shirt covered his thin, nut-brown chest and baggy jeans emphasized his bowed legs, but his casual conversation—as if there hadn't been two days and a world between them since they last talked—was a dead giveaway.

"The Barrier Panel is older than the Fremont painting by at least fifteen-hundred years. And the Fremont painting," Pat indicated the solitary drawing on the left, "is nearly twelve hundred years old. That makes that big panel somewhere around twenty-seven hundred years old."

July turned back to the cliff. He couldn't care less about the history lesson. "Do you happen to remember that one of your buddies tried to kill me the last time I was here?"

"I thought you believed this was all a dream."

July proffered his cast, still looking at the cliff. "That changed when I woke up with this. As far as I can tell, there are three options: both my world and this one are real; I'm brain-damaged or comatose from the car accident and dreaming everything that's happening to me in both worlds; or that car killed me and both of these worlds are my own private hell."

July looked over his shoulder, trying to find some clue in Pat's face. A furtive breeze teased Pat's black hair, which hung straight and thin past his shoulders. The pores on the old man's bulbous nose were so large that July could see them from where he sat.

"What do your instincts tell you?"

His instincts told him that both worlds were real.

"I don't know, because you won't give me any information." He stood and walked to Pat. "Tell me then, *is* this hell?"

Rheumy brown eyes contemplated him. "No. Not in the way you mean, anyway."

"Not in the way I mean? Do you talk in circles just to piss me off?" Pat looked at him with such solemnity that July's anger lost some of its momentum.

"You don't have to be dead to be in hell, July."

"Whatever. Okay, let's say for now that both worlds are real. Is that psycho, Bill, here again?" July waved a hand at the landscape.

Pat nodded.

"So if that maniac manages to kill me this time, will I die in the real world too?"

"Yes. If you die here, you die there also."

"Then help me!" July raised both arms in frustration. "Why do I keep coming here? What the fuck *is* this place and who *are* you people?"

"This is an opportunity, July."

"An opportunity for what? To lose my marbles flipping back and forth between two realities?"

"A way for you to accept that where you came from is a

part of who you are."

"Fuck you and your psychobabble. I know who I am and where I came from. Better than you ever will. And I've dealt with it better than anyone else I know."

"Until lately."

Pat was right—his control had been slipping of late. The more the cards had stacked against him, the worse his responses had been. So maybe he was headed for some kind of supernova. Maybe he'd end up drinking his life away, or die a meth-head working for his uncle in Las Vegas. But he'd worked his whole life at avoiding those pitfalls. Whatever this weird-ass place was, it wasn't going to do more for him than he could do for himself.

"I don't want to be here, do you understand that? I don't want to be here! Tell me how to get the hell out of this place and I'll be happy." His control over his anger was as fragile as a snowflake in the sun. July felt violence building within him and turned his back on Pat.

"I had hoped to have more time," Pat said, "so you could prepare better for your journey, but Bill's aggression has changed that."

July turned back suddenly. "What journey? Bill told me you'd send me back. I thought he meant back to my own world, but he seemed pretty adamant that I shouldn't do it."

Pat shook his head. "Your only way out of here now is to keep moving forward."

"What?"

Pat was looking down the road, his expression sad.

"So, what, I can just walk out of here? Why didn't you tell me that before?"

"It isn't as easy as that. I wanted to help you to be ready, but there's no time for that now. You need to get started before

Bill finds you again. Once you start your journey, I don't believe he'll follow."

"So what's the part that isn't easy?"

Pat stood silent as the desert around them, his old eyes filled with sorrow. *Or was that pity?*

"Walk always to the west and always forward," Pat replied, nodding down the road. "That's very important. You mustn't ever backtrack. Not a single step backward."

"What happens if I do?"

"You'll be here forever."

He watched Pat for some sign that he was joking or exaggerating, but Pat looked deadly serious.

"Do I have to take some specific route?"

"No. Just always west and always forward."

"How far?"

Pat shrugged. "It depends."

"On what? Is there a trick to this?"

"No. No trick. But there will be obstacles."

It was starting to sound like some stupid reality show contest. July nearly laughed. He wished the explanation for all this insanity could be that simple. "Should I take supplies? Food, water, sleeping bag?" He gestured to the bags by the cliff.

"All you need is yourself."

July wanted nothing more than to get started, and yet he hesitated. "I just walk until I walk out of here and then I never come back?"

Pat said nothing.

"So what, this is the last time I'll see any of you?" The thought of walking off into this bizarre world without Pat disturbed him more than he would have guessed.

"You'll see me again." The old man stepped close and

patted him on the shoulder. He left his hand there a moment then gripped July's shoulder as if he didn't want to let go. The touch conveyed more genuine caring than July might ever have felt from anyone.

The dirt road next to the pictographs ran west. He left Pat without another word and started walking. The sooner he was out of here the better. To whatever degree this place was real—real as in some parallel world he'd landed in or just some reality his brain had latched on to, making him walk around like a schizophrenic writing on his own cast—if what Pat said was true, then this was his only way out of here. Besides, it felt good to be moving in this world. At least while he was walking he felt a sense of purpose.

The good feeling lasted about thirty minutes.

He'd been following the road for maybe a mile when it curved sharply to the south. He wasn't sure how precisely he needed to walk west, or even how well he could with no compass, but decided he'd better travel as straight a line as possible, just in case. Pat had been adamant about him not deviating.

Standing at the turn in the road, he surveyed the sand and rock ahead. It wasn't easy to step off into the wilderness beyond. He had thought, like Dorothy in Oz, the road would lead him all the way to his destination. He'd been naïve on more than just that front. When Pat told him to walk west, July had imagined a fairly brief trip. Pat sent him off without food or water and he'd figured that he would encounter some obstacles and move on, without ever needing to eat or drink or stop to piss. Home by dinner and all that.

He'd only been walking half an hour and he was already

thirsty and feeling the effects of the sun that had fallen from its midday perch to dance glittering and shimmering in his eyes. Walking into the unforgiving desert with nothing suddenly felt pretty stupid.

A State Parks marker stood at the corner of the road next to him. It was the first sign he'd seen; a strip of brown plastic on the shoulder that indicated he was in this world's version of Utah. It sported the numbers 22.4, which told him nothing except that there might be another road 22.4 miles behind him or ahead of him.

Standing here wasn't helping. July stepped off the road.

The sand was hard-packed and easier going than he'd feared, though the land had more vertical lifts and drops than he'd anticipated. He soon found himself scrambling over rocks, down into shallow ravines and back up again, keeping the sun always annoyingly in his eyes.

The colors here were vibrant; a dozen shades of red against the ochre sand, and an occasional startlingly green bush or tree along a dry watercourse. After a while his thirst diminished, though he knew it to be a temporary adaptation by his body. His lips were dry and his skin already felt too warm.

A couple of hours later, the thirst returned with a vengeance. July saw a patch of shade in his direct line of travel and resolved to take a short rest. His forearms sported a mottled reddish hue over his olive skin, and he was pretty sure his face was worse off than his arms. Reaching the shade of the boulder, he turned carefully in place and sat with his back against the rock. He experienced a moment of panic when he wondered if turning around to sit violated some rule, but nothing happened. "Screw it," he said to the vast, blue sky.

He twisted his left arm to look at the writing on his cast for another affirmation of all this craziness. The warning was still there, scrawled in black marker, with bloody smudges for emphasis. July sought for any explanation that would negate Pat and this journey and everything here, but he had nothing. Even if he'd written upside-down on his own cast it didn't explain the bloody fingerprints. After a few minutes, he got up and kept going. He may not accept life's curves gracefully, but he'd never been one to give up easily.

He walked on for maybe four hours when the land in front of him dropped off sharply. Looking ahead he saw the floor of a small wash not far down. He walked to the edge, confident that he would find an easy scramble down. It wasn't until his toes were a foot or so from the rough edge that he saw his mistake.

The rocky ground he stood upon dropped sheer for thirty or forty feet before cascading another fifty feet in a jagged, bulging cliff face. The wash lay at least a hundred feet below him. He'd misjudged badly. Now he stood inches from the edge, unable to backtrack according to the guidelines he'd been given. Looking to either side, he saw no way to skirt the canyon and still move forward.

He stood on the ridge for a few minutes unsure what to do. He guessed that this was his first obstacle. Pat had implied there would be a way through them, but with his rules of travel restricting him and the threat of being trapped here forever as punishment if he broke them, he saw no way out of his predicament. July sat, careful not to scoot any further forward, and stared into the bottom of the canyon.

Twilight began to erase the sandy floor below him and July still hadn't come up with a solution. He needed food and water and it was rapidly getting dark. If he held to the rules, he'd have to sleep at the edge of this maw. The obvious answer was to call bullshit on Pat and go forward or backward or sideways, or whatever the hell he felt like, until he woke up in his own reality again. Just to the east of him was a good place to sleep, soft sand sheltered by a jut of rock.

He didn't move.

"Okay, whatever," he said, making up his mind. If he slept where he was there wasn't really much chance he'd roll over the edge. He'd never rolled out of his bed after all, although his bed wasn't a hundred feet off the floor. He was grateful that his history of working at heights had long ago erased any trace of acrophobia in him.

July lay on his side, facing the canyon. He shifted twice before admitting he was as comfortable as he would get. He tried to swallow a little moisture into his raw throat and ignore his stomach growling like a predator. His mind paced restlessly back and forth, keeping him from sleep for a long while. He wouldn't die from one afternoon and night without food or water, not this time of year especially, but he sure as hell didn't want to go through this again tomorrow. What he expected more than anything was that he'd wake up at his campsite outside Flagstaff.

If he didn't, he'd deal with it in the morning.

Chapter 12

July woke frequently during the night, cold and uncomfortable, hunched into a ball to conserve what little warmth his body generated.

When morning finally came, the sun on his back eased the tightness that a night on the hard rock had written into his muscles. He sat up and rubbed his arms to generate a little warmth and circulation. Morning hadn't returned him to his own world and his obstacle lay gaping before him.

Ignoring his rising frustration, he tried think his way through the situation. When that failed he heaved small rocks into the canyon, along with a number of curses. "A little help here," he said loudly when he'd used up all the rocks in reach. No help came.

He couldn't fight or yell his way out of this, and he certainly wouldn't get anywhere by ignoring it. If he didn't eat or drink soon he'd be forced to start walking back, regardless of the consequences. He wondered if anyone would be there when he got back to the pictographs or if they'd all bugged out for some other location, leaving him alone in this strange not-Utah.

The sun lifted above the horizon and the morning grew warmer. His sleepless night, his forced immobility, and the silence of this empty country lulled him. His mind wandered.

He wondered how Valerian was coping, a world away in Flagstaff. His hunger and fatigue were ample evidence of how physically he existed in this world, but he knew that his real body must be lying unconscious at his campsite. He hoped the situation didn't frighten her, but she didn't seem like someone who frightened easily. Just his being out of work for a while had been enough to frighten Mia right out of his life. He remembered the day Mia had left him, the note he found on the table when he came home from job hunting.

Other girlfriends came to mind, one by one. July didn't want to review the litany of unsuccessful relationships and tried to shut the thoughts out, but the quiet and the space and his fatigue defeated his normal control over unwanted memories. Instead, the memories steadily gained clarity and detail. The images that came seemed less and less by choice.

He felt as if he was being forcefully dragged backward through all his past girlfriends, his mind hijacked. The vista before him vanished. He sank into a specific memory, as sharp and clear as if he lived it all over again.

July spun the combination, right, then left, then right. He opened his locker. The items taped inside the door were the ones he had brought from his locker at his last high school: a poster for a Stone Temple Pilots concert, a pen and ink drawing of a tattoo he wanted, and a newspaper clipping of a white German Shepherd at a rescue facility. The picture was nearly a year old. The sad but hopeful eyes of the dog had faded with time. His last stepmother hadn't allowed him to adopt it, but he had kept the clipping anyway.

The door at the end of the hall banged open and Rob Brady made his entrance, Janie McCreedy at his side. It surprised July to see Janie with Rob. In the month or more that July had been dating her, she'd never mentioned sharing a class with him.

Rob's locker was only two down from July's. "Who are you taking to homecoming?" he asked July, dialing his lock open. If possible, Rob looked even more smug than usual.

July looked from Rob to Janie. Until now, he had thought that he was taking Janie.

"I don't know," he said, truthfully.

"You could take your sister, and make it official." Rob said, tossing one book in his locker and removing another.

July was used to being teased about his closeness to Alice. It was her first year at the school and everyone knew he watched out for her. He didn't care what Rob's opinion of their relationship was—he'd never much cared much about what others thought of him. July ignored the barb and turned to Janie.

"Did you say you'd go to the dance with him?" he asked her.

She had the decency to look embarrassed. "Yeah."

Janie wasn't the most popular girl in school but, to July, she was the prettiest. Rob Brady must have thought so as well. Apparently July's serious honesty and small tokens of urban daisies and amateur origami hadn't impressed Janie as much as Rob's letter jackets for football and basketball.

He wanted to punch the smug expression right off Rob's face, but he doubted he could take him. Rob was taller and heavier, and July's spring baseball at his last school wouldn't have put him in the kind of shape Rob would be in with his current football training.

"He won't treat you right," July told Janie. She should know that

already from Rob's ass-hole reputation.

"Says who?" Rob said, slamming his locker shut. He approached July, trying to intimidate him with his size, like he did with everyone.

July wasn't intimidated, he was just pretty sure Rob could win a fight. He looked at Janie, willing her to see what she was getting into. Her expression said that if July fought Rob and won, he could have her. She was the type who would always need the winner. No matter how cruel they were.

July knew he sat on the edge of a cliff, though he could neither see nor feel it. Before he could reach up to his face and check to see if his eyes were open or closed, the high school hallway faded and another memory began...

He sat at a small table near the back of the bar. Taking a sip of his overpriced club soda and lime, he glanced over his shoulder, yet again, toward the bathrooms. The dark hallway behind him concealed the doors marked hombres and señoritas, a pay telephone cubby, a utility closet, and a back exit. A man emerged from the hallway. He was perhaps in his early fifties with small, tight eyes a shade darker than his brown cowboy hat. A neatly trimmed salt-and-pepper mustache and beard framed his mouth. July had seen him here before. The man stared at July as he walked past, but continued out the front door and into the warm El Paso night. Sarah reappeared a moment later.

"Whatcha doin'?" she said, plopping into her seat next to him.

The answer was too obvious to bother saying it over the loud country music, so July said nothing. Sarah picked up her beer and set it down again without drinking. She drummed her fingers on her glass and looked around the bar as if waiting for something to happen.

"You were gone quite a while," he said.

"You know, girl stuff."

She circled her face with a finger indicating makeup and fluffed her hair, smiling. Sarah tipped her chair back on two legs, looked around the bar again, and let the chair fall forward with a loud thump, acting more like a hyper sixteen-year-old than her twenty-four years. Her eyes darted everywhere but to him. "No, I'm just kidding. I had to make a phone call, too. Sorry. Why, did you miss me?" She leaned across the small table, close to his face. "Were you lonely? Huh? Were you? Were you lonely?" She tried to tickle him.

July didn't smile. It wasn't funny. She never told him the truth, though the effects of the cocaine were plainer than words. She always used it when she was nervous or when things were going badly for her, even though they both knew it only made things worse. When he tried to talk to her about it she denied everything. Since he couldn't confront the issue head-on, July had tried to make her feel safe, so maybe she wouldn't need it, and he had tried to keep her from the places and people that tempted her. She always found a way back to them.

His mind jumped forward two weeks in time to a new memory.

Sarah canceled their date at the last minute. It surprised him, because she'd been anxious lately, and she usually wanted him around when she got anxious. July went over to her house anyway. He parked his truck at the apartment complex across the street and watched her front window to see if she was home. About fifteen minutes later a Dodge truck pulled up. A man with a brown cowboy hat and neatly trimmed salt-and-pepper beard stepped out of the truck. He carried a fanny pack. July watched as Sarah opened the door and let him in. She greeted him with a kiss. July had assumed the man was her dealer. He hadn't guessed until then that he was more. Stupid of him.

The parking lot faded as a new memory began…

July's cell phone vibrated in his pocket. He moved away from the crane and around a partial concrete wall. Holding a leather-gloved finger to one ear he answered it, tipping the phone to fit under the edge of his hardhat.

"July? Are you there? Can you hear me?" Mia sounded impatient.

"I can hear you now," he said.

"I need you to pick up my prescriptions on your way home from work today. I have a headache and I don't want to deal with standing in line at the store. Don't forget, okay? There are three of them, so make sure you get all three."

He didn't forget and Mia was right, the line at the pharmacy was long. He shuffled forward with the coughing and sniffling children and the terminally elderly. July wished Mia didn't need the Ambien and the Imitrex, but she was a light sleeper and prone to headaches. The anti-anxiety pills were what bothered him most, almost as much as alcohol and street drugs. It felt like a failing on his part that she couldn't trust that he was strong enough to take care of them both, but the more he took care of her the more she seemed to worry.

July thought he heard his name. Turning, he saw a flash of brightness, like a blazing globe of flame. He scanned the corner where he thought he had seen the fire, looking for a display with artificial flames or bright golden objects but found nothing. Fire. The image tickled at his memory, reminding him of something—or perhaps someone.

The images stopped. The vista of the canyon stretched out before him again, the sun higher in the sky.

He shivered, though not from the cold this time. Like the times he had fallen unconscious, it both frightened and angered July to have not been in control of his body. He assumed that Pat, or something else in this strange world had been responsible for the images, but why? And why those memories? What did past girlfriends have to do with anything?

If Pat wanted July to face his past, he'd missed the target by a good margin. July wasn't proud of losing every girlfriend he'd ever dated, but there were a hell of a lot more traumatic memories buried in his head. Missing Mia stung, but if Pat had wanted to hurt him he would have dragged out July's last conversation with her. The one they had on the phone while she was on her way to Big Sur and another man.

Janie's need to attach herself to that Neanderthal, Sarah's addiction, Mia's crutches. He was sorry he hadn't done better by them all, especially Mia, but then he doubted he ever could have done enough to change things for any of them. Hell, his own mother hadn't given up her drugs and alcohol for him or for Alice. Why would Mia have been any different?

He'd always been drawn to women who needed something, he knew that, but in the end, he was never enough to fill that need. Their demons were too strong for him to vanquish for them. It was something they had to do for themselves, he supposed, though it never stopped him from trying.

Maybe it was the desert that stirred him to think of his mother. It was a novel sensation, though, looking at Mia and his mother side by side. They were so very different that he'd never once equated them. He'd been attracted to Mia *because* of the differences, her career with an insurance company, her normal life. But looked at in another light, the similarities were there. If he hadn't pushed the memories of New Mexico away so hard, he would have admitted the wellspring of his attraction to troubled women years ago.

He thought of Valerian again, so different from the others. He couldn't deny that he felt an attraction to her, but he didn't picture them together. Their lives seemed destined to intersect here then move on their different directions. Or maybe he was *making* it happen because he didn't see himself caring for a woman who could care for herself.

The stiff breeze picked up and a gust prowled the canyon, howling like an animal on the hunt. He heard it echo through caves and crevices below. The sound seemed a perfect backdrop to his thoughts; a lonely and sad melody. He looked across the expanse to the ridge beyond. The sun rising behind him was slowly reaching down into the canyon, illuminating the shadows at the bottom by degrees.

A soft clanking yanked him out of his reflections. He turned toward the sound, his heart picking up speed; his first thought that it was Bill. Even before he'd fully turned, his mind rationalized that if Bill had managed to sneak up behind him, the crazy fuck would have probably heaved him over the edge by now.

A woman squatted on the ground behind July. She was lighting the camp stove with the bandaged leg, and setting a coffee pot on it to heat. She looked up when he turned. "Would you like some coffee?"

"Water, if you have any left." The words croaked in his throat. She slid a canteen to him. He drank nearly all of it before he could stop himself. "Sorry," he said, recapping the container. "I hope that wasn't all you had."

She shook her head. "I can get more."

He squinted, looking at her closely. She didn't have the mannerisms of Patty. This woman was too calm, too composed. "Pat?" he said, uncertainly.

She laughed, quietly and good-naturedly. "No. We don't change gender." She shifted to a cross-legged sit and wiped her hands on her nylon hiking pants. Her skin was dark, but not Native American, more big-city-melting-pot light brown.

"Have we met before?" he asked.

"No."

"What should I call you?"

She shrugged. "Nothing. Anything. It doesn't matter. If it's easier for you, 'Pat' suits us all, really."

"I'm glad there aren't many of you," he said. To keep them straight, he dubbed her Patricia. "So why does that suit you all?"

"We're all primary patterns."

That stopped him. He hadn't expected an answer and now that he had one, he wasn't sure what it meant. "Primary patterns for what?"

"For humanity, of course." The battered aluminum pot hissed and spat. "Ready for some coffee?" she asked. She poured into two tin cups and leaned forward to hand him one.

He remembered just in time not to scoot closer in case it constituted going backward. Leaning back on one elbow with Patricia leaning far forward, he reached the cup. The metal burned his hand. He twisted it quickly to grab the little handle.

July watched her over the rim of his mug as he sipped, trying to process what she'd told him. Pat's penchant for art made at least a little sense now. If they were in some way the patterns for the human soul, or mind, or whatever made people human, it was reasonable to assume they would be interested in how humanity represented themselves. He thought about the people he'd seen walking in and out of Coit tower; how different they all seemed.

"Are you the patterns for our personalities?"

She nodded. "Essentially," she said. "It's a bit more involved than that, but that's an adequate summary."

"Did you create us? Are you gods?"

She smothered such a sudden laugh that she spat a few

drops of her coffee. "No," she said, when she'd swallowed and wiped her mouth, "we're not gods—or angels, before you ask that. We search for the same answers about our creation that your people do. Same as you, all we can do is theorize. Most here believe in a divine creator though. Evolution seems unlikely when you take both your people and ours into consideration."

July had never believed in God. His mother had worshipped a bottle and a spoon and his father had worshipped a succession of women. Life was too hard and too mean to believe in a loving God. If one existed, he didn't think he wanted to get to know Him.

"Are there other worlds too?" he asked. "Other planes of existence, or whatever this place is?"

She shrugged. "All that I'm aware of is our world and yours, but who's to say?"

Patricia rummaged in a red day-pack behind her and unwrapped something from a piece of waxed paper. "I have food with me, if you want some." She handed it to him. It looked like a huge, square granola bar. His stomach growled fiercely just holding it. He took a bite. It tasted as good as anything he'd ever eaten.

They were both quiet while he devoured the dense oatcake-thingy and drank his coffee.

When he finished eating, he wiped the crumbs on his pants and wished she would produce another from her pack. She didn't. "Patty said once that she wasn't Mia, that Mia was her," he said. "Is that what she meant? That Patty is the pattern for Mia's personality?"

Patricia nodded.

July mentally scanned the personalities he'd met so far. If

118

Patty was Mia then maybe Patricia was Valerian. Perhaps that was why he hadn't met Patricia on his previous visits before picking Val up on the road. Pat seemed to be the one in charge here, his spirit guide or whatever, but that still left July with one question. "Who is Bill the pattern for? Crazy people?"

Patricia stared into the depths of her coffee cup. He thought she wasn't going to answer and he was forming his next question when she spoke softly.

"He isn't a pattern. He's from your world."

A dozen new questions popped into his head. July felt afraid of them all. "Did he try to walk out of here?"

She nodded and lifted her head to meet his eyes straight on. Suddenly July didn't want to ask any more questions.

Patricia stood and packed the coffee pot, the stove, and both cups.

"Are you leaving? Wait. I'm stuck here. Tell me how I'm supposed to keep going west with this big-ass canyon in front of me."

"You should find it easier now," she said, shouldering her pack. "Inertia works against you here, July. You should try to keep moving as soon as you can." And with that she turned and walked east, a direction he couldn't follow.

He watched her until she disappeared over a small knoll then scooted around until he was facing the canyon again. The things he'd learned were confusing, like trying to put a jig-saw puzzle together with only half the pieces. He didn't want to think about his obstacle either. His thirst slaked and his belly filled, he felt tempted to lie down in the sun and push all thoughts of this crazy place out of his head. He didn't.

July assumed Patricia could have brought him food and water at any time and yet she had let him go hungry and thirsty through the night. Perhaps they'd needed proof of his commitment to this journey before giving him some aid and a few more answers. He looked at the emptiness of the land around him and the skin on his back prickled at the 'what ifs' that occurred to him. It would have been so easy yesterday to say *the hell with it* and walk back to the pictographs in search of food and water. If he had, he could be stranded here already, like Bill.

July looked again at the canyon, wondering why it should be easier now. Perhaps she meant that he could walk on air or defy other laws of physics in this place. If so, he wouldn't find out—he wasn't about to step off that edge to test the theory.

The wind brushed his face and made his forearms prickle. He scrubbed his hands through his hair, as if he could rub away the clutter of memories he'd been subjected to this morning and the uncomfortable sensation of analyzing them. He took a deep breath of clean air.

Knowing he needed to act on Patricia's advice, he stood and stretched. He stepped forward to look down over the lip of the canyon at the wash below, studying his adversary. Realizing what he'd just done, a jolt of panic ran through him. His guts clenched. He hardly had room to sit at the edge now and couldn't step backward.

"Idiot," he said aloud, pressing his palm against his forehead in frustration.

With no choice now but to go backward or forward, he squatted at the edge and peered over. From this new perspective, he saw that the rock just below the lip wasn't as sheer as he had thought. It was textured into lumps and cracks. Perhaps forty feet below, the wall sloped at a steep but far less dramatic angle toward the valley. If he could climb the first section without falling, he might even make it down alive. Directly across from him, the far side of the canyon had a deep crevice that presented possibilities, and if the crevice didn't work, that side had a mirror image of the sloping bottom and steep top that he could probably navigate.

He'd always been more of a doer than a thinker.

He tried to memorize the best hand and foot holds for the first ten feet or so, and before he could talk himself out of it, rolled onto his belly and eased his legs over the edge.

Chapter 13

Shimmying the lower half of his body over the edge, his jaw tensed and his stomach fluttered. There was nothing to hang onto with his hands and he spread his arms across the lip of the canyon, nails digging into the soft dirt covering the rock.

He felt blindly with his left foot until he found the rock jutting from the wall that he had marked for a first foothold. He eased his weight onto it. The rock was just large enough for the ball of his foot and gave him a solid platform. He felt around with his other foot, trying to remember the steps he had plotted while squatting at the rim.

Sweat prickled his forehead and dampened his hands. The thoughts came unbidden: what if his hands became slippery with sweat, what if there was no footing below the first few steps, what would it feel like to fall to the bluff below? He tried to block the thoughts and focus.

His right foot found purchase. To move down any further he had to ease his elbows off the rim and grab at handholds, committing himself to a vertical position on the cliff-face. He groped near his face until he held a small knob of rock in his right hand and had the fingers of his casted hand wedged painfully into a small crack. The cliff still lay in shadow, but a trickle of sweat ran from July's forehead and made his skin itch as it dripped past his right eye.

He was perhaps fifteen feet below the rim when his left foot reached for a foothold and found none. July tried instead with his right foot. Still nothing. He told himself not to panic. Looking up, he wasn't sure he could make it back up the rock—and even though it was vertical, it would probably constitute going backward. He looked down between his arms, trying to see a foothold. What he saw wasn't comforting. The rock fell away, steep and deadly, for another thirty feet before any real contour began.

Reaching farther to the right, July discovered a shelf of rock large enough to wrap his fingers around. He swung his foot the same distance to the right, and finally felt a small protrusion, no larger than a piece of gravel. Holding as much of his weight with his hands as possible, he eased his foot onto the small bulge. He let his left foot drop down and searched again, finding a small jut. The tiny rock gave way under his right foot but his left foothold held him. He continued to ease his way down the cliff face.

Looking up a few minutes later, July judged he had come perhaps three-quarters of the way down the vertical section. Not far below him, jumbled and piled rocks spread in a rough spill to the bottom of the wash.

The sweat on his palms had dried and he was feeling more confident. His cast made his grip awkward on his left side, but he was moving faster now, anxious to reach the easier section.

Grabbing a firm handhold, he swung his leg downward again. Without warning, the rock in his hand broke away from the canyon wall. His weight shifted hard onto his left leg and his foot slipped. He was sliding.

July clenched back a yell. His hands and feet wind-milled against the cliff, searching for any hold. One foot hit a boulder, but momentum bounced him from his momentary safety. His chest struck the same boulder and he wrapped his arms desperately around the rock.

He clung to the rock, panting. He'd bruised his knees and chest. His right forearm burned, and when he inspected it he saw a laceration about an inch long, slightly curved, and deep enough to create a flap of soon-to-be-dead skin. The cut was bleeding at a decent clip, but not enough to be serious. Otherwise, he seemed to be okay. He'd slid at least a dozen feet to the lower section. The rubble of boulders that had long ago peeled off from the wall above were strewn against the base and piled high in a chaotic jumble, like the toy blocks of a giant's child. If July hadn't checked his fall, he could've bounced to his death down this rough skirt of the cliff.

He worked his knees under him until he could take his weight on his legs, but waited until his hands stopped shaking before letting go of the boulder. Slowly, he started down again. In a dozen more feet he was able to turn and scramble the rest of the way down to the valley floor.

He was hot, thirsty, and tired when he reached the bottom. The sun had crept over the rim of the canyon and it shone down on him, spotlighting his trek across the wash. He hoped Patricia might show up again to bring him food and water, but there was no sign of her. It had been stupid of him not to ask her to leave the canteen. It had been stupid of him not to ask her lots of things.

The canyon floor was narrow, divided down the middle by a dry watercourse lined on both sides with dried brush and dead trees. In the center of the old riverbed he found a small puddle of murky rainwater near a leafless cottonwood. July lay on his belly and drank gratefully, then pulled his T-shirt off. There was a tear near the hem of the shirt, from his slide down the rock face, and July used that as a starting place to pull a strip of cloth free.

He dipped a corner of the cloth in the clearest part of the puddle and scrubbed at the wound on his arm, but was unable to remove all of the sand and grit from the lips of the cut. Too late, he wondered if the questionable water would make things worse instead of better. He wrapped the strip of cloth around his still bleeding forearm, using his teeth to tie it off. That done, he soaked up most of the rest of the water into the fabric and wiped the dust and sweat off his face before pulling the wet shirt back on. He wanted to stay in the meager shade of the cottonwood and rest, but Patricia had warned him that inertia was his enemy.

July crossed the rest of the wash and scrambled fairly easily up the first thirty or forty feet of rock on the other side. When the going got steeper, he stepped into the wide crevice. The rock inside the crevice was jagged and stair-step-like but covered in loose sand. It was hard going as his climb became steeper. He was sweating and breathing heavily by the time he reached the last few feet. Near the top, the slit narrowed enough that he used opposing pressure with his arms to work his way up the final section.

Crawling above the rim, he fell, panting, on blessedly flat ground.

This side of the canyon looked much like the other: flat, sandy landscape with small rolling undulations and dramatic rocky outcrops. Hoodoos, with their large, blocky heads, watched him from atop hundred-foot-tall columnar bodies of rock. Like calving glaciers, they had splits dividing them vertically from the main outcrop, and clung precariously, attached only at their stubby bases. Unlike impulsive and dynamic ice, though, the hoodoos gave the impression they may dangle for millennia before gravity at last peeled them away with a massive and thunderous split that would send their tonnage crashing down.

July rested only a short time at the rim before he pushed himself to his feet. He did his best to gauge direct west, and began walking again. The sun half-blinded him as it marched down the last quarter of the sky, and he amended his wish for things he had asked of Patricia to not only a canteen but sunglasses, too. When the sun finally dropped below the horizon, July found a nice, safe spot to stop. No cliffs in sight; deep, comfortable sand on which to sleep.

He was exhausted. Despite Patricia's warning, he couldn't walk forever. He rationalized that it wouldn't be safe to continue after dark anyway. Making himself as comfortable as he could, July sat with his back against a rock and looked out at the deepening twilight. He wished he had his supplies from his campsite in Flagstaff. If he could have any one thing from there, though, he would want it to be Valerian.

July realized he had dozed off when a noise woke him. He opened his eyes to see Pat standing in front of him. The old man was looking past July to the horizon. He lifted one arm and did a side bend, then lifted the other arm and bent the other way. He squatted with his arms in front of him, then stood and reached for his toes, making it as far as the middles of his shins.

"I'm the one who should be sore," July said.

"It's good to stay limber," Pat replied.

"Did you happen to bring any food or water with you?" July saw no sign of a pack or camp stove.

"You won't be needing it."

"Bullshit. I need it now."

Pat said nothing. He sat down near July.

"You know I could've killed myself today," July said.

"I didn't think you would."

Pat sat cross-legged in the sand. Silence filled the night between them.

"Was that canyon impassible yesterday?" July asked suddenly. It sounded crazy to say it out loud, but he'd thought about it all day. He was sure that cliff had been sheer when he first looked down that rocky wall. Changing his perspective by moving a couple of feet closer shouldn't have shown him anything that substantially different. "Did what I thought about this morning, about Mia and the others, have something to do with my being able to get through that canyon?"

"It had everything to do with it."

"So this isn't just about me walking out of here. What then? Is this some alternate-world *This Is Your Life?*" Am I your entertainment for the week?" For all he knew about these people, this was how primary patterns got their kicks. Angry at their machinations and manipulations, as well as his inability to do anything except play along, he heaved a small stone out onto the sand.

Pat gave him that look again—the one that said July was a child in an adult world—though there was sympathy in the old blue-brown eyes.

July leaned back against the outcrop. "Okay, I get that I'm reliving memories on this journey, but I still don't understand why. My childhood sucked. I know that. Lots of people's have. I've moved on. Why don't you bring someone like my Uncle Eddie here and see what you can do with him?"

"Because most people won't learn."

"And a lot of people probably would."

"I don't know the criteria or algorithm that brings some people here and not all the rest. I suspect some risk to reward ratio might be a part of it. We don't want people to fail. Bill was our first." Pat looked off into the dusk, maybe toward Bill. "It's possible destiny is involved, something you have the potential to do, or a child of yours, or someone you influence. What I do know is that this is a chance for you to become what you were meant to be."

July bristled. "Who are you to say what I was meant to be?"

"We're the only ones who can." Pat shrugged. "We know who everyone was meant to be."

"So this is what you do? Bring people here who got screwed up along the way and show them slices of their lives?"

"We don't bring you here. We just provide the venue for the journey. Very few people have ever come to us. Very few. Perhaps saving that banker tipped the scales. Do you remember how your anger was getting harder to control? What do you think would have happened if your confrontation with Robert Vegas hadn't been interrupted?"

July looked at the ground. He grabbed a handful of sand and let it pour through his fist, remembering his volcanic anger that day at the bank.

Pat continued. "I think you saved yourself when you made the decision to save Robert Vegas. You proved yourself again when you poured that bottle of bourbon down the drain. And you didn't turn back last night. You have it in you to do this, July. Remember that as you go."

"So what happened to Bill?"

For the first time since July had met him, Pat seemed unable or unwilling to look July in the eye. The old man stared out into the desert instead. "He came to an obstacle he couldn't surmount."

"Physical or emotional?"

"Both," Pat said.

"They're one and the same, aren't they?"

"Yes."

July shifted and sat forward. "So the walking-back-the-way-you've-come thing, is that literal or figurative?"

"Both," Pat said again. "When someone goes back literally, they're giving up, they're not pushing through. They won't succeed on either level."

"How long has Bill been here?"

Pat shrugged. "I don't know. Time has little meaning here."

"Is he crazy?"

"More or less, depending on the day. He was unstable to begin with. Being trapped here has made him worse."

"What if I'd refused to start this journey?"

"You would have kept coming back."

"Why couldn't you have told me all of this from the start?" July asked.

"Would you have listened then?"

He didn't answer. They were both quiet for a long time. July leaned his head back against the rock again and thought until he couldn't think anymore. He was tired and thirsty and hungry, and didn't know why Pat couldn't have brought something for him to eat or drink. July dozed. When he opened his eyes, Pat hadn't moved. July shifted to lie on his side and fell into a sound sleep.

Chapter 14

July opened his eyes slowly. His mouth was as dry as an old sock and his head hurt like hell.

"Hey there. How are you doing?" A feminine voice was speaking. The voice was familiar, but he couldn't place it. "No, don't turn your head," she said quickly, as he tried to see her. "The doctor said moving your head will make the headache worse."

A figure leaned over him and Valerian slowly came into focus. She was perpendicular to him and he realized he was lying in a bed. He raised his right hand to brush at a fuzzy sensation at his right temple and a length of IV tubing trailed behind. His fingers stroked a gauze bandage on his forehead.

"You've had surgery and you're in the ICU now."

"Is there water?" At least that's what he tried to say; only the word 'water' croaked out clearly.

"Let me check with the nurses first and make sure it's okay."

Valerian pulled back a curtain, revealing a glass wall. His seemed one of a number of individual rooms that formed a large square around a central nurse's station. She came back in and poured water into a plastic cup for him, putting a bendy straw in it and holding it so he could drink. A nurse followed her in to chart his vital signs, and ask him how he was doing.

"How long?" he asked Valerian, after the nurse left. As soon as he said the words he remembered asking them the last time he had woken up in a hospital.

"You passed out about five hours ago. It's ten o'clock at night now. The paramedics brought you to the hospital and the ER sent you straight up for surgery. Dr. Weslyn was on call for neurology tonight, so he did your operation." July reached for the cup again. She handed it to him and he took another drink. "The nurse came in just before you woke up and said the doctor was on his way to see you. He should be here any time now."

July didn't remember falling asleep until Dr. Weslyn's hand on his shoulder woke him. Val stood on his other side.

"How are you feeling?" The neurosurgeon looked almost as dapper in surgical scrubs as he had in a suit.

"Tired. My head hurts."

"Both of those things are to be expected." The doctor studied the monitor above July's bed, tracking the bevy of readings coming from the leads attached to July. He glanced at the dry-erase board on the wall where the nurse had written the most recent vitals. "The surgery went very well," he continued. "The clot was removed with no complications. I'll have the nurses give you something more for pain, but be careful about moving your head for the next few hours." He leaned over July to check the dressing on his head. "Once the post-surgical headache passes, this shouldn't even be too painful, as there aren't many sensory nerves where we operated. We'll keep you in ICU for a couple of days just for observation, then move you to a regular ward. You should be able to go home in about three or four days."

No he wouldn't, July thought. He didn't have a home.

"I'll see you again tomorrow," Dr. Weslyn said.

July noticed Valerian watching the debonair doctor as he left the room. When her turquoise eyes turned back to him she took his hand.

"Thanks for everything, Val," he said. "I don't like to think what might've happened if I'd been out there alone." He looked down—embarrassed at his injury, his weakness and his need for her—and noticed the gauze wrapped around his right forearm. It covered the exact spot where he had cut himself falling down the cliff face.

It all came back to him... The desert. Walking west. The canyon.

Valerian let go of his hand. Her gaze had followed his and was fixed on the same patch of gauze. She seemed lost in thought. "It's late and I should go," she mumbled. "You need to rest."

"Where will you stay?" he asked.

It took a moment for his question to sink in. "The campsite is still set up," she said, as if shaking free of a dream...or a memory. "I thought I'd go back there. I hope you don't mind, I followed the ambulance here in your truck."

"No, that's fine, of course. Drive it as much as you want, but I'm not sure I like the idea of you camping out there by yourself. I'll give you the money to get a motel room."

"Thanks, but I'll be fine. I don't mind. I'll see you in the morning, okay?"

She seemed upset and he wasn't sure why. "Okay," he said.

She leaned over and kissed him on the cheek, then turned quickly and left.

After she had gone, a nurse came in to give him the extra pain pill.

"What's this on my arm?" he asked, pointing to the gauze bandage. He was hoping she would say it was from an IV site put in by the ER or surgery, but he doubted she would.

"You had a cut on that arm that was quite deep. You must have injured yourself when you passed out. It should heal up nicely, though. The ER said it was as clean as a surgical wound when they stitched it up."

July woke the next morning to find Valerian sitting at his bedside reading his copy of Pericles.

"Good morning," she said, smiling her big country smile when she saw he was awake.

"Morning."

She waved the booklet. "You had it on the seat of the truck, and it's better than the magazines in the lounge. I've never tried reading Shakespeare for fun before. The last time I read anything like this it was because I had to for high school English."

Her strange mood from last night had evaporated. Perhaps it had just been the stress of seeing him pass out and having to deal with the ambulance and the hospital and all. Whatever, he was glad that she seemed to be back to herself today.

"I used to feel the same way," he admitted, "but I enjoy it now. I still like seeing the plays more than reading them, though."

He listed the plays he'd seen and she told him the ones

she'd read. Their conversation flowed naturally into high school, and best and worst teachers, then on to cafeteria food and hospital food and favorite foods, herbal remedies for headaches, and caffeine addictions and construction and math and the places they'd lived. She helped steady him when he walked to and from the bathroom and up and down the hall, and said nothing about his indiscreet gown. When he got tired she left, and in the evening, when she came back from getting dinner for herself, she climbed onto the bed with him. They lay shoulder to shoulder and hip to hip, reading Pericles.

They'd been reading for about an hour when Dr. Weslyn walked in. He was in scrubs again, wearing a surgical cap over his close-cropped hair. His hazel eyes were hooded and he looked fatigued. Valerian blushed at being caught on the bed and moved quickly to a chair in the corner. The doctor lifted the bandage on July's head and checked the surgical site.

"All looks well," he said. "How are you feeling?"

"Not bad, actually. Tired mainly."

"Fatigue is common after this surgery. The brain is very sensitive to physical insult. You're doing well, though, and we should be able to move you to a regular room tomorrow."

The doctor turned to leave. He was at the door when July blurted out the question he had been afraid to ask. "Do you think I'll pass out again?"

Dr. Weslyn turned back. He looked surprised at the tension in July's voice. When he answered, he was serious and reassuring. "No, I don't. The pressure of the blood clot was causing your syncope. I'm surprised that it happened at all actually, as things looked pretty stable when I examined you and when we had a look around during surgery. The swelling from your initial accident had already resolved. Now that the clot is out and the surgical area is well cauterized, there's really nothing left that should cause you to lose consciousness."

The rush of excitement July experienced made his heart race and his hands tingle. If he didn't pass out then they couldn't take him back to that other world. Bill had said to be vigilant, to avoid anything that might cause unconsciousness. If that was the only way they could take him, he would be careful every day for the rest of his life. July felt truly happy for the first time in a long time.

"How soon can I travel?"

Valerian made a little noise of protest. "There's no rush," she said.

The doctor shrugged. "As soon as you feel up to it, I suppose. I'd prefer to see you in the office in a few days, but if you need to, you could have another neurosurgeon do the follow-up. Just use common sense." He turned to include Valerian in the conversation, probably assuming she was his significant other. "Don't drive until you're cleared to do so, don't go out and play rugby or anything, but normal activity is fine."

When the doctor left, Valerian gave July a high-five, then looked at the clock on the wall. "It's pretty late, I'd better get going."

"You sure you're okay camping out there on your own?"

"I didn't see another soul there yesterday. And if I do, I have my staff and my poi. Did I tell you Steve and I met in a martial arts class?"

"No. What else don't I know about you?"

"Lots." She winked at him. "I took a Tae Kwon Do class my first semester at ASU just for fun. Steve was a red belt. He said martial arts made him a better fire dancer. Within a month

I was taking Tae Kwon Do four nights a week and practicing fire dancing every day. And now *I'm* a red belt. So there. Does that make you feel better?"

"A little," he said. "But I'd still pay to have you stay in a motel the next couple of nights."

"I'll be fine. See you tomorrow," she said. She kissed him on the cheek, same as she had done the night before.

After two days in the ICU and a day and a half on a regular ward, July was more than ready when Dr. Weslyn did his final check-up and wrote out his discharge papers for release from the hospital.

"I have all the camping stuff in the truck already," Valerian said, as she wheeled him down the hall to the exit.

"Why are you so good to me?" July looked up, smiling.

"Because you're so darn pathetic."

She drove him to a small and older looking motel, with a rate that was surprisingly inexpensive. It was set apart well away from the big chain hotels, in an older section of town near a little strip mall. Valerian tried to insist on paying half, but July refused; he didn't know if his credit card had been canceled yet, but even if it had been he resolved to pay out of his small reserve of cash.

"You're staying around here for my sake," he said, as he held the lobby door open for her. "It's only right that I pay. If it wasn't for me, you would have been in Vail days ago."

"If it wasn't for you," Valerian said, "who knows where I'd be right now. I'll tell you a secret," she leaned both elbows on the check-in counter and spoke in a stage whisper. "I hated the idea of hitchhiking."

"Really? You looked pretty comfortable with it."

"I just wanted to get as far away from Steve as I could, as fast as I could."

A heavy-set, dark-skinned woman emerged from a room behind the counter, handed July a check-in form and ran his card. She spoke over her shoulder the whole time in a foreign language, Indonesian maybe, to a man in the apartment behind the office. The conversation seemed to be an ongoing banter between them, and not about his card, but July was still relieved when the little machine coughed up the receipt for him to sign.

He felt a twinge of guilt as he handed it back, knowing his credit card cancellation would come any day now. The charges would catch up with him soon, but maybe by then he'd have the insurance money to make good on it all. He and Valerian left the office and walked down the sidewalk to their first story room. July slid the card in the lock and opened the door. Neither of them went in.

One double bed looked back at them.

"I swear I asked for two beds," Valerian said.

She was such a pretty shade of red that he had to believe her. "It's okay. We'll see what else they have."

They went back to the front desk but the clerk was nowhere in sight. July rang the little bell on the counter. A TV played what sounded like a soap opera in the apartment and July could hear the man and woman, still talking, over the thump of pots and pans. He wished he could go back to the room to lie down and let Valerian take care of this. It was the longest he'd been vertical in days and he felt exhausted, though it was only ten o'clock in the morning.

"Look," Valerian said, "don't take this the wrong way, but I'm okay with it if you are. I mean, we were sleeping closer in the tent then we'd need to in that bed."

He looked at her, wondering if she'd heard his tired sigh while they'd tried to get the clerk's attention. Either way, she looked like she meant it.

"You're just saying that because you know I'm harmless right now." He touched one finger to the bandage at his head. He wasn't lying either. If she took him back to the room, ripped off his clothes, and mounted him, he probably wouldn't be able to manage more than a chaste kiss before falling asleep.

Agreed, they went back to the room and stacked her backpack and his duffel bags in one corner. July took his antibiotics and some Tylenol, and gratefully collapsed on the bed. Valerian sat up against the headboard on the other side.

"Hey," she said suddenly. "I forgot to tell you, I got a gig fire dancing tonight. There's a fall festival and crafts fair starting today over by the University. I talked to the event organizer yesterday, and she said I can go on in between bands."

"That's great," he said.

"Do you think you'll feel up to going with me?"

"I don't know. I sure couldn't right now, but I'll see how I feel later today."

July spent most of the day alternating napping with watching TV. Valerian came and went. She wanted to see where the event was being held and get the layout of the stage. July had a feeling she wasn't much for sitting around anyway, and she'd been doing a lot of that since she met him.

By evening he felt restless. The event wasn't far from the motel and July decided to go with her. While Valerian was setting up, he wandered around the booths. He tired quickly and sat on a little knoll in the grass where he had a good view of the stage.

The band finished their set as twilight was giving way to

dark. Valerian took the stage. She started with the poi he had seen her use before, lighting them from a metal container at her feet that sported a small flame. She swirled the poi in bright and intricate patterns to recorded music. When the song changed she switched to a long staff with fire at both ends. For the third song she used something like a hula hoop with two wicks on short stems sticking out at opposite ends of the hoop. By the end of the song she was spinning one hoop around her waist and two smaller ones up and down her arms.

The audience that had given a smattering of applause for the band whooped and applauded loudly as Valerian took her bow. July felt proprietarily proud, in a "that's my girl" way. The feeling surprised him. Not that he wasn't aware of his attraction to her—like moths and crows, men were usually attracted to bright things, and Valerian's spirit was certainly very bright—but this ran deeper than attraction, all the way to caring.

She found him after the show. He hugged her with his good arm and told her what a great job she'd done. They stayed for a while, listening to the next band, sitting shoulder to shoulder in the grass. The day caught up with him suddenly. As soon as he mentioned how tired he felt she herded him immediately to the truck.

Back at the motel, Valerian channel-surfed through the networks, annoyed by laugh-tracks and commercials, until she found a movie that showed some promise. July took a shower, careful to keep his head dry, brushed his teeth and came out to bed wearing his T-shirt and underwear.

"Boxer briefs," Valerian said approvingly, "good choice."

"You're not supposed to be looking. It's not my fault that we can't afford two rooms."

"I saw more than that in the hospital," she said.

"That you really weren't supposed to look at." He climbed into bed, exhausted.

"Do you mind if I watch TV for a while?" she asked.

He didn't, and said so.

In the ironic way that silence can wake someone who has slept through the explosions and loud music of an action movie, July woke when Valerian turned the TV off. She went into the bathroom, and also came out in a T-shirt and her underwear, with that odd felt tube holding her dreads back. The lights were off, but he could see her clearly by the light of the halogen street lamps that wiggled through the gap in the motel curtains.

"Nice sunflowers on those panties," he said, as he rolled away from her onto his side.

"You weren't supposed to look," she said.

He was nearly asleep again when he heard her voice. It came to him, soft and unsure, out of the darkness.

"July?"

"Yeah?"

There was a pause. "What happened to your arm?"

He stopped breathing for a long moment. "You should know better than me," he said, finally. "I was unconscious. I figured I cut it when I fell." He had hoped he cut it in the real world too, though he'd doubted it.

"I've been trying to tell myself that for three days, but you didn't fall on anything. I know you didn't. You went down on your knees and then kind-of keeled over. I rolled you over onto your back and I'm sure I would have seen if your arm was cut. You were just lying there and then your arm started bleeding. It was weird, July. And I can't convince myself anymore that it didn't happen."

He didn't know what to say. He wanted to get her to Vail,

see her safely there. He wanted to stay with her a little longer. He didn't want to scare her away now. But he wouldn't keep her with lies.

"Something's been happening to me since that car accident," he said, grateful for the darkness of the room though his back was still turned to her. He stopped and she waited silently for him to go on. "I don't know how to explain it. I thought it was a dream at first, but then somebody in my dream wrote those words on my cast and I woke up with them still there. It's like I go somewhere when I'm unconscious and I have to do something while I'm there or I'll keep going back." He rolled onto his back and looked at her in the semi-darkness. "I really haven't been entirely sure I wasn't crazy. In a way, it kind of helps that you saw what you did."

"Where do you go?"

Not *what do you mean* or *what are you talking about*, just *"where do you go?"* He could have hugged her.

"I don't really know. The people there aren't big on giving me answers."

"What do you have to do?"

"I'm not sure I have that completely figured out either, but when I'm there I'm on some kind of journey. The cut was from a fall I took trying to climb down a cliff. And by the way, I have to say you're taking this remarkably well."

The shadow figure next to him shifted. She rolled onto her side facing him, head propped on one hand. "I'd do better if you could put it in an equation for me, but I've been dealing the last three years with abstract math principles. Some people think that's kind of out there too. Besides, you should hear some of the things I've heard from other fire dancers. One gal swears every time she dances that she's a vessel for an ancient

Polynesian warrior. At least with you, I have some empirical proof."

"Well, whatever, thanks for believing me."

"So how will you get back there to finish your journey? The doctor said now the blood clot is gone you won't pass out anymore."

"I'm counting on it. If I never go back, it'll be too soon."

He had a fair idea of what was in store for him there if he went back. The thought of digging deeper into the attic of his mind terrified him. There were too many terrible things that he had hidden there years ago, meaning for them never to see the light of day again.

Maybe Valerian felt his fear. She said no more, but scrunched against him until he moved his casted arm to make room for her. Resting her head below his repaired collar-bone, she wrapped one arm across his chest. They fell asleep holding each other in the darkness.

Chapter 15

"So do you still want me to go to Vail with you?" July asked. He kept his back to her and punched the buttons on the microwave to warm the water for their instant oatmeal. The little coffee pot in the room hissed and bubbled, producing some very weak looking coffee.

"Of course I do. Why wouldn't I?"

July shrugged. He hadn't been sure how his revelations of the previous night would look to her in the light of day.

"Who would take care of you if I left now?" she asked. He turned and smiled at her mock seriousness. "But I still say we don't go until you feel up to it."

"If all I have to do is sit there and look pretty, I think I'm okay with leaving this morning. We can see on the way if we want to try and make it all the way there in one day or camp out somewhere tonight. As long as you don't enter me in any rugby games along the way, I should be fine."

He wasn't certain he was ready for a day of vibrating down

the road in his old truck, but he didn't want to give her too much time to think either. If he did, the things he'd said last night and the things she'd seen at the campsite might propel her into leaving him and striking out on her own again.

Valerian offered to load the truck and he let her. They traveled north through the early morning commuter traffic, driving in comfortable silence as they left Flagstaff behind. Ranch homes and horse corrals were nestled in the pine trees in the rural outskirts of town, but the houses stopped abruptly after they passed their campsite turnoff. The Arizona mountain scene changed, and they lost elevation quickly enough to make July's ears pop. Sage and scrub re-emerged, and by the time they leveled out they had descended to the flat plain of the desert, and a wide expanse of bare, sandy land.

July felt tired again already, and leaned back against the door frame to rest. He fell asleep to the rocking vibration of the truck and the lullaby of its loud hum. In his dream, he was riding in his father's semi, but instead of being a child or a teenager— as he had been the times he had ridden in that truck—he was an adult. July asked why his father had no oxygen tank or tubing with him, and his father answered that it was piped into the cab of the truck. Soon after, his father began to wheeze, and July knew the oxygen must have run out. He crawled into the back compartment, where the bed was, looking for the oxygen system. The lack of air began to affect him too, giving him a splitting headache.

The truck swerved and July woke.

Valerian was arched partially over the seat, stretching to keep a foot on the accelerator while her right arm rummaged in the back, blindly groping the floor.

"What do you need?" His mouth was fuzzy again and he

had a bad headache.

"I think I remember seeing an atlas back there."

"I'll get it."

His head nearly split lengthwise down the crown as he knelt and reached over the seat to grab the tattered atlas. Twisting back into his seat, he sat with his eyes closed a moment until the pounding lessened. When the pain had dimmed back to a steady ache, he opened the atlas to Arizona, glad that Valerian hadn't seen his discomfort. "Where are we?"

"Just about to pass Cameron. I think we turn off on 160 toward Tuba City, but I'm not sure."

"Who the hell would name a town after a tuba?"

He scanned the map and found Highway 160. "Yeah. Right on 160. That's the straightest route into southwestern Colorado."

The billboards for the Cameron Trading Post became more enthusiastic and soon a large adobe building and matching hotel came into view. "Hey, why don't we pull in there?" he said. "I could use a cup of coffee."

They were nearly past the driveway when he pointed and Valerian had to brake quickly to make the turn into the trading post parking lot. Cameron looked to be in the middle of nowhere, but it was only a mile or two from the turnoff to the Grand Canyon, and the lot was filled with RV's, busses, and cars.

"Are you feeling okay?" she asked. "You look a little rough around the edges."

He nodded. "It'll pass. I just need some stronger coffee to wake up."

They went inside together. The Trading Post was an immense building with an acre of trinkets, T-shirts, jewelry, candy, and postcards. There was a restaurant near the back. He ordered coffee and handed her the menu while he headed for the restroom. When he returned, she'd already paid for his coffee and her herbal tea. They made their way back through the maze of departments and sales counters to the front doors.

The coffee was hot and black and tasted good despite the Styrofoam cup and plastic lid. He finished it as they drove, but about twenty miles down the road his stomach began to churn.

"Pull off the road."

She looked at him.

"Seriously, pull off the road now." He had one hand on the door handle, ready to bail out.

Valerian downshifted and maneuvered the truck to the paved shoulder, taking two wheels onto the sandy dirt to be well off the highway. July threw the door open while she was still coming to a full stop. He made it three steps before the coffee and the morning's oatmeal came up, staining the sand a mealy yellow.

He stayed bent over, hands on his knees, for a long moment to be sure he was done. July heard the door on the far side of the truck squeak open and slam shut. He wiped the stringy rope of mucous from the side of his mouth. When he stood, the road and desert swayed. His vision blurred and he blinked to clear it. The headache intensified with the rush of blood from his brain as he straightened, and it hit him like the brain-freeze of drinking something too cold, too fast. It hurt enough that it immobilized him. He squeezed his eyes shut against the pain.

Valerian's hand gripped his upper arm.

"Tell me what to do."

"Nothing," he said. July opened his eyes to her furrowed

brow and her turquoise eyes tight with concern. "I think it'll be okay now. Maybe coffee wasn't the best idea."

She left her hand on his arm as he walked back to the truck. When she got in and started driving north again he took her sweater from the seat, put it behind his head in the corner of the cab and leaned back again.

"I'm sorry I've been such a rotten ride for you," he said with his eyes closed. "You could have been in Colorado days ago instead of babysitting me."

"Well, at least it's been interesting." She reached over and patted his knee. He opened his eyes at her touch but she already had both hands back on the wheel, and was looking out the big windshield at the road. "It's okay, July," she said. "My life attracts weirdness too. I mean, really, is this how you expect a Kansas farm girl to end up?"

She spread her elbows in a wide shrug, displaying her retro-hippiness, her fire dancing, PhD self to him. He smiled and closed his eyes against the bright glare of the morning sun. Nausea was still worrying at his belly, gnawing at the bottom of his stomach, cramping and contracting it. The headache was less sharp, but still viciously strong. He was genuinely grateful for Valerian's company.

"You're missing some beautiful desert." she said, cheerfully.

"Desert isn't beautiful," he replied, keeping his eyes closed.

"Really? You don't think so? I don't know, the vastness, the contrasts... I've always thought it was beautiful. The Painted Desert is only a little way from here, and some of the rocks here have the same amazing colorations and bands. You can read the millennia like a book."

He still didn't bother to look. "I think it looks like the land died right down to the core of the earth. People and animals have no business trying to live out here."

"Did you live in New Mexico for long?"

"Longer than I wanted."

The bitterness must have leaked into his words. Valerian changed the subject.

"160 was our exit, right?" she asked.

He cracked his eyes open to slits as they passed a sign announcing the turn off in half a mile. "Yeah, right at 160." He bent to pick the atlas off the floorboards. The top of his head exploded with pain. A stifled yell pushed out of his throat and both hands went to his temples. He threw up on the floor.

"Oh, shit," Valerian said. "Look, we're only four miles from Tuba City. Can you make it that far?"

He nodded as he sat up again, eyes watering with pain. He felt her accelerate to an unsafe speed. A few minutes later they pulled into the small town on the vast Navajo reservation they had been traversing since Flagstaff. A strong buzz whined in his ears and he held the heels of his hands pressed to his eyes.

"Stay here," she commanded, and jumped out at a gas station. "Good news," she said when she climbed back in the truck, "they not only have a medical center here, they have a small hospital."

Valerian drove a short distance. He felt the truck bump up into a parking lot and slow to a stop. The smell of vomit at his feet made his nausea worse. He pulled his hands from his eyes and tried to blink his blurry vision away. Valerian ran around to his side and pulled his door open. "Should I get a wheelchair or something?"

"No. It's okay. I can make it."

He slipped off the seat and stood in the open truck

doorway, feeling shaky. The buzzing increased and July knew what was coming. Before he could drop to his hands and knees, his world tunneled to black.

Chapter 16

July woke lying on his side in the sand. He pushed himself to a sitting position. The jut of rock at his back was the same one he had been leaning against when talking to Pat the last time he was here. All that remained of Pat were scuff marks in the sand.

He put his elbows on his knees and his head in his hands. He'd hoped this nightmare was over, that having his surgery had cut him off from this place. He lifted his head and looked around. The wind blew over the empty landscape. No Pat or Patty or Patricia, and thankfully, no Bill. After spending so much time with Valerian over the past few days, it felt odd to be alone in the empty expanse of desert.

The sun was in the east and a morning chill still hung in the air. All trace of headache and nausea were gone, just as his wrist and shoulder always felt healed when he was here. With nothing else to do, July stood and gauged west. He wanted to reach his next obstacle, get it over with, and get the hell home.

If his life had been more normal, he might have even believed that was possible.

He expected the deprivation of a long hike in the hot sun with no food or water, so it didn't bother him much when that was exactly what happened, though he questioned why it was necessary. If he was here to deal with things, why couldn't he deal with them in an alternate world that had fast food joints along the way? Was this supposed to help him build character? Make him tough? Give him time to reflect so he was more likely to succeed? Whatever it was supposed to do, it wasn't doing it. He resented the walk, he resented being here, and he became more frustrated with each mile.

About mid-afternoon, July came to another canyon. This one was shallow and easy to scramble down, but the big surprise was the creek at the bottom. July had seen plenty of dry watercourses out here, but this was an actual running creek.

He walked to the edge and took good drink. It was hard to scoop a mouthful with only one hand, but even if his wrist was healed while he was here, he didn't want to deal with a wet cast for the next day or so. The creek looked no more than calf-deep and easy enough to wade. He debated taking off his boots, but decided that a cut on the bottom of his foot would be worse than walking in wet shoes. He stepped into the water.

The shallow creek became a raging torrent. Vertigo rushed at him as water splashed up to his hip in powerful waves that threatened to throw him from his feet and carry him away. He threw himself backward and landed on the sand with his legs still in the water. The current was forceful enough to torque his body, tugging his legs downstream. He hauled himself the rest of the way up onto dry land and stared at the creek babbling down the gully, looking no more than calf deep.

July's heart hammered in his chest. His right side was wet almost to the armpit where the water had splashed high on his body, and his left leg was wet to the crotch; proof enough that he hadn't imagined the event. He panicked a moment when it occurred to him that stepping backward to the shore might have been a mistake. Perhaps he was supposed to push through the obstacles as he encountered them, but it was too late now and, anyway, he didn't see how he could have made it across.

He took off his soaking wet boots, socks and jeans and laid them out to dry in the sun, then sat down with his arms around his knees. Confronting his relationship choices and the reasons behind them the last time he'd been here had been relatively painless. The rest of his past was not, and he dreaded what might come up this time. He wondered if he was supposed to do something to trigger the memories. He tried thinking about his past, waiting for his thoughts to be pulled one direction or another. Nothing happened.

Disgusted with everything and hating the process of thinking anything at all about his life, he lay back in the sand and crooked one arm over his eyes. He tried to fight the anger that always seemed to come with frustration lately.

Lying in the sand while the sun dried his skin and clothes, he finally began to relax. His mind drifted. He realized he hadn't called his dad since he'd left San Diego. It wasn't like him to go a long time without calling his father to check on him.

With a jolt, he realized that his thoughts *were* being led down a path. He instinctively shied away and suppressed the thoughts of his father. He thought nothing at all for a while, and let the quiet of the desert and the babble of the creek fill his mind. Of course, the quiet of the desert and the babble of the creek would never stop. He could be here on this bank forever, listening.

"Let's get this over with then," he said aloud, and opened himself to whatever was in store.

Images and memories came smooth and fast.

July slipped into the straps of his Spiderman backpack as the school bus doors opened to let him off. He held the picture he had drawn gripped in one hand while his other waved up and down for balance as he navigated the steep steps. The humidity hit him like a wet blanket when he stepped off the bus and out of the comfortable air conditioning. His dad had moved them to Louisiana after his mother died, and the moist air still felt foreign and stifling after the dry heat of New Mexico. The bus doors clattered closed and the bus pulled away, spewing a great gout of black exhaust.

Two children who had gotten off at the same stop were greeted by mothers waiting for them. July wished that his mother was there to greet him too. He looked up and down the busy street for landmarks. It was only the first day of first grade, and he wasn't as sure of his way home as he thought.

He walked the two blocks without error and found the apartment building of his dad's new girlfriend. Wilma was on the couch, watching Jerry Springer, and didn't look up when he came in. He knew she was there because her stiff blonde hair was teased high enough to show over the back of the couch and a fog of cigarette smoke plumed up as she exhaled, like a pale gray version of the exhaust from the school bus. Her hair looked as dry as the nest in the cage where his little white mouse lived, and he wondered if her cigarettes would ever catch it on fire, waving so close to the hair-sprayed strands.

July came around the couch and shrugged out of his backpack. "Mrs. Lucy made us draw a picture today of the place where we live," he said, lifting the paper to show her his rendition of the apartment building, complete with stick figures on the sidewalk and the tree out front.

"Pick that pack up," Wilma said in her deep drawl. *She pointed to the backpack on the floor. "Do you think you live in a barn?"*

July set the pack on the far end of the couch before returning to the picture. "See, there's Denny and Michelle from down the hall out front, and Baxter too." The dog was the four legged stick figure with pointy ears.

"Can't you see I'm watching my show?" she said. "Here, give it here," Wilma said, holding out a hand for the picture. *"I'll look at it later." She set it on the end table and took another long drag of her cigarette, staring at the TV.*

They were all 'her shows' and it was hard to know when it was okay to talk to her. July slid off the couch and went to his room. Alice was still taking her nap in the other twin bed. She was only three anyway, too little to tell about his first day at school. His father was coming home today. July would tell him.

His father wasn't home by dinnertime and the anticipation had upset July's stomach. Wilma got angry with him for not eating all his dinner. It was nearly bedtime when the front door finally opened. July ran to his father, with Alice tottering behind. His father picked them both up, one under each arm, and swung them in a big circle, making July laugh with excitement.

His father kissed Wilma, still holding July and Alice, then set them down and kissed Wilma harder. "How's my boys and girls?" his father asked, still holding onto Wilma.

"The kids are fine," Wilma answered for them all. "They got me takin' care of 'em all day. It's me that's all lonesome, Walter."

"Aw, I'll make it up to you baby."

He picked up his bag and carried it to the couch. July ran after him, knowing what was coming next. His father pulled two small packages from a side pocket and handed them to July and Alice. July ripped his open to find a brown plastic dinosaur, and his father helped Alice unwrap her tiny teddy bear sporting a floral hat that said Florida, though Alice was too young to know where Florida was or what the bear's hat said.

"And where's my present?" Wilma asked.

"I got something extra special for you," his father said, grabbing Wilma around the waist and grinding against her until she laughed. "Come on, baby. I'll take you out and we'll paint the town red. How's that sound?"

Wilma called the neighbor's teenage daughter to babysit and changed into a dress. A few minutes later July's dad kissed July and his sister goodnight, and then he was gone. It wasn't until the door closed that July saw his school picture on the end table and realized he hadn't told his father about school…

The image faded and another began…

Brenda rummaged in the freezer. "Who wants popsicles?" she asked, in the sing-song voice she used when company was over.

"I do!" Alice dropped Unger, her toy hedgehog—named for the deep "ung-ung" grunting sound he made when squeezed—and ran to the kitchen. "An orange one." She was five years old and obsessed with popsicles and Otter Pops.

"July, orange or red?

"Orange," he said. He didn't run to the kitchen; he kept an eye on the man sitting on the couch.

Brenda came back to the living room and pawed through the cabinet below the TV until she came up with Peter Pan, a movie that both July and his sister liked. Popping it into the DVD player she pointed to the couch and July and Alice sat.

"You be good while Dan and I talk insurance, okay?" she said, still in her sing-song voice.

July didn't answer. Brenda's happy-happy talk and abrupt mood shift whenever Dan came over and made July uncomfortable. It was how she had acted before marrying their father, but following the courthouse ceremony, July and Alice had seen a side of Brenda that their father never did. The bad-temper and impatience came like a storm when their father left and vanished when he returned—or when Dan visited. Her changeable mood made July wary of her at all times, and he knew it wasn't right that she took another man into his dad's bedroom to talk.

The movie froze up after just a few minutes and July went to the TV to try and fix it. Alice slid off the couch to come see, but she stepped on Unger, who gave a mechanical grunt of protest at her sudden weight. July heard the hedgehog's grumble followed by a thump and turned to see Alice holding her head and crying. He went to her and checked her head, which she had hit on the coffee table.

"You'll be okay Alice," he said, though he wasn't entirely sure she would be. She was crying very hard and a red circle had formed on her forehead where it had struck the table. A small cut trickled blood from the center of the red circle. July got a wet paper towel from the kitchen and dabbed at her head. He needed a Band-Aid and the ointment you were supposed to put on a cut, but they were in the bathroom off his dad and Brenda's room.

July stood close to the bedroom door, listening. He was afraid to knock as Brenda had told him before never to interrupt her and Dan talking. The sounds from within weren't the sounds of people talking, they were muffled grunts and wet sucking noises that made July even more afraid. He opened the door quietly, thinking that it would be better to look first and see if it seemed safe to disturb them.

Brenda and Dan were at the foot of the bed, with Brenda facing July. Brenda was naked and Dan was wearing only his underwear. He was kneeling on the floor with his head pressed between Brenda legs. Brenda's face froze in a horror as deep as July's own. She regained her ability to move before July did, and snatched her dress from the foot of the bed. Holding it to her chest, she reached July in two steps and grabbed him by the arm. She yanked him into the room and slammed him against the wall so hard that his head snapped back and struck the wall with a loud crack. Her grip crushed his upper arm.

"I told you never to come in here when Dan was here. What we're doing here is private, you little shit. Don't you never tell your dad nothing about this." She punctuated each sentence by thumping him against the wall until his teeth rattled. "I've told you before he might think something bad if you told him. And if he thinks that, then he'll not only leave me, but he'll hate you for telling me, and he'll leave you too. He'll leave you and Alice with me, and he'll drive away and he'll never come back." She let go of his arm and stood up straight, trying to smooth the dress to cover her nakedness. Dan stood silent behind her.

July told his father everything as soon as he came home. He cried and begged his father not to leave Alice and him behind. Brenda's sudden rage at July and her pleading with Walter only served to confirm July's story. A week later, Walter, Alice, and July moved from South Carolina to Nebraska. A new home, followed shortly after by another new girlfriend, and another new school...

He was reliving these scenes as the child he had been, but the part of him that was sitting by a creek-bed in Utah observed and wept inside for the little boy he had been. A new image began...

"July, have you finished your homework?" Anna called through July's closed door, raising her voice to be heard over the loud music.

"Yeah," he lied.

"You'd better have. Your father called me from Sioux City. He'll be home in a couple of hours you know, and I'll make sure he double-checks that it's done.

She should look to her own kids, July thought. Tyler never did his homework when he was told to and Jack was so dyslexic he never got any of his right.

When his father walked in the door, Alice ran to him for a bear hug, then bounced up and down waiting for her gift. It was another snow-globe paperweight, but she loved all her different ones. July always wondered what his dad would bring, but he cared less about the gift than about having his dad home. Anna barely let him say "hi" before she started in.

"You need to check on July's homework tonight. I told him to get it done but he's been playing that damn music since he got home from school. I swear Walter, if I say black, that boy has to say white just to be contrary."

"Aw, hun, it's just a phase. He's almost twelve, and you oughta know how boys are at that age."

"Tyler was never like this. I'm tired of it, Walter. I'm tired of him being disrespectful and doing whatever he pleases."

July was disrespectful to her. Anna had tried harder and treated him and Alice better than any of the others, but somehow that just made it easier to be mean to her. He was tired of the stepmothers and girlfriends. He didn't want them anymore. He didn't want them telling him what to do when he knew that in a few months or a year they would be out of his life.

His father gave him a friendly slap between the shoulder blades. "He's a good kid. He just needs something to do. July, how'd you like to go outside and start learning the shift patterns on that old truck of mine? You'll be driving age before we know it. Might as well start learning now."

July couldn't believe his ears. "Really?" He ran to the truck ahead of his father.

When they came back half an hour later, Anna was sitting at the kitchen table holding a small piece of paper. The spaghetti water was boiling furiously, though there was no pasta in the pot.

"I unpacked your things," she said to Walter. She tucked the small card into a pocket of her sweater before his father saw it, but not before July

noticed that it was a business card for a motel.

"Oh," Walter said, sounding surprised. "Well that was awful sweet of you, babe, but there wasn't much need. Jimmy told me yesterday I gotta do another quick turnaround. I leave for New England Wednesday morning."

"Wednesday morning? That's barely more than twenty-four hours home."

"I know, hun. But I gotta take the work when it comes. It's been good money these past couple of months, hasn't it?"

July knew the fight that was coming by heart.

"I don't care about the money. I make a decent income too, you know. Please, Walter. I need some help here at home once in a while. Tell Jimmy you need to go back to a regular schedule. Maybe if you're home more, you could look for a local route to drive."

"You know the local routes don't pay shit," his dad answered. "I've driven long-haul all my life. I ain't about to quit now. Look, how about I take you out somewhere nice tonight, huh?"

"I don't want to go somewhere nice. You need to stay home with your kids once in a while. Maybe they wouldn't act out so much if you were around more."

His father left a day and a half later. Anna kissed him goodbye with less enthusiasm than usual. "How's that bed in there?" She nodded to his truck idling out front. "Do you need me to shop for linens or a new mattress or anything?"

"No, no. It's in fine shape. Good as new and comfy as a bear's den." He patted his beer belly. "And you know I'm just an old bear."

He kissed Alice and shook hands solemnly with July. "You behave, you hear?" he said. "Listen to your mom."

Anna wasn't his mom. His mom had died seven years ago.

That night, Anna put thirteen-year-old Tyler in charge and left without saying where she was going, though July thought he could guess. He had pulled the card out of her sweater that first night his dad was home, and it had advertised a motel in Sioux City. His dad sometimes needed more love than one woman could give him. It was like trying to fill a bathtub with the drain plug pulled out. He just needed more than he could ever get.

Anna came home four hours later, crying and calling Walter a bastard. July went up to his room and packed his things, then helped Alice with hers. When his dad divorced, or even just broke up with a girlfriend, it wasn't enough to leave the relationship. He always had to put distance between them...

July lay back in the warm sand. He wanted to bury his feelings out here, where no one would ever find them, and say people were just people and everybody did the best they could.

But he couldn't anymore. The selfishness and flaws in his father that the unfiltered memories had shown him were too large to hide again. He had never forgotten those incidents, or dozens more like them, but he had blamed the women and clung to his childhood belief that his father embodied security. When his father was home, July and Alice were safe and happy. He brought presents and swung them in the air and he loved them.

The bitter truth that July had always turned away from was that his father had continually dumped the two of them on a series of women who cared nothing for them. He could have looked for work that would have kept him home after their mother died, but he didn't. He was a jolly man who loved his children, but he was also a selfish and flawed womanizer. His father's childhood had been no picnic either, based on what little July knew of it and the cavernous needs of both his father and his uncle. But Walter Davish was a complex man, like everyone else, not a fragment, and July would never think of him quite the same again.

He lay there until nearly dark. He was sure he could cross the creek now, but he didn't have the will or energy to try. When he finally sat up, there was a flickering light on the other side. July heard the faint pop and crackle of a fire. He stood to pick up his clothes, and walked to the edge of the creek. He stepped in up to one ankle and paused. Nothing untoward happened. He stepped in with his other foot. Walking carefully, alert for any sign of danger, he waded across the creek.

"Here for my debriefing?" July asked Pat. At least he assumed it was Pat. He pulled on his jeans and sat to put on his socks and boots.

A boy sat at the fire. He was perhaps twelve or thirteen years old, dark-haired and athletic-looking. July recognized him as a boy from one of his schools, a farm boy who had never been cocky or mean, but a kid whom none of the others ever challenged. Most of the girls had had crushes on him.

The boy's mouth quirked in a smile. "I'm not qualified to debrief you. But you are. If you don't close this off again, July, it'll sort and sift itself out over time. Don't let your emotions do a submarine dive again, and you'll be fine."

July's feelings were as raw as if a power sander had been taken to them. His skin hurt and he felt nauseous. "It doesn't change things, seeing all that again. I still love him."

"Good. That's healthy. Do you want something to eat?" the boy asked. "I have a can of stew in my pack."

"No thanks." The appetite that had raged at him this afternoon was gone.

July looked up at the stars coming out. They looked out of place, like a giant hand had reached up and rotated the sky a quarter turn so that nothing was where it should be. "Will I go back soon?"

Pat nodded.

"So how does this work? Am I going to keep coming back here and living my life in reverse?"

"You're not living life in reverse. It's just coincidence that it seems that way. The memories will progress from the least traumatic to the most difficult."

"How many more?" July's voice broke as he asked.

"I'm not sure. We don't control the memories."

"Who does?"

"You, I imagine. I wish I could tell you more." Pat poked at the fire with a stick, his mannerisms utterly boyish even if his words weren't.

"Do you know what's coming next?"

"I can guess. But I think you can too."

July wasn't as ready to contemplate it as he had thought he was when he asked. He changed the subject.

"So if you guys are the patterns for all the personalities in the world, how come I keep showing up in Utah? Why don't I ever show up in Bangladesh or something?"

"Your realm of experience is in America," Pat replied. He was becoming less solid in the contrast of growing darkness and flickering firelight, giving him a wraith-like aspect. "If you were from Indonesia, or Cape Town, or Morocco, then you would go to a representation of those places." He rested his chin on his knees and poked at the embers again until the end of the stick caught fire. He pulled the stick out and blew on it, extinguishing the little flame.

"How is it you know so much about me? Patricia said you weren't god or angels. Do you watch us somehow?"

"I know you because I am you." Pat looked up from the

fire.

"What the hell does that mean?"

"I'm your pattern," Pat said, poking the stick back into the flames.

July was speechless.

The confident, easy-going farm boy in middle school; Pat was saying that's what July might have been without all the shit he was going through at that age. The mellow, self-assured man that was the adult Pat, the one July instinctively trusted as a leader, that's who Pat was saying July was under the solitude and the walls.

The silence stretched out between them. July finally broke the quiet in a voice that sounded too unsteady to be his own.

"I'm not you, though. And I'm not sure I can handle it…you know…if I have to keep coming back. If things get harder than the stuff today and last time." There was another long pause. "I don't want to end up like Bill."

The boy nodded in understanding, but said nothing.

Chapter 17

"July!" Valerian ran around the truck to July's unconscious form, lying on the parking lot tarmac outside the ER. "Oh, shit," she breathed. She didn't know whether to arrange him so his airway was open like last time, or to run thirty feet to the entrance and get help.

An old Cadillac pulled into the parking lot. A woman and young girl, both wearing their hair in long braids, got out of the car. The woman stared at Valerian and July, apprehensive.

"Get someone to help me, please," Valerian called to the woman.

She hurried past, pulling the little girl by the arm while the girl kept turning back to stare at July.

July's body and his features were so slack that he looked dead, which only increased Valerian's anxiety, even though she could see the rise and fall of his chest. It seemed a long wait, though it must have only been a minute or two before a man and a woman in scrubs came out the front door.

"What happened?" asked the woman.

"He had surgery two days ago to remove a blood clot from a head injury. He just got sick in the last few minutes and passed out when he got out of the truck."

"I'll get a gurney," said the man, and vanished back inside. He returned a moment later pushing a wheeled bed. Another man walked beside him, bald to the crown of his head with short, spiky gray-blonde hair. He also wore scrubs, but with a white lab coat over them.

"I'm Dr. Tafoya," said the man in the lab coat. "Let's get him inside," he said to the others.

Valerian stepped back as the three clinic workers lifted July from the pavement onto the gurney. July's head lolled back as they lifted his shoulders. His Adam's apple was prominent in that position and somehow made his neck look even more vulnerable. His arms flopped to the sides, prevented from winging out further by the bodies of the man and woman lifting his torso. The position, head back, arms out, made Valerian think of a painting in a Mexican restaurant in Phoenix, an artist's rendering of a loin-clothed victim being carried to a Maya alter for sacrifice.

It was the second time she had seen him unconscious, his body moved and handled without his knowledge. He looked so defenseless. The white gauze wrap on his head and the pink cast on his arm and the pink scar over his collarbone were enough; to see him unconscious was somehow too much.

The female nurse, a short, rotund woman, had difficulty lifting July. She dropped his shoulders heavily onto the gurney, her plaited hair swinging into his face as she did, and Valerian worried for his head injury. They wheeled him inside and Valerian followed the gurney down the hall until an older woman called her back to the registration desk.

An aide brought July's wallet from his jeans, and Valerian filled out the paperwork and fished out his insurance card for the clerk. She verified his San Diego address and had barely finished with the registration process when the doctor came out again.

"He's doing fine. He's awake and seems alert and oriented. We're sending him for a CT scan. When he gets back, we'll let you go in with him."

Valerian waited, pacing the tiny waiting room from the desk to the magazine rack to the front door, where she stood and stared out at the monochrome landscape. She read a pamphlet on the history of Tuba City, which explained that the name came from an Indian Chief in the area, Tuuvi, who converted to Mormonism in the late 1800's. Finally she was called back to a small exam room.

July was still on the gurney. The skin at the corners of his hazel eyes crinkled as he smiled. She walked to his side and took his hand, not sure if he had reached for her or she had reached for him.

"You scared me again," she said.

His brow furrowed in sudden concern and he looked down at his arms.

"No, nothing like that. I just mean it's scary watching you suddenly fall down unconscious like that."

"Sorry," he said.

The doctor walked back into the room, interrupting them. "Good news," he said. "The scan looks normal. There's no sign of hemorrhage or swelling."

"What caused him to pass out then?" asked Valerian.

"Probably some vasovagal effect."

Valerian quirked an eyebrow and waited for the translation.

"The body sometimes sends out a sort of panic signal that causes the vessels to dilate and the heart to slow. It can cause unconsciousness. There are a lot of things that can bring it on. It can be something as small as sudden nausea or an aversion to needles. Even a strong emotion can cause it. In light of Mr. Davish's recent surgery, it was probably just due to post-surgical nausea and fatigue."

"Does that mean it's going to keep happening?" July asked, sounding concerned.

"I wouldn't expect it to," the doctor said. "This was probably an isolated incident, some combination of unique factors. Do you feel well enough to sit up?"

"Sure," July said. Valerian let go of his hand and stepped back while the doctor offered an arm and helped July to swing his legs over the side of the cart.

"Any dizziness?" the doctor asked.

"No. I feel fine. I think maybe all I needed was to throw up and then not stand up so fast."

Valerian wasn't so sure. July had a haunted look that worried her.

She wondered if he'd gone to the other world again, though he'd only been unconscious for a few minutes. It was weird even thinking such a thing, but she believed his story. Sure, she hadn't known him very long, and maybe she was being gullible. He might be crazy as a bedbug, whatever that meant; but if he believed in this alternate world, then unless a better explanation came along, so did she.

She remembered staying at her aunt's old farmhouse as a little girl. She'd hated it, always believing it was haunted. Sometimes the cupboards would be open in the morning when she was sure they had been closed the night before. At night in her room, she would sometimes hear dishes rattle in the cupboards, and the old gas stove tap, tap, tap, like someone repeatedly trying to light a burner and failing. Her aunt, who slept upstairs, had been oblivious to the nocturnal going-ons in her kitchen and never believed Valerie's stories.

The fire-dancing friend she'd told July about, Bella, who said she channeled a Polynesian warrior when she danced probably *was* nuts, but there had been others: a girl in her high school who always had panic attacks two days before a tornado came through the county; the Ouija board at that party in junior high that *really had* moved by itself. And Valerian had seen the cut appear on July's arm.

"Where are you folks from?" the doctor asked.

Valerian and July looked at each other. "San Diego," Valerian answered.

The doctor pursed his lips. "Well, we'd be happy to keep you here for observation, but I'm not sure you really need it. Towns are a bit few and far between out here, though. You might want to consider staying overnight in a motel before you travel on."

"No, I think I'll be fine now," July said, before Valerian could say anything.

"Okay, let's stand you up and see how you do."

Valerian held one arm and the doctor held the other, as July slid off the gurney. "Still okay?" the doctor asked. July nodded. The doctor had a nurse give him a shot of Phenergan in his ass to stop the nausea from coming back. Valerian hovered at July's arm as he walked to the registration desk and checked out.

The doors hissed closed behind them as they left. The heat of midday sun made the outdoors feel stuffier than indoors had.

Valerian stepped in front of July, stopping him, and faced him with her arms folded across her chest. "Okay, the truth now. How do you feel?"

"Really, I feel fine, Val. Come on. I'd like to get out of here."

She liked it when he called her Val. With Phoenix and Steve far behind her, she didn't even feel like Valerian anymore, and she hadn't been Valerie in a very long time. "Okay," she said, still uncertain. She could tell there was more behind his words than he was saying.

They got as far as the front bumper of the truck and she suddenly stopped. "Oh. I didn't think to clean up the puke while I was waiting. Hang on a minute." She went to the passenger side door, but his hand on her arm stopped her.

"Oh, no you don't. I'm not going to let you clean that up for me. Besides I'm the one who got the anti-nausea shot."

"No way, José. If I get sick cleaning it, the only downside is that there'll be two piles to clean up. If you try, you might end up face first on the parking lot blacktop again."

She opened the passenger door and wished she had rolled down a window when she parked. "Ummph," she mumbled involuntarily, then brightened when she realized most of the puke had landed on the atlas. "Oh, hey, that's not so bad." She looked back for the nearest trashcan and saw one by the front door.

"Seriously," he said, "I'm not letting you do this." He was blushing.

July tried to stop her, but stepped quickly out of her way when he saw she what she was carrying. Tearing the first few pages off the atlas, she tossed them into the waste can, then balanced the atlas on the edge and went inside to borrow a wet rag to swab the passenger floor mat.

When they got back in, she started up the truck, and drove back to Highway 160. The rag must have had some kind of disinfectant on it, and with the windows rolled down partway she hardly noticed either the puke or the disinfectant smell.

"So, do you feel like telling me what happened?" she asked, as she turned left onto the highway.

He looked at her, puzzled.

"Like why *you* think you went unconscious, and if anything happened while you were out."

He had a serious face at the best of times, handsome in a rugged way, but very serious. Now it went positively grim. His brow furrowed and his hazel eyes went cold. He stared out the window at some middle distance that she knew she wouldn't see if she looked.

"No," he said. "I mean, I will, but not right now."

It confirmed her suspicions. "That's fine, I didn't mean to push. I just want you to know that you can tell me, okay?"

"Okay. Thanks."

They were both quiet as they drove through the north eastern corner of Arizona. A little while later she asked if he felt up to eating and he did, so they pulled into the Burger King in Kayenta. She opened her door and nearly hit a little basset hound mix. The dog had teats that almost brushed the ground, but no puppies in sight. It slunk back from her as she stepped out of the truck, then approached again, the need for food overcoming its apprehension.

"Oh, poor thing." She bent to pet it, but it skittered away.

"There's another one over there," July said, as he came around the truck to her. He pointed. Another mutt was scraping at the paved lot with its front teeth, worrying at some French fries that had been smashed into the blacktop.

Valerian didn't want to go inside. She wanted to pick both dogs up and put them in the truck and drive all four of them somewhere safe. July looked as sorry for the dogs as she felt, but convinced her that picking up every stray they passed would be impractical. In the end, she had to settle for buying two extra hamburgers and feeding them to the dogs before they left.

She pulled into a gas station and July insisted on paying for the gas. Valerian climbed out and retrieved the atlas that had been relegated to the truck bed. It was still a little soggy on the first few pages, but she hadn't wanted to tear off any more as they might need the United States map at the front, and the Arizona map was only a few pages down. She studied the atlas and talked to July across the truck bed.

"There are a couple of ways we could go from here. We could cut north up 191 through Utah and catch I-70 east, or we can stay on this highway into the southwest corner of Colorado. From there it would be smaller highways until we connected with I-70. It looks about six of one, half a dozen of the other. I wouldn't mind seeing the Utah Canyonlands, though, if you want to go that way.

"No," July said roughly. "I don't want to go anywhere near Utah. And I've had enough God damn desert to last a lifetime."

"Sure. Okay," she said. The vehemence of his response took her back. It was a sharp reminder that no matter how close she was coming to feel to July, she was still essentially traveling with a stranger. Not that she didn't trust her instincts—and her instincts had told her from the first moment she climbed in his truck that he was one of the good guys—but, still, it was a good reminder.

Driving out of town, they passed half a dozen thin horses,

feeding on the sparse weeds in the bar ditch next to the highway. "Do you think they're wild horses?" she asked.

July shook his head but said nothing. He seemed so melancholy. Whether it was the desert, which he obviously hated, or the endless desolation of this reservation, or something that had happened to him while he was unconscious, she couldn't guess.

They crossed into Colorado less than three hours later and stopped at a grocery store in Cortez to pick up some food from the deli. Valerian had mentioned as they came into town that there was forest service land near the Anasazi Indians sites by Mesa Verde and Hovenweep. She thought there might be pictographs or cliff dwellings that they could find even if they didn't go into the National Parks. July was as adamant about not staying there as he had been about Utah.

They took their bagged deli dinner and left Cortez heading northwest. After a full day of traveling through desert, the difference in landscape from Cortez onward was startling. Even a canyon that they traveled through was green and vibrant. Once through the canyon, there were grassy pastures and ponds and hills with green pine trees and golden aspens. Valerian found it monstrous that with all this so close, the Native Americans of the 1800's had been herded onto miles of arid land that had virtually no hunting, no water, and no agriculture potential.

By the time they reached the town of Dolores, the sun had dropped behind the big hills. They scanned both sides of the road for forest service signs. A couple of miles later July said, "There," and pointed to the right. Valerian turned off on the little dirt track. A few hundred yards back they saw an open, primitive campsite, but someone was already camped there.

Looking past the truck with the pull-behind camper they saw a little one-person tent in the next site and, beyond that, the dead-end of the road.

"How about going up the hill a little way," July suggested.

Valerian turned the truck around and drove up the hill. They expected there to be pullouts along the way, but she drove higher and higher without finding any. The road dropped steeply to the right into thick trees and banked straight up to her left. Kansas and Phoenix had nothing like this and, though she would never admit it to July, driving the big truck on the narrow road made her uneasy.

She asked for the second time if she should turn around, but July wanted to see what was up ahead. After nearly six miles of steadily climbing, the road leveled out into an immense aspen forest, glittering in fall yellows and golds. The forest was so dense that there were whole groves where many of the trees were only arms-length apart. The trees towered atypically tall for aspens—at least, as far as she knew—perhaps sixty feet tall or more, and limbless all the way up to their bushy, golden-headed tops.

They found a set of well-worn tire tracks leading up to a little meadow with a fire ring, and the truck jounced up the rutted, makeshift road until she found a level spot to park. They were efficient at setting up camp by now, and had the truck unloaded and the tent erected in no time.

"Feel like going for a walk?" July asked her. His mood had improved steadily since entering Colorado.

"Sure," she replied, glad for a chance to stretch her legs.

Twilight made the most of its short time in the sky while Valerian and July walked. The deep blue Colorado canopy dimmed to hazy purple painted with the pinks and oranges of sunset, and onward to bluish gray with the first stars dotting the sky.

They walked up the road side-by-side. Their fingers brushed once and she thought he might take her hand but he didn't. She wanted to ask him again if anything had happened to him while he was unconscious—though she was pretty sure she knew the answer—but she held her tongue and took comfort in the fact that he seemed to be feeling better.

The road was lined on either side with aspens but, where there was a break in the trees, the vistas were breathtaking. Immense hills undulated one after another to the horizon. They were shadowed in the early dusk but she could still make out that they were heavily blanketed in either pines, golden aspens, or a combination of both.

They walked until the uphill climb, the altitude, and the dark contrived to turn them back. July was still quiet but seemed peaceful. Back at their camp, they started a fire and ate their fried chicken and potato wedges mostly in silence, talking only about the little tangible things, like gathering wood and the chill air and the tall trees.

As darkness shadowed July's face against the firelight, he began, haltingly, to talk about more substantial things.

"Thank you for taking care of me again, Val."

She nodded, unwilling to intrude on what he seemed ready to say.

"I know you've been wondering," he continued, "and, yes, I went back to that other world. I was sure I would. I think I'm going to have to keep going back until I finish the journey or until I fail."

"The journey is the thing there that you have to accomplish?"

"Yeah. Basically."

"I'm sorry. I'm not trying to push." Whatever was happening to him there, it had rattled him more this time than the last. She was trying to let things come in their own time and didn't know which would help him more, her silence or her words.

"It's okay," he said. "I think the more I can talk about things the better. It's just hard for me. I've never talked about my family or my childhood or anything like that. Not to anyone, not even Mia. It's how I keep it from overwhelming me, you know? And now it's all kind of in my face and I don't want to go back again, and I don't think I can stop it."

"I'll listen to anything you feel like telling me, no matter what. If I ask anything that you don't want to answer, you don't have to answer."

He nodded. "I still can't understand why you believe me, but I'm glad you do. You have no idea how glad I am."

He paused a long while with his knees hugged his to his chest and his arms wrapped tight around his legs. The fire played with the shadows of his face, hooding his eyes like a mask and making the planes of his high cheekbones and strong jaw stand out. His five o'clock shadow added to the already rough face that he showed to the world, but the few times she'd seen him smile it transformed him. He rested his chin on his knees and stared into the fire, lost in thought. Just when she was certain that was all he was going to say, he spoke again.

"Some combination of factors brought me there: my background, saving that banker...I'm not sure what. It's a weird place, unnerving. Not like being transported to some other world isn't unnerving enough." His body relaxed a little, unfolding, as if starting had been the hardest part. "It's like our world, except there are very few people there. There's one guy who's sort of a guide for me. I don't know if he has a name or not, but I call him Pat. I think he wants to help me but he's not allowed to very much."

Hearing him talk about the other world gave her the heebie-jeebies, like camp kids sitting around the campfire telling ghost stories, only everyone's telling the truth.

"The journey is taking me through some bad parts in my past. And my past is pretty fucking bad. What happened today was tough," he gave a small shrug, as if ridding himself of the feel of it on his back, "but if I go there again it'll get worse."

It shocked her to see tears in his eyes. One rolled down the hardness of his cheek and into the stubble of his beard. She couldn't help reaching out and wrapping her hands around his arm. She rested her head on his shoulder and said nothing.

July tipped his head until it touched hers. They stayed that way until the fire burned to embers.

In all his life, July couldn't remember anyone taking care of him, not really taking care of him. He had cared for his mother when he was small, fended for himself when he was a child, and watched out for his sister as best he could. He had been the grown-up when his father wasn't, and had tried to protect the women he'd loved. In the week that he'd known Valerian, she'd done more for him than anyone in his life.

The pressure of his emotions pushed out against his skin, making his body tight, and when Valerian silently leaned against him a dull ache clenched his heart from fitting in one too many feelings. He wondered if he would fragment into shards, as sharp and jagged as the emotions roiling inside him. Memories that hadn't seen the light of day in years crowded his thoughts.

After years of suppressing them, now they seemed all he could think about, even in the quiet times when he first woke or he and Val drove in silence, the presence of those dark times remained foremost in his thoughts. There were times over the past few days when he'd felt he couldn't breathe, like the involuntary contraction and expansion of his diaphragm had ceased to work properly. This wasn't the path to healing; this was a path to madness. And if he didn't follow it to its end, worse consequences awaited him.

He felt weak from his injuries, and weak that Val had to drive because he couldn't, and he felt weak letting her see him cry. He couldn't remember a time as an adult that he'd cried in front of another person. She felt sympathy for him, he was certain of that, but part of him believed she would leave him at the first opportunity for his weakness and problems and part of him hoped he was wrong. She did believe him, though. And for that, he'd be forever grateful to her no matter how this all played out.

They sat silently in front of the dying fire until the chill mountain air finally galvanized them both.

"I could really use some sleep," he said.

She nodded and stood, and they made their way to the tent. Slipping into their individual sleeping bags felt to him like taking the one body they had been, huddled at the fire, and splitting it into two again. It felt lonely. He wanted to tell her how she made him feel, how grateful he was.

"Hey, Val, I just…I just want you to know…" He didn't know how to finish without giving her more reason to run from him.

She reached from her bag and touched him on the arm. Her touch felt good, as always. "It's okay," she said.

July nodded in the dark. He rolled onto his back, crooked his arm over his eyes. Thoughts of his experience today at the creek and the memories generated there came out like ghouls from behind gravestones in his mind. He viciously dissected the memories, all the way to the bones of his relationship with his father. There wasn't anything he hadn't really known all along, but he stripped the pretty ribbons from the childhood memories. Pat told him that he mustn't hide from his memories and so he wouldn't.

Valerian shifted next to him, still awake, and he enjoyed the sound of her moving in the dark. He wondered if his growing desire for her was born of nothing more than the weakness and need that had enveloped him ever since his accident, and decided that it wasn't. The first lesson on his journey had been that it was okay to care for a woman who could care for herself. He didn't know if Val had real feelings for him, or felt the same for him as she had for those dogs on the reservation. Whether she did or not, he resolved that he wouldn't let his old patterns of loving women who needed saving or his new insecurities sabotage whatever might be happening between them.

His mind drifted back to his father and his step-moms, the moving and the endless bouncing from school to school. But never to New Mexico. Or worse.

Chapter 18

July felt a lightness of spirit when he woke. The morning seemed brighter, more hopeful. Valerian woke a moment later, as if his wakefulness had awakened her. She sat up and removed the felt tube from her dreads and rubbed a hand through the ropes of her hair, like fluffing a pillow.

He laughed. "You give a whole new meaning to bed-head."

She blushed. "Yeah well my morning-mouth is giving it pretty stiff competition right now."

Neither of them had washed, or even brushed their teeth last night. The evening had been too emotionally exhausting for routine things. July crawled out of the sleeping bag needing to pee like a racehorse, so used to being in his underwear in front of her that he hardly thought about it anymore. Putting on his boots without his jeans would just look too stupid though, so he held his bladder long enough to get dressed, crawl out of the tent and make it to the huge old aspen standing by itself near their tent.

The thing must've been ancient. Its trunk was easily three times the diameter of the hundreds of trees on the other side of the meadow, which had grown close together and thin as spider's legs.

Feeling better, he zipped up and gathered a few sticks to make a fire to heat water for coffee and oatmeal. Valerian climbed out of the tent looking surprisingly put together. She headed off past his aspen and into some oak bushes. When she returned, she brushed her teeth and washed her face before joining him at fire.

Val suggested a walk after breakfast to stretch their cramped muscles. They found a little trail on the other side of the road that led steeply down to a barbed wire fence, then paralleled the fence, winding slowly toward the valley far below. The climb back up to the road was tougher on him than July had expected. The last month of infirmity had taken more out of him then he realized, and he vowed to start working out as soon as he was settled—wherever that might be. Flagstaff he guessed. The thought sent a little pang through him. Flagstaff didn't sound nearly as enticing as it once had.

Valerian chatted about the mountains and Colorado and fire dancing in Vail, and left all the things they had talked about the previous night in the night's darkness. Her happiness was infectious. She was wearing the patchwork skirt and backless top she had worn on the first day they met, along with her heavy wool sweater, and was as lithe and graceful in her movements as any ballet dancer. He watched her bouncing dreads as she climbed the narrow trail in front of him, grateful that she was here with him.

They packed up camp when they got back. He doused the fire while she fought with the tent to push the air out of the folds. When she tried to wrestle the bulky roll into the tent bag, he took the bag from her and held it while she stuffed the unwieldy mass inside.

"Mobius Strips are less complicated," she muttered.

He didn't know what a Mobius Strip was and he didn't care. He tossed the tent, still poking out of its bag, onto the ground. She looked up at him, perplexed.

July slipped his hands behind her neck, almost without thought, and kissed her. It wasn't until their lips touched that he wondered if this was something she wanted. Apparently she did. Valerian slid her arms around his waist and kissed him back. Her mouth opened under his, as she accepted a deeper kiss from him. When he released her, she looked up at him with a soft wonder.

"Well, you're full of surprises," she said.

"That I am," he agreed.

An hour after leaving their campsite, they drove over the oddly named Lizard Head Pass. At the bottom of the pass, a sign announced the ski town of Telluride to the right, but the highway made a hard left.

"This is a pretty place," he said, craning to peer out her window toward little village at the top of the hill. "Why don't you want to settle here?"

"It's pretty isolated from the other ski areas. Vail and Aspen are only a couple of hours from each other. And just east of Vail, toward Denver, there are a whole bunch close together. That way I can try a few places out and decide where I want to stay."

"Aren't you supposed to be looking for a real job?"

"I'll do that over the winter. I figure by spring, I'll grow up and start my daily grind."

They stopped in the little mountain town of Ridgeway for a snack and to gas up the Silverado again. July looked around as he filled the tank. He'd lived a lot of places in his life, but couldn't ever remember seeing so much beautiful country in one day. By early afternoon they were at I-70, had a quick lunch in Grand Junction, and less than three hours later they were pulling off at the main Vail exit.

"First order," Valerian said, "a place to stay. I didn't much like the idea of you sleeping on the ground last night after your surgery."

"It wasn't bad." It really hadn't been. There was less pain than he had expected. He had to sleep on his back to avoid the dressing on the right side of his head or the collar-bone injury still healing on the left. There was still a lot of fatigue but, all in all, he was feeling better every day.

They pulled into a gas station to fill the truck again, picked up a local free paper and found out in short order that they wouldn't be able to afford so much as a broom closet in Vail, and cheap motels were non-existent.

"Well," Valerian said, "we can stay at the Four Seasons and have valet service, doormen, a suite of rooms, and spa facilities, or we can go back the way we came and get a regular room for the night while we look for something that I might actually be able to afford to rent."

"I wish I could treat you to the Four Seasons for all you've done," he said, "but I think we'd better go with plan B for now."

They decided to walk around Vail for a while before leaving, and enjoy the Swiss-Alps feel of the town. The village, the mountains, the mansions, the flowers everywhere despite the late season—he'd never seen anything like it. Even with the masses of touristy shops, July thought it was one of the most beautiful places he'd ever been. He'd been right, though, about the off-season. Most of the shops and restaurants had signs that they would close for the month of October or longer, and the wide roads and sidewalks were sparsely peopled with locals and childless tourists who had the freedom to travel see the trees changing on a weekday in late September.

They picked up some local papers, found their way back to the truck, and traveled west again through progressively less elegant towns. They pulled off in Eagle, a normal looking town with slightly more affordable hotels. July tried his credit card again, but the inevitable happened and it finally declined, either maxed out or canceled for non-payment. Valerian tried to pay, but he refused and paid the clerk in cash, then treated her to Chinese take-out, which they ate in their room.

They spent the evening pouring over the newspapers and she found some possibilities for a rental. After phone calls and appointments had been made for the next day they cuddled on the bed while they watched TV. July enjoyed the feel of her closeness but wondered if he might have misread her reaction to their kiss this morning. Valerian had been the one to suggest a room with one bed, and she had been the one to curl up against him, but she watched TV with the same nonchalance as at their last hotel room.

July dozed most of the evening. He woke to Valerian getting ready for bed and he did the same. They climbed into bed and turned off the nightstand lights. Valerian snuggled her face against him in the dark. She felt so damn good. July put an arm around her and stroked her back. His hand slipped up under the T-shirt she had worn to bed. He brushed the smooth, soft skin with his fingertips and let his hand slide over her hip and trail back up her side. Valerian began to shift under his ministrations, stretching against him, nuzzling his neck with her lips.

"Are you sure you're up for this?" she asked, her voice a whisper in his ear.

In answer, he took her hand from his chest and slid it down to his crotch.

"You know that's not what I meant." He could hear the smile in her voice.

"Are you planning to play rugby?"

"No," she said.

"Do you have any hidden sadistic tendencies? I mean, if you're into some dominatrix thing, I'd like to know now."

She laughed.

"Well then, I think this falls under the heading of normal daily activities."

"Daily?"

"You never know."

His lips found hers in the dark, and he kissed her long and deep. His good hand roamed her body, brushing her breasts, feeling the soft outlines of her hips and her buttocks, and tracing the crease between her legs that he could feel beneath the cotton of her underwear.

He ran his hands up her sides, careful not to scratch her with his cast, and lifted her T-shirt. She sat up to accommodate him and he eased the shirt over her head. He pulled off his own T-shirt, careful not to dislodge the gauze bandage still around his head, and rolled to his knees. He leaned over her until she lay back, and he hooked his fingers in the waistband of her underpants.

In the gap of the curtains—that seemed to exist in every hotel and motel in the world, no matter how heavy the material—the light of floodlights lit the room enough to see her clearly. He watched as she lifted, allowing him to slide her panties off, and saw no hesitation in her face.

July learned her body with his hands, and then with his mouth. She responded to each new caress with increasing intensity. Her body was lithe and athletic. When she stretched and moved under his touch he felt her ribs, like the ribs on a lean and muscled hunting hound. Her legs were nearly as long as his, graceful and toned as a swimmer's. He wished his cast wasn't in the way, so he could run the palms of both hands down the lengths of her thighs.

Despite his healing collarbone, he didn't want to be on his back. He wanted to cover her and make love to her and feel like a man again. He raised himself over her keeping most of his weight on his good arm. She slid his underwear down so he could kick them off. He entered her slowly and teased her with short strokes and long, shallow and deep. Her hands moved down his ass, and she pulled him into the rhythm she desired, keeping him there until finally the beast within him took over. Orgasm was the only time in his life where he truly let go. He let go now and came deep and hard.

July woke to the sound of the shower running. He stretched and rubbed his eyes, feeling more relaxed than he had in months. When Valerian stayed in the bathroom overly long he began to worry, imagining that she didn't want to come out, that she was avoiding him. The door finally opened and she emerged with a white towel wrapped around her nakedness. She rubbed her newly-cropped, blonde hair with a second, smaller towel and smiled at him sheepishly.

"Oh, wow." he said. The dreads had been cut all the way to their bases, leaving a cap of short pixie-like hair. He loved it and said so.

"It took forever with that little motel razor and my pocket knife." She laughed.

"So what inspired that?"

"It just didn't feel like me anymore," she said.

July donned a weathered Padres baseball cap, which mostly covered the bandage wrapping his head, and they left the hotel. They read the new set of morning papers over breakfast, finding one or two additional listings, and set out to look at potential rentals, though both of them were still shell-shocked by the costs. The little towns between Eagle and Vail had more than their share of luxury homes, but also run-of-the-mill apartments and trailer parks because the house cleaners, gardeners, waiters, and all the other support staff for the obscenely wealthy had to live somewhere. Scouring the low-end housing, though, they found that even sharing a 'cheap' apartment was as high-priced as renting a whole house in the Midwest.

They started down Val's list of addresses that seemed to have the most potential. There were four places on the list. At the first one the tenants spoke Spanish only, another had four people looking for a fifth, and the third was a dump. The fourth place they went to turned out to be a nice condo in Minturn, a little town on a turn-off not far from Vail. A thirty-something man opened the door. He looked dude-like cool and athletic, and July felt an instant jealousy that Valerian might end up living with him.

Travis, as he introduced himself, opened the door wide and invited them in. The condo was clean, but piles of clutter stood in every corner. Boxes of biking shoes and motocross boots were stacked by the living room window, decals and medals and posters covered one edge of the dining room table. When he showed them the rest of the place, July glanced into Travis's bedroom to find so much sporting goods equipment and memorabilia, that it was hard at a glance to see the bed and the desk.

Travis noticed July scanning all the piles. "I race under sponsorship, downhill in the winter and motocross in the summer," he explained. "Between races I sell shit on eBay. You wouldn't believe how much crap I come into during a season. It's pretty wild what people will pay for it too." He waved a hand at the other bedroom. "This one would be yours. My last roommate didn't get re-hired at the ski area for the winter season, so he moved over to Breckenridge last weekend. You could move in right away if you wanted."

Valerian looked to July for his opinion and he shrugged, leaving the decision to her.

"I'll take it," she said.

"Cool," Travis said. "I'm out of here this evening and I'll be gone for the weekend. Some of my buddies and me are headed for Moab, so make yourselves at home." He seemed not to care whether July was part of the bargain or not.

Valerian wrote him a check on the spot and signed the generic rental agreement. Travis took a spare key off the fireplace mantle and handed it to her. July and Valerian unloaded their pathetically few possessions into the empty bedroom then headed out to drive around and familiarize themselves with the area.

"Val, are you sure it's okay for me to stay here for a bit?" he asked, as she pulled back onto I-70. "I'm feeling pretty decent now. I could head back to Flagstaff if you wanted me to. You know, so you could get settled here or whatever."

Her turquoise eyes went momentarily tight, forming the crease of a worry line between her brows. "No, I don't want you to. Not unless you *want* to leave, that is. But even if you don't want to stay with me, I hope you'll at least stay at the hotel for a bit. I mean, it was only yesterday that you passed out again."

"I wasn't saying that I want to leave," he amended, realizing how she had taken what he said. "I was just making sure you still want me around."

"Sheesh," she exclaimed, flapping one arm in the air in exasperation. "Don't do that to me! I thought maybe you were one of those guys who want someone until they get them and then do anything to get away. No, stupid, of course I want you here. You promised me you would stay a few weeks until you're fully recovered."

"I can't work though, and now that my credit card is no good my money won't last very long. I don't feel right about being dead weight."

"Recovering from brain surgery is not the same thing as being dead weight," she pointed out. "Get over it."

She pulled her phone out of the tapestry bag she called a purse and handed it to him. "Okay. Next order of business. We need to find you a doctor before your follow-up is due, and I'd like to hit the local chamber of commerce offices to see if there are any upcoming events."

"Yes ma'am," he said, taking the phone.

They were leaving the Vail chamber of commerce when Valerian spotted Steve. The shock of seeing him caused her brain to lock up momentarily, like a car hitting the brakes. Her heart thumped with a quick extra beat.

Steve did a double-take at her short hair, not seeming to know for sure if it was her. "Valerian?"

"Oh, shit," she said. July, walking hand-in-hand with her, tensed at her tone.

Looking more certain, Steve jogged across the wide cobbled path that ran through the center of the village.

"What the hell are you doing here Steve?" she asked when he stopped in front of her.

"What do you think I'm doing? I'm looking for you."

She should've never told him where she was going when she left. She was angry, that last time they fought, and she'd wanted to throw it in his face.

"Who the hell is this?" Steve asked, thrusting his chin at July. "Is he the reason you cut your hair? I can't believe this, you've been gone one God-damn week and you're all hand in hand with some guy already. Or were you fucking him before you left? Is he the reason you split?"

"Ease up, ass-hole," July said, letting go of her hand and moving between Valerian and Steve.

"July, don't," she said. He didn't listen to her. July and Steve stood face-to-face, like two bad-tempered badgers quarreling over territory. Steve turned red, the way he did when he was about to lose it. He was a second-degree black belt, and July was in no condition to take him on anyway.

"Steve, don't do this," she said, moving to July's side. "I didn't know him in Phoenix. I left you because of *you*, nothing else, and being an ass is most definitely not going to improve my opinion of you."

Never taking his eyes off July, Steve said, "Valerian, let's go somewhere and talk."

"It doesn't sound to me like she wants to talk to you," July said.

Valerian would have gone with Steve, just to tell him to go back to Phoenix, but she didn't have the chance to say it. Steve punched straight at July's face. July moved quicker than she would've thought he could, dodging back and bringing his cast down on the bony protrusions of Steve's wrist. It had to have hurt like hell, but Steve never paused. He threw a roundhouse kick at July's head.

"Goddammit Steve, he just had brain surgery!" she yelled. "Stop this."

At some super-aware level she felt July tense at her words. Sandwiched in with her fear for July and her anger at Steve, came an awful guilt that she had diminished July in front of an adversary, breaking trust with him by exposing his weakness.

She was a red belt herself and capable at sparring, but the two men were engaged in such close conflict that there was no way to come between them. She moved with them, remaining in their circle of conflict, looking for an opening.

July threw a wicked and fast punch to Steve's head and caught him on the chin before Steve could fully dodge it. Steve threw himself backward, going with the momentum and turning it to an advantage as he dropped to a three-point support and swept one leg behind July's knees, taking him down. She saw July flail as he fell, trying to protect both his left shoulder and the right side of his head. He took the brunt of the fall square on his shoulder blades, but his head succumbed to gravity and bounced back to hit the sidewalk.

He went limp.

Chapter 19

July knew what was going to happen even before his head made contact with the cobbles.

One moment he was lying on the sidewalk in Vail, and the next he was lying on the warm sand of the pseudo-Utah desert.

He closed his eyes, unwilling to look at his surroundings, though he could feel it did nothing to change them. His blood raced and his arms tingled, still amped from the fight. Adrenaline coursing through him increased his anger at being pulled back to this world again. It burned through him as hot and relentless as the desert sun in mid-summer. He didn't want to be here. He didn't want to leave Val with that ass-hole. He didn't want to be forced into yet another journey through the dark places in his head.

July rubbed at his eyes as if he could rub away the landscape in front of him. He sat up and looked out at the now familiar vista of scrub plants, rock bluffs and sand. He shouted a guttural cry of frustration at the blue sky above. Raking a hand through hair that no longer possessed nor needed the gauze bandage, he took a deep breath. He needed to get back to his own world as quickly as possible and knew only one way to make that happen. Twisting his neck to find the sun, July did his best to gauge west.

If time ran differently here it could be mid-afternoon instead of mid-morning, which would mean his sense of direction could be off by a hundred and eighty degrees, in which case he was fucked. He got up and began walking the direction that seemed most likely to be west, wondering why they couldn't just show him what he had to see and let him get on with it already.

It was nearly midday when he caught a movement at the corner of his eye. He stopped and scanned the bluff to his right. There had been a coyote in this world at Coit Tower; perhaps there were mountain lions in Utah. The dozen shades of reds and tans in the rock could camouflage any number of things. He watched until he felt convinced that nothing was moving.

July walked perhaps twenty minutes more before he saw something again. Scanning the horizon, he studied what looked suspiciously like a figure hunched near a bush. When he stared at it long enough, it turned out to be a boulder. He searched 360 degrees, looking for any living thing besides himself. Maybe Pat shadowed him as an animal, or had to trail him secretively to seem to appear out of nowhere. Maybe, but July doubted it.

He had just started walking again when he heard the swish and scrape of boots running across the sand. He spun to see Bill launching at him. July had just enough time to wonder why the universe—both universes apparently—wanted so badly to hurt him, before Bill grabbed July by the shoulders and pulled him down.

July hadn't been in a fight in years and now found himself in his third in as many weeks. The reflexes built in the cockfights of his youth, and the occasional job-site scuffles and bar fights inherent to construction workers served him well. Bill rolled him in the sand and scrabbled for a hand-hold on his throat. July tried to twist away, but Bill was stocky, and stronger still with the strength that insanity can lend to a man.

Unlike the fight with Steve, July didn't need to worry about his head injury or collarbone—although the ridiculously pink cast still hampered him. He worked his left arm up between them and pressed his cast against Bill's throat. Face-to-face, July could clearly see the crazy in Bill's eyes. He pushed the cast harder against the sensitive Adam's apple until Bill gave a strangled roar and rolled free. They both came to their feet breathless and wary.

"Bill," July panted, "you don't need to do this. I'm trying my best to get the hell out of here. Why don't you just ease up and let me be on my way."

Bill hadn't changed at all. He was the same as he had been the last two times July had seen him, except that he was sans the oiled duster in the desert heat, wearing only the tattered T-shirt and jeans.

"I told you not to come back," Bill said, "but you did anyway. You keep coming back. I have to stop you."

July put his hands up, placating. He backed away two or three steps. "Look, maybe there's another way for you to help me. Maybe you can tell me something that might help me get through this. If I finish my journey, then I'll be gone. You won't have to see me here anymore."

"No!" Bill yelled. His voice reverberated off the bluffs and hoodoos. "You'll fail. That's what we do, we fail. We failed there and we fail here. You're leaving me no choice." His voice dropped and his head bowed. "It's too late for me, but it's not too late for you."

"What do you mean?" July asked, trying to keep Bill talking.

"They won't let me kill myself," he said with a sad whine. "I can't even do that."

July lowered his hands and looked at the man, really looked at him. Bill might be crazy, but he was also a kindred spirit; a man who had carried his own too-heavy baggage of traumas and failures in the real world. Someone who had lived in his own borrowed hell, like July had, and then had been kept here against his will to live in another kind of hell. One that had driven him mad.

"Do you remember anything of your other life?" July asked quietly. He didn't know where the question had come from, and he hoped, belatedly, that it wouldn't ignite the man to violence again.

The question caught Bill off-guard. He looked for a moment like an overgrown child, lost on a busy city street. "I dream about it sometimes. I think I do anyway." Bill pressed the heels of his hands to his eyes and pushed hard enough that July worried he might hurt himself. July thought he heard a sob.

He squatted, the same as he might have done with an unpredictable dog. "Look, Bill," he said, "I get it. You think I'd be better off dead than stuck here like you, but I finally have something in my life that makes me want to get through this so I can go back to my own world. There's a woman I met. I need to get back to her."

Bill lowered his hands. Perhaps his eyes were only watering from the pressure of his fists, but the fight had gone out of him. For now, anyway.

"I learned some things about myself here," July continued, standing again slowly, "and I think I might have a chance finally at making a relationship work. I might fail here, but at least I want the chance to try."

Bill shook his head slowly side to side. "You will fail. You'll never get your girl. You'll never escape your demons."

Bill stood to the west of him now. He approached slowly, watching the man's body language carefully. It was wrong what they'd done to him. They had no right to pull people out of their lives and put them through this obscene and unasked-for ritual. The least they could've done was return Bill to his own world, even if their test hadn't molded him into the man they wanted him to be.

"Is there a way that I can help you from the other side?" July was within arm's length of Bill again, but the big man stood morose and unmoving. "Is there anything I could do to help you get out of this place?"

Bill shook his head. The moisture in his eyes brimmed at his lower lids. He dropped his head until his long hair covered his face.

July reached out and squeezed Bill's thick arm. "If I make it through this," he said, "I'll look for a way to get you out of here. I promise." Bill looked up at him with a puppy-dog-pleading look. "I'll ask Pat," July told him, "and if he doesn't know, I'll ask God himself."

July knew he was one step east of becoming just like Bill. Empathy swelled in him for whatever the man had suffered in the real world and his punishment here for not being strong enough. With a rush of emotional solidarity, he stepped closer and gave Bill a rough bear hug. Bill stiffened but made no move to pull away. July was letting go when he felt meaty arms wrap around his back and squeeze.

July let the man bruise his ribs. It was the least he could do and it wasn't enough. He couldn't remember ever having prayed in his life, but he prayed now, to whatever might be listening, that somehow they would both find a way out of this madness.

Bill released him and turned away. He walked to the east, looking back over his shoulder only once.

"Don't give up," he said.

Chapter 20

July watched Bill walk over a small rise.

He set off again, hoping he wouldn't have much further to go, but as he trudged onward the hope faded. The land began to rise to either side and July was funneled into a dry riverbed running between the bluffs. The riverbed had deeper sand and the grains worked under the tongue of his boots, small enough that they weren't worth stopping to remove and large enough to be irritating. The noon heat beat down, and the sweat on his face mingled, grimy and sticky, with the layer of fine dust coating his skin.

After twenty or thirty minutes in the riverbed, he stepped out of the watercourse when it turned abruptly to the north. He climbed up onto a bulge of rock, smoothed eons ago when the river must have run higher. He judged west as best he could with the sun nearly overhead, and continued onward.

His course seemed to run conveniently between the rocky bluffs to either side, down a wide path that narrowed as the bluffs began to form a V. Soon he was walking between walls that he could have reached out and touched on either side. The bluffs were low, perhaps twenty feet tall, but as he walked deeper into the cleft between them, they grew taller. Soon they were fifty feet high or more, with smooth, insurmountable walls.

The sun tumbled into the wide crack overhead, illuminating what had become a shoulder-wide slit in the rock. Ahead, the walls curved to the right, hiding whatever lay beyond. The narrow path woke July's old claustrophobia, and it squeezed at his chest as if the walls of the cleft pressed against him physically. He pushed away a sudden fear that he might encounter his obstacle in this confined space and be stuck in here.

Slot-canyons. The name came to him. He'd seen them on some TV show or movie, but had never seen one in person. The formation seemed too tall and narrow to have been made by water; it looked more like some tremendous pressure had simply split the bluff in two with enough force to separate the halves by a foot or two.

July's breathing grew short and shallow. He tried to breathe deeper, slower. He could control his anxiety; he knew he could because he always had. *Except in tight spaces,* the reminder niggled in. His sister had been the same; they had shared their fear of confinement all through their childhood, though Alice had probably picked it up from him. He tried to calm himself by reasoning that if this was the path he had been led to, then there would be a way out. The thought was harder to hold onto in the sections where the walls narrowed enough that he had to twist his body and crab-walk.

He squeezed past yet another tight bend in the path and

scrambled over a boulder blocking his way. Besides the variations in the path, the rock itself changed from section to section. One curve exposed a deep, cavernous whorl, another, a flat stretch of rock pocked with a thousand pigeon-sized caves. The striations twisted agonizingly in places, where uplifts had pushed the rock like liquid. Sun and shadow played with the ever-changing angle of the walls. *Slow breaths, keep moving,* he repeated in his head like a mantra, as he continued to make steady progress.

He'd gone perhaps a quarter of a mile or more into the bowels of the sundered bluff when the trail suddenly narrowed to half the width. In the space of a few heartbeats, he was stuck; unable to go forward and forbidden to turn back, with walls too sheer to climb.

His claustrophobia ratcheted up a couple of notches and July braced to resist the panic that thundered at him like a rapidly approaching train. There was no end in sight to the slot canyon, and the walls were too close together to place his feet against one side and his back against the other to chimney-climb up, even if he had the nerve to try it on this tallest-yet stretch of wall.

Why did his obstacle have to be in the middle of this God-damn thing? He had played along with everything they'd thrown at him, showed determination, walked west; why couldn't they give him a break for once? They wouldn't though, and this was where he was going to have to deal with the next set of memories. He had guessed it some time ago.

July reassured himself that all he had to do was control his fear long enough to see whatever he had to see, and then a way out of this place would present itself. That was only half his battle, though. If the memories thrown at him progressed from the least to the greatest of his emotional issues, then this could only be one of two things.

July took a few more deep breaths, as much to prepare for what was coming as to push back the claustrophobia. He turned and leaned against one wall, sliding down into a sitting position, with his knees folded nearly to his chest in the cramped space. He looked to his right, to the east and the way out of all of this. He closed his eyes against the temptation.

The thought of Bill haunted July as much as the thought of what was coming. Running back out of this canyon wouldn't be an escape, it would be a trap worse than the one he was in already. It would confine him forever. July steeled himself to be strong, and remembered Pat's words that he had it within himself to do this. He opened to the memories. The pictures came immediately.

He was a child in the barren and dry desert of southeastern New Mexico. In front of him stood an ancient aqua-colored, single-wide trailer, with peeling aluminum trim. He could smell the garbage piled in the burn barrel behind the trailer, waiting for someone to take the time to pour lighter fluid over it and drop a match on top.

Flat desert stretched in all directions, nothing but an occasional yucca plant jutting out of the ground. One of his mother's friends had told July that the plants were hands clawing out of the ground, and they'd grab him by the ankles and pull him under if he went close. July knew they weren't really hands, but he still walked well clear of the one in front of him as he made his way to the front steps.

Trash was strewn around the trailer, things that had been dropped or had blown out of the burn barrel, or had gained their freedom from the trailer thanks to the gusty New Mexico winds. Among the cigarette wrappers and empty tin cans, was a white, stuffed bunny lying near the steps, one glass eye missing. Baxter Bunny was his favorite toy of all the things he could ever remember his father bringing home for him. He picked Baxter up out of the dirt and stroked the long ears, then climbed up the precariously tall trailer steps.

The front door was closed and his small fingers tugged at the metal latch to pull the door open. His mother lay on their old couch, with its faded orange and gray check pattern, the stuffing oozing out of the arms like cotton candy. Alice sat on the floor, half under the coffee table. She thumped her pacifier on the dirty floor.

His mother woke when the trailer door banged shut. Her black hair was un-brushed and haphazardly caught up in a clip, and her pink, flowered housecoat contrasted violently with the couch.

For the adult July, living the scene somewhere in the recesses of his mind as he sat in another desert and his body lay unconscious in his own world, it was a shock to see his mother with clarity and vividness. She looked older than her years, but must have only been his age now. Perhaps even younger.

His mother lifted her head and saw July standing at the foot of the couch. He was hopping Baxter across the cotton candy stuffing. "Bring me my Jimmy, July," she said in a groggy voice. "There's a good boy."

He was five years old, but knew already that 'her Jimmy' was one of her medicines that made her feel better. July set Baxter down and obediently went to the kitchen to retrieve the half-full quart bottle of Jim Beam from under the sink. He carried it awkwardly, one hand on the neck of the bottle, the other wrapped around the body, holding it to his chest so he wouldn't drop it. He set it on the coffee table in front of her, next to the brimming ashtray, then went back to the kitchen for the short, round glass she liked. The sink was full of dirty dishes and the cupboards were too tall for him, but he found a tumbler on the counter. It had a sticky brown coating at the bottom, but she didn't seem to mind when he brought her those. He handed her the glass.

A car ground and crunched its way from the paved road across the gravel and sand to the door of the trailer. With a jolt of apprehension, he stared at the door; the same apprehension he always felt when people came over. Four car doors slammed.

July went to Alice, dragging her out from under the coffee table. She cried at his awkward handling but he hushed her. He wasn't big enough to lift her, so he half-carried, half-walked her to their bedroom. From his room, he heard the voices of four men and a woman as they entered the trailer.

"Hey, Estella," one of the men said. "I tried to call, but your phone's shut off. This is my friend Miguel. He don't have no place to stay tonight. I told him maybe he could stay here."

"Sure, yeah. Sure he can." July's mother answered. Her voice was low and rough from cigarettes and alcohol. She had the same accent all the adults in the room did, a little Apache, a little Spanish, a little West Texas influence. "Have you seen Sebastian?" she asked.

"Sure have honey, and he sent you a little present."

July pulled his door open a crack and watched. He saw his mother smile as she took the package.

Alice and July went hungry that night. Alice cried sometimes, but July insisted they stay in their room while the six adults partied late into the night. Probably no one would've cared if he'd gone out to get some food from the kitchen, but he had seen enough of these parties to be cautious. He knew that the happiness went away, changing to an unpredictable phase, before his mother and the visitors eventually passed out. There had been times July and Alice had been enticed to interact with the visitors, and it frightened him how they shouted everything they said, or tried to dance with him and Alice, or stumbled, sometimes falling into them. Alice cried again, and he whispered to her that they had to wait until it was quiet.

The scene shifted.

The partiers were gone. It was another day. July was watching cartoons on TV. Alice was on the floor by the couch. She was too young to watch TV, but she liked to watch the pictures move. When she got excited she would flap her arms and talk baby talk at them.

July's mother was on the couch again. She asked July to get her 'special things.' She'd been better the past few days while their father was home, she only needed 'her Jimmy' now and then when he was there, and never her 'special things,' but their father was never home very long.

July went into her bedroom and opened her nightstand drawer. He took the little wooden box out of the drawer that held the medicine she needed when she got really sick. She had told him many times that she would die without it. His finger traced the cutout flower pattern carved into the top that he liked so much, and he walked back to her, still transfixed by the feel of his finger in the grooves of the petals and vines.

His mother opened the box and took out the rubber thing that looked like a noodle, the spoon, the lighter, and a little foil package. She took one end of the noodle and handed the other end to July to hold while she wrapped it around her arm. July watched as she heated the spoon over the lighter until the thick brown goo bubbled. When it cooled, she drew it up into the syringe and hunted for a vein that would still accept the prick of a needle.

She nodded with the needle still in her arm, and he thought she had gone to sleep, but her eyes flicked open and she pulled the needle out. His mother dropped the things back into the box then tipped the lid shut with one finger. July tugged at the rubber noodle, reminding her, and she pulled it, releasing it with a pop.

Near evening, his mother opened the box again. It wasn't like her to take her medicine more than once a day and July worried that she might be more sick than usual. He helped her again and waited while she gave herself a shot. This time when July tried to remind her about the noodle, she didn't wake up. He pulled on one end and it snapped free.

"Mama?" he said, when she still didn't wake. July had never touched the needle, but he tugged it from her arm and placed it in the box, shutting the lid like she always did. "Mama?" he said again, but she didn't respond.

She remained sitting up, but July pulled a blanket up under her chin to help her sleep. She was still—so still that fingers of fear pulled at his stomach and his heart beat faster watching her, though he couldn't have said why. July climbed up onto the sofa next to her and laid his head against her arm.

He napped there a short time until a sound from his mother woke him, it was like the sound a snake might make, a hiss of air. A bubble of saliva formed between her purpling lips and stayed there for minutes. Everything about her felt strange and frightening. July tugged at her hand. It felt cold to touch, with a texture like the rubber of the noodle. He cried and yelled for her to wake, but all he accomplished was to wake Alice, who was sleeping on the floor, and then she cried too.

The adult July cringed from the memories, from the searing, awful reality of seeing that event in life-sized detail, every tactile sensation relived, every emotion felt anew. He pulled back and felt the connection to the memory stretch like taffy. He knew then that he had the power to break the connection, to refuse, to run. To run east.

"Don't give up." Bill's single piece of advice. July clung to the thought. He gritted his teeth and allowed the memory to continue.

July and Alice slept hungry that night. In the morning, his mother looked so rigid and mottled that he was afraid to go near her. He'd never made a phone call but he had talked to his father on the phone and thought maybe he would be there. The rapid beeping in the earpiece was loud when he picked up the receiver. July tried to talk over it, "Daddy?" he said, but no one answered him. He didn't know when his father would be back, but it always seemed a long time in between his leaving and his coming home.

July took Alice's hand and left the trailer. He scooted down the steps and had his sister do the same so they wouldn't fall, but his sister fell off the last step anyway and cried. Holding her hand, he walked out to the road but no cars were coming. He waited a while longer, but still no one came along. July took Alice back to the trailer and helped her up the stairs.

He hurried out to the road every time he heard a car, but by the time he got outside they were gone, leaving only a cloud of dust. Once, two cars in a row went by. July waited at the road for the second car but it never slowed, and he stood there, watching it drive past.

By mid-morning he was so hungry that he opened all the cabinets he could reach. There was never much food in the refrigerator when his father was gone. He and Alice ate a can of potato chips and all the string cheese he found. He wasn't allowed to use the gas stove, but that evening he found a step stool in a closet, put a pan on the stove and cracked two eggs into it, picking out as much shell as he could. He fiddled with the knobs until the stove hissed but it never did light and he turned it off. Climbing down, he went to the little flower-covered box on the coffee table. He didn't like being so close to his mother now. Her face looked blue and she smelled like the burn barrel outside. He tried not to look into her half-open eyes.

He took the lighter out of the box and tried the stove again, but his little fingers couldn't make the lighter come to life. He and Alice tried to eat their eggs raw and share a glass of milk, but the milk had a bitter taste and Alice wouldn't eat the raw egg. Alice cried more often.

The following day some of his mother's friends came by to visit. They found her bloated body still sitting up on the couch. A woman stayed outside with July and Alice while one of the men drove to town to use a pay phone. Other people came then, a policeman and more people that July had never seen before. They took him and his sister away and July and Alice stayed with an old couple. He kept asking for his father. When his father finally came, he scooped them both up and hugged them and promised that he would never leave them again.

The pictures stopped. The memories he'd always suppressed from childhood had been bad enough. The harsh reality of those experiences, seen again as an adult, was the kind of ugly no one should ever have to face.

He wanted to rage at this Utah. He took a perverse pleasure in his claustrophobic hatred of the slot canyon; like he had hated the confines of that trailer for those few days. The punishment seemed apt for watching his mother die, for helping her. He wanted to curl up in the canyon like he might in a womb and never leave. The tears finally came. July cried for his guilt and for his innocence, he cried for his mother's wasted life and the demons that took her from him, he cried for the child he had been and the cost to him for witnessing her death. A cost he'd carried all these years. He cried until he had no tears left and then he cried some more.

The tears finally dried, but still he sat against the rocky wall, unmoving. Nothing changed. Pat didn't come, nor did Patricia. Bill didn't come back. July dozed but he woke up again in the pattern's world. He hadn't eaten or drunk since breakfast in Vail and he was hungry and thirsty. Looking more closely at the narrow cleft, he thought that he might be able to squeeze through the opening after all. It was only the first few feet that looked too constricted, after that it seemed to open at least a little bit more. He didn't care. He didn't want to squeeze through the opening. He wanted to wake up in his own reality, or to rot here in this slot canyon, but he didn't want to think about what he'd seen and he didn't want to take another step in this world.

He sat curled where he was until sunset shadowed the cleft. Stubbornness came and went. He hadn't moved forward, and he knew that nothing would happen until he did. He knew that he was cutting off his nose to spite his face.

"Don't give up," Bill had said. Not moving forward was just another way of giving up.

July's face was crusty with dried tears and sand. He scrubbed at it roughly. In the same way that seeing his father without rose-colored glasses hadn't changed anything, neither had this, not really. He'd never forgotten his mother's overdose, nor the two days he and his sister had spent, afraid and alone, living in the trailer with her dead body.

His mother's alcoholism and drug abuse had made a wreck of his childhood, but she had grown up in poverty, the child of two alcoholics. She'd hardly stood a chance. Like so many others, she had chosen a false escape route over true freedom. Her friends, the ones that July had hated so much as a child, had been just like her; people who felt they had no options for change, nowhere to go, and people who, just like his mother, dealt poorly with their inertia.

His whole life, July had avoided the worst of his memories out of fear that reviving them might change him. Without them he wasn't crazy, he wasn't an addict, he wasn't suicidal. With them riding around in the front of his thoughts he didn't know who he was going to be. Dealing poorly with the lot he had, though, would serve him no better than it had her.

July looked at the narrow way through the cleft again and pushed to his feet. He wriggled his chest and shoulders into the gap. He squeezed his hips through the small opening. He pushed toward freedom and an uncertain future, like being born anew.

He was too numb to feel his claustrophobia. He squirmed and writhed his way past the narrowest section until he could stand again without his shoulders rubbing the walls. Darkness filled the cleft, and he brushed both hands along the walls as he walked, until the walls spread to the point where he could only touch one side at a time.

The images he had relived from his past flashed like a zoetrope in his mind. At each new frame his mind flinched, but he fought the impulse to hide them away again. He found to his surprise that the memories lost a little of their power as he visited them over and over.

July came out of the slot canyon as gradually as he had entered it. The moon crested the horizon behind him. It was full and harvest orange. July couldn't remember if the moon had been full his last time here. In its pale glow, he could see the land rising up before him. He walked up the slope and the exertion felt good. It flushed his arteries, blowing out the rusty pipes in his body and his head, easing his pounding headache and nausea.

When he looked up again, Pat was standing there. He was middle-aged and Asian-American, well-muscled with short, dark hair. As July came closer, he saw the eyes were lighter than he expected, green perhaps. The light of the moon shimmered on tears standing unshed in those eyes. July wanted to hate Pat for what the man was putting him through, but he couldn't. Pat looked as hurt and beat up as July felt.

"I'm proud of you," he said to July.

"You don't give me many options except to keep going."

"There are always options. I'm just glad you picked the right one." Pat moved closer to him. He slid one arm across July's back and when July didn't pull back he wrapped his other arm around July and hugged him. It was the same thing July had tried to do for Bill, but July didn't want to be like Bill. He didn't want to be the one who needed comfort, but the strong arms enfolding him made him feel safe, made him feel cared for. Hot tears burned his eyes again.

July pushed back from Pat and wiped his nose on his cast. "It was hard to watch her doing that to herself," he said.

"And to others," Pat added.

July shrugged and nodded. He sat, tired. Night had brought a chill to the air. "Why do there have to be so many types of people in the world. Why couldn't we all just have been made from you and Patricia? Think of all the bullshit in the world it would have prevented."

Pat sat as well. He pulled a bottle of water out of a pack that July hadn't noticed before. He uncapped the bottle and handed it to July. "Variety, I guess. Why is there more than one species of animal or tree? Besides, being based on my pattern or Patricia's doesn't mean someone won't have issues, or won't deal with them poorly. It just means you start with a different set of tools. It can be as much of a handicap to believe in yourself too strongly as not at all. It might make you think you can handle everything alone."

Pat relaxed into the cross-legged position he seemed to prefer in every incarnation of himself. He took the bottle back when July had finished drinking and took a swallow himself before continuing.

"The psychologists in your world have Jung's models, the Big Five, eight base personality models, sixteen base models, and so on. But the truth is that no matter what you start with, life boils down to insecurities." Pat held the bottle out to July again, but July shook his head. He screwed the cap back on and continued. "You come into the world wrapped in individual skins and isolated in your own brain from everyone else, then you get yanked through the physical, emotional and hormonal changes of maturation. Nobody's getting out of all that without issues."

Pat gestured, palms up, arms wide, still holding the bottle in one hand. "From there, it's all how you chose to deal with them. Base personality has a lot to do with it, but for better or for worse, most people try to incorporate the methods parents or role-models used: class-clown, class bully, shy, whatever. Add to that mess all the negative things people encounter as they grow up. Genetics complicates everything further. But at the end of the day, it's all about insecurity. The drive for money, perversions of the sex drive, crimes and posturing and fears and addictions. It's all ways to try and deal. Your mom just dealt with it in one of the ways that doesn't stand a chance of working."

"Maybe my way hasn't been that much better."

"Maybe not. Denial is like any other crutch, it only works so long."

July changed the subject. "So, is Val's ass-hole of a boyfriend going to manifest here somehow?"

Pat quirked an eyebrow in question.

"Of all the people here in this world I've only met four: Patty, who's like Mia—or Mia's like her, whatever—and she seems not to have been around since I quit thinking so much about Mia. Patricia, who showed up after I met Valerian; Bill, who comes from my world; and you, my pattern. So, now that Steve has jumped into my life and tried to beat the shit out of me, is his pattern going to be drawn to me here?"

"Perhaps. It depends how much of an influence he is on you there. Speaking of Bill, though, I wanted to tell you that you dealt with that situation well, July. Really well."

July shrugged, uncomfortable. "I didn't do anything. He's still crazy, and he's still stuck here. It was wrong of you to bring him here, to do that to him."

"I've told you, we aren't the ones to bring people here."

"Is there any way for him to get back to the real world?"

"I don't know. He's the first to be stranded here like this. I'm not sure what will become of him."

A thought suddenly occurred to July. "What about the coyote? What was that all about?"

"Coyote?"

"At the tower, the first time I came here. I saw a coyote in the doorway. It was looking right at me and it kind-of play-bowed and wagged its tail and then it ran off."

Pat shook his head. "I don't know what it meant. Something from your real life, I suppose. You're still there as much as you are here. An emotion or an event in your real life that's powerful enough might mirror itself here."

July tried to think what in his real life could have caused the coyote to appear, and remembered thinking of Robert Vegas as a coyote. And Robert had come to the hospital while July was still unconscious to drop off the coin and the card to thank him.

"Huh," he said. He remembered the globe of flame in the pharmacy.

July looked at up at the stars covering the night sky. He was dead tired and emotionally drained. His eyes felt like the dusty sand beneath him. All he wanted was to get back to his own world. He closed his eyes and Pat fell silent. Within minutes, July drifted toward sleep.

Chapter 21

July sat up and wished he hadn't. His head hurt at the back where he had hit the pavement and at the side under his surgery incision. His baseball cap had rolled off, exposing the gauze bandage around his head. They were in the middle of Vail Village, and the few locals and workers in the nearby shops were coming out to stare. One had a cell phone to his ear.

Valerian must have understood the implication as well as July did. "Are you doing well enough to get out of here?"

He nodded. "How long was I out?"

"I wasn't even sure you'd passed out. It must have been just a few seconds. Your eyes were open by the time I got to you." She searched his face, aware of what passing out meant for him.

"I'm sorry, babe," Steve said behind her. "I just wanted him to lay off so we could talk."

"I'm not the one you need to apologize to," she snapped.

Steve didn't apologize, but he held out his hand to help July up. Wary, July took it. Once he was on his feet, he bent to pick up his cap, making his head throb.

"We should go before the police get here," Valerian said.

Steve patted July on the back, putting on a show for the small knot of people watching them. "It's all good," he said in a loud voice, looking toward the man on the cell phone. To Valerian he said, "I have a hotel room not too far from here. Let's go there for now."

"July, do you need to go the hospital?" Valerian asked.

"No, I'm okay. Let's get out of here." July didn't want to go anywhere with Steve but he was disoriented from the jump back into his own world and numbed by the emotional storm he had suffered in the other one. Besides, he was as eager as they were to move away from the stares of the little crowd they had attracted.

The three of them crossed the street, leaving the village behind, and walked into an area with apartments and condos and timeshares mixed in with hotels and the ever-present shops. Behind them, the police pulled up at the corner and walked the other way into the village, toward the caller.

July followed Steve and Val wordlessly for about two blocks, away from the police and away from his truck. Steve had taken a room in a nearby lodge, and he opened the door to a small room not much different than the motel room July and Valerian had stayed in the previous night, except that it had a small deck off the back. July guessed the view from that deck had cost him a lot more than his and Val's hotel room had.

The tension between the three of them was palpable almost to being electric and July wished he was anywhere but here. Steve probably wished that for him as well. What Val thought was anyone's guess. July needed to go somewhere quiet. He needed to think and he needed to sleep. From his perspective, he'd been up for the past twenty-four hours—and a fucking rough twenty-four hours at that.

"Listen, Valerian, just let me talk to you," Steve was saying to her as he closed the door. "I came all this way to find you. At least let me say what I came to say."

Val shot July a look. He wasn't sure if it was a look of regret or apology. "Fine," she said to Steve. "Say what you have to say."

"Out here," he said, leading her to the back of the room. She followed him onto the deck. July sat on the couch wishing he could just take off, but not willing to leave Valerian here with Steve unless she told him she wanted that.

Steve slid the glass door firmly closed behind them, and July was left with only murmurs and body language. Steve looked younger than July, more Val's age, or maybe life just hadn't beat him up as bad. July had heard more than once that he looked older than his thirty-one years.

Steve's sandy-blonde hair was cut short. He was deeply tanned, well-muscled, and handsome enough to look like a performer despite the long scar above his left eyebrow. He kept touching Valerian as he talked to her, reaching out and brushing her arm, running his fingers through her short-cropped hair, reaching for her face. She pulled back at first, then stood still for his touch. He leaned in and gave her a gentle kiss.

Val didn't appear to object.

When Steve pulled back, Val brushed a tear from one eye. She let him keep his arms around her waist and spoke earnestly to him, one hand still on his arm, never glancing toward July. She stretched up and gave him a kiss on the forehead.

July felt like one of those eggshells where all the egg has

been sucked out through a tiny pinprick, leaving something that looked whole and normal, though it was empty inside. But really, what had he expected? He'd known Val for less than two weeks. Steve had been with her for years.

It was for the best, he told himself. He'd been relying on her too much and it was making him weak. The hollowness rattling in his chest and belly showed how little of him was left without her. If he was going to survive what was still to come in that other world, then he needed to learn to rely on himself again. Besides, Val didn't need him. She'd be okay on her own, and if Steve pissed her off she'd probably leave him even easier a second time. It'd probably just been a simple misunderstanding anyway. If he stayed here until they came in, he only put her in the position of having to explain and him of waiting around to be handed one more loss in his life. After reliving his mother's death what seemed only hours ago, more loss wasn't something he could handle right now.

July got up and let himself out.

He walked the long way around to the parking garage, taking the main road in case the police were still in the village. Once in his truck, July sat there a long while, unwilling to start the engine and drive away. He hadn't even gotten a chance to tell Val about his last journey to the other world. July turned the truck over, but didn't put it in gear, waiting just a little longer to see if she would show up.

She didn't.

He drove back to the condo in Minturn. Travis was in the garage, loading his motorbike onto a trailer and told July that the front door was still open. July gathered his stuff from the bedroom, threw it in the truck and got back on the interstate. He debated driving straight back to Flagstaff, but was too damn tired. He pulled off a few exits west of Minturn, in the town he and Val had stayed in the night before. He would have camped out to save money, but he wasn't sure he should be too far from other people, having just hit his head again this morning. He didn't think he had the energy to look for a campsite anyway.

July checked back into the same motel and paid for the room from his dwindling cash—nearly one-sixth of all the money he had left in the world. He didn't recognize the room number until he stood in front of the door. Sleeping alone in the bed that he and Val had just shared seemed like salt in the wound, but he didn't have the reserves to change it out for another.

He was glad the gold Kugerand Robert Vegas had given him lay in a side pouch of his duffle. It probably wouldn't be enough to get him by until he could work again, but at least it would help. Thinking of being released to work reminded him that today was the day he should have seen a doctor for his post-surgical checkup. He'd head back to Flagstaff in the morning and make an appointment with Dr. Weslyn when he got there.

Once in the room, he tossed his bags in a corner and lay down on the bed. The sheets had been changed, the dirty towels taken away, and all traces of Val vacuumed and dusted and emptied from the room. His head spun with too many things: his injury, money, work, Val. His next obstacle.

July had never been suicidal, it just wasn't in his nature. He thought about it now, almost wistfully wishing that it could be an option. There was only one memory left worse than all the others. If anything could trap him there, this would be it, and suicide was the only sure way out. Bill would applaud the idea.

The images from New Mexico re-played in his head. It

renewed his desire to share the experience with Val. He had never been one to talk about his emotions or his past, but now that she knew some of it he wanted her to know all of it. Maybe telling her would have helped him get through the next one.

He didn't know how he was going to cope. He'd told Bill that Val was the reason he wanted to continue, to succeed. The hollowness he'd felt in Steve's room expanded. It seemed to fill not only him but all the room. He sat up on the bed, reached for the phone, and dialed his father's cell phone number.

"Howdy," a hearty recorded voice greeted him. "I'm on the road somewhere, maybe even on my way to your neck of the woods, but if not, I'd sure like to talk to you. Leave a message and I'll get back as soon as I can."

July hung up.

He didn't know if his prayer, his first ever—that he and Bill escape that world for good—would have any effect, but he tried again now, praying as hard as he could not to be taken back again. There was no answer to that call either.

The memories that had been brought to the fore in his previous visits kept rattling through July's head. They felt unfamiliar there, and couldn't seem to find a place to rest. Everything had been easier waking up with Val, walking hand-in-hand with her. The demons seemed quieter with her around. It had been good when they made love. Caring for people had always given him a sense of purpose and filled the empty parts of his life. Forced to take a long hard look at his childhood it was easy to see why.

The thoughts circled 'round, and 'round, and 'round in his head, keeping him from sleep. He got up to go into the bathroom thinking to check his head for any new damage from the fight this morning. His ears buzzed when he stood.

No. Not yet. *Oh God, no. Don't let them take me again so soon. I'm not ready.*

He reached out to steady himself against the wall as his world tunneled to black. His hand slid down the wall as he fell.

Chapter 22

He was standing at the top of the bluff where he had last seen Asian Pat.

The sky was wide and blue. It was just after dawn. He looked to the east, to the newly risen sun, and wondered if he should just turn around and walk that direction now.

Don't give up. Bill's last words rang through his head again.

July sighed and started west. He braced himself for another long trek and determined to spend the time steeling himself as best he could.

He'd been walking for an hour or so, when he scrambled up a sloping rock face and reached a rocky top. The sun warmed him and the wind cooled him and the silence gave him a quiet peace. Given what had happened with Val, he almost enjoyed the feel of this empty world. He took in the view. In the vast stillness of this land it was hard to believe that it had all been formed in violence: canyons by rushing water, hoodoos by the wind and erosion, uplifts and outcrops by the earth shrugging its great shoulders.

He walked across the flat, rocky surface until he came to a sudden deep but narrow crevasse. The slice in the rock looked like a knife cut. The gap in front of July was perhaps twenty feet deep or more but only a foot and a half wide, easy enough to step across. July lifted his foot to do just that when his perception changed and he realized the crevasse was actually three or four feet wide. Off-balance, he teetered, struggling to bring his center of gravity back over his supporting foot. His arms windmilled. Getting his balance under him so he would neither step forward nor backward, he set his foot down again at the edge of the split in the rock and waited for his heart to slow to normal.

Mother-fuckers could give me some warning.

Anger welled up inside, but he knew there was a better way to fight them. He was at the precipice of his last obstacle and if he made it through this he would never come here again.

"Give it your best shot," he hollered up to the sky.

Nothing happened. July sat and tried to clear his mind, resentful that he not only had to endure this, but had to want it.

The breeze tickled his scalp and neck. There should be red-tailed hawks floating on that breeze, and turkey vultures too. Other than the coyote, he had never seen an animal in this world: not even a lizard or a rabbit. He guessed animals didn't need patterns, but then why would they? It was human personalities that were screwed up; animals were pretty damn perfect. Maybe if there was a heaven, people would be based on animal patterns when they went there.

"I'm as ready as I'll ever be," he shouted.

As he expected, the memories that came were of his sister,

Alice.

July was at the kitchen table doing homework though it was his bedtime. A half-eaten pork chop, cold mashed potatoes, and some heated up frozen vegetable mix sat on a plate at his elbow.

"Don't you think about getting up until all that food is gone," Denise, his third stepmother, had told him over an hour ago.

His father was asleep in his recliner, snoring despite Roseanne Barr's strident voice and the sitcom's laugh track. Uncle Eddie and Denise were talking in low voices on the couch but July caught snippets of the conversation. He could see them through the open arch of the kitchen if he leaned forward just a bit.

"You're just too damn pretty," Eddie said.

Denise wasn't pretty, July thought, she was pudgy and mean.

"Hey," Denise said, sharply. July eased forward and saw Denise slap Eddie's hand away from her breast. July's father snored on.

"Well, you can't blame a guy for trying." Eddie smiled in what July guessed was an attempt at friendly. It looked feral. If you don't want me here, I guess I'll go tuck Alice in. Maybe read her a bedtime story or something."

Denise watched him get up and go. She looked sorry he'd given up so easily.

July wished Eddie would take one of his business trips to Las Vegas. He wished they hadn't had to move in with his uncle, but his dad said it wouldn't be for long. And, at thirteen years old, he didn't get a say in much of anything anyway.

Eddie opened Alice's door without knocking. July wanted to follow him into Alice's room, though he couldn't have said why. He looked at his plate of food then out to Denise who was staring at him.

"You best finish that before you think about getting up," she said again. "I'll not have food going to waste…"

The scene changed…

July opened the liquor cabinet. He had already tried most things in there at one time or another: red wine, whiskey, tequila, rum, vodka. He didn't like the taste of any of them but he liked the feel of getting drunk. Zelda and his dad would be out late tonight; Walter was always out late when he had a new girlfriend. July could get a good buzz on and be in bed before his dad got home. He pulled out a bottle of tequila and poured himself a shot. Alice stood, as always, at his elbow.

"Dad will be mad if he finds out," she said, sounding like the twelve-year-old snitch that she was.

"How's he going to find out?"

Alice shrugged.

"You aren't going to tell him, are you?" July asked, pretty sure she wouldn't.

"What will you give me if I don't?"

July had a few dollars from his lawn mowing job; in Florida, there were always lawns to mow. "I'll give you two bucks."

"Five," she said.

"Two bucks and I'll let you try some of this."

"Okay."

He tossed back the shot like he'd seen his dad do. It burned his throat and made him cough.

"My turn," Alice whined.

"Wait. You won't like it that way." He rummaged through the cabinet until he found the margarita mix.

He got down a large water glass and a small glass that used to be a jam jar. He poured the tall glass half full of tequila and added a little bit of the mix for himself. In the jam jar he put a generous dollop of mix and little tequila and handed that to Alice…she took her first ever drink of alcohol and made a face.

Same house, different month…

The doorbell rang, announcing Danny and Wes. They'd brought their own drinks in Mason jars, so July's dad was less likely to notice the missing alcohol if it was only July drinking it. He loaded a video game he'd bought recently, then slopped a little of his drink into a cup for Alice, knowing she would insist. If she felt left out she'd bug them all night. Her first drink had been two months ago, but ever since then, she insisted on having some of his each time she saw him drinking.

Wes had introduced July to pot and hash, but usually they only got high when July went over there, so July was surprised when Wes pulled a joint out of his backpack and they passed it around.

"I want to try," Alice said, plaintively.

"No. This isn't for kids."

Alice flounced into the kitchen to pour herself another drink. July followed her and took the bottle from her.

"Quit it," he said. "You'll end up drunk like the last time. You only get this if I give it to you, understand?"

Danny and Wes must have been drinking before they came over. They were buzzed already, and started roughhousing. The two of them wrestled on the floor over control of the joystick for the game. Danny, got the upper hand, grabbed the joystick, and scrambled up and ran. He'd forgotten it was plugged in and nearly jerked the TV off the stand.

Wes came after him. Danny dropped the joystick and ran behind Alice, who was just coming out of the kitchen in a pout. He grabbed her around the throat with the crook of one elbow. "Give up, or the girl gets it." It was a line from a B-movie they had all watched the other night.

Alice squirmed but couldn't get free. "Ooh, do that again," Danny said, pushing his hips into her backside and laughing. Unstable on his feet to begin with, he lost his balance and fell back with Alice on top of him.

July had been putting the bottles out of Alice's reach, but came now from the kitchen at a run. He jerked Alice by one arm and freed her from Danny's drunken grip.

"Go to your room," he said to her, sharply, shaking her a little by the arm. "Now." She went.

Feeling stone-cold sober, he hauled Danny to his feet by the collar of his shirt, his anger giving his strength a substantial boost. He cocked back and punched Danny in the face, knocking him down to the floor again, then straddled him, ready to punch him a few more times. Wes grabbed July by the arm.

"He was just kidding around," Wes yelled. July elbowed Wes in the chin and got up off Danny. He grabbed Wes's backpack and threw it at the boy. Then he picked up the Mason jars and threw those at both of them, making them duck to avoid getting hit. "Get out," he said. "And don't come back."

"No wonder you don't have any other friends," Danny yelled, holding his nose. "Freak."

When the boys had gone, July went into Alice's room. She was sitting on her narrow bed holding her stuffed Cheshire cat. An Alice in Wonderland doll decorated a shelf and a couple of cheap plastic flamingos watched from the corner of the room. And, of course, her collection of truck stop trinkets decorated the remaining surfaces, her collection as big as July's own, though more organized.

He sat down next to her, not sure if she was more upset by the fight or by Danny grabbing her like he had. Maybe it was just the drunken rowdiness getting out of hand, like it used to with their mother's friends when he and Alice were little, but he felt pretty sure she'd been too young to remember those days. July remembered, though he tried not to think about that time.

"I'm sorry," he told her. "It won't happen again…"

The scene shifted…

July heard shouting from the downstairs of Zelda's two-story townhouse. Alice was fighting with her again, as she had almost daily in the six months since they'd moved in with her. The front door slammed.

Alice would be on her way to her friend Lisa's house, or maybe Marguerite's. July didn't like either of them. They were a bad influence on her. July hadn't touched alcohol or drugs in nearly a year, not since that night when he realized how much his drinking influenced Alice, but he had realized too late.

July ran out the door and down the street after his sister. He caught up with her two blocks from their house. "Hey, I was thinking of going to a movie this afternoon. You want to go?"

"I'm going to go to Lisa's," Alice retorted. She was angry and bit her words off as she spoke. "She and some of her friends are going to be hanging out tonight."

"Lisa's a bimbo," he snapped back. "All you do when you go over there is smoke pot and do stupid things with that group of idiots."

"Lisa's not a bimbo! You take that back! And her friends aren't idiots either. You're just jealous 'cause I'm hanging out with cool people finally, and you don't even have any friends."

He didn't have any friends. The only friends he'd made in their new school were Danny and Wes, and they hadn't spoken to him since the fight at his house. They were wary of July, but from a distance they pointed him out to other boys at the school and laughed at him. July didn't care, they were all losers anyway. He'd started over in so many new schools that solitude was nothing new for him.

July stopped and Alice walked on. "Fine, go get high," he yelled after her. It wasn't heroin after all. Still, it bothered him. He walked back to the house but felt too frustrated to go inside. The suggestion of a movie had just been a bribe, but he decided maybe he'd go anyway. It wasn't a far walk to the strip mall and the three-plex; he was bound to find something there he wanted to see.

When he got back from the movie it was dinner-time and Alice wasn't home yet. July went into her room and rummaged through her nightstand until he found Lisa's number. He called but there was no answer. The scummy boys Lisa had introduced Alice to usually hung out in one of two places, the cemetery or down at the junkyard that was owned by the dad of one of the boys. He wished he'd followed Alice. If he'd kept an eye on her he'd know where she was now. His sister was the youngest in her group of friends, and she was often teased or left behind somewhere to fend for herself when the older kids tired of her.

Inner city cemeteries in Florida were rare; most had been dug up and the bones or ashes, or whatever else was left in the old graveyards, had been moved out to the suburbs. For some reason this tiny graveyard, less than a city block big, had hunkered down behind its short iron fence as the city grew around it. It was left mostly unmolested except for the kids that hung out there over generations of dares. He jogged to the cemetery and reached it, breathless, only to find it empty.

The junkyard was the opposite direction from the house.

The junkyard was small also, smaller even than the cemetery. It stood on a double lot in an old warehouse district behind a tall chain-link fence with barbed wire around the top. The yard was filled mostly with junker cars. Appliances, mattresses, old pipe, wire cable and other trash was stacked high against the walls of a one-story office building covered in flaking blue paint. The mattresses were where the older kids had sex, Alice had confided once, and the cars were another place to make out or do drugs, or a place for the girls to giggle and hide themselves and talk about the boys.

It was after six on a hot and humid, summer evening when July finally got to the junkyard. He hooked his fingers in the chain-link wire of the locked gate and scanned the yard for Alice. They could be at somebody's house, they could be walking around the neighborhood, or Alice could be safe at home wondering why July wasn't there.

He heard a muffled thud from the yard, a sound so soft he wasn't sure he was hearing it. The sound came again, and he narrowed the source to somewhere near the building. Searching the cars and piles of junk he still saw nothing moving. A soft thump came again. The sound occurred on a regular interval. One thump. Silence. One thump. Silence. Waiting for the sound to come again, he finally pinpointed the location—a refrigerator near the front door of the building.

He scaled the chain-link fence and faced the barbed wire at the top, coiled in large, loose loops. It offered no stability when he placed one hand carefully between the barbs. The thump came again. July tried reaching over the wire, grabbing the chain-link on the other side, thinking that maybe he could somersault, but the barbed wire dug into his belly catching his shirt and arm, pricking the skin beneath. He pulled his shirt free and climbed higher, so he teetered in the air, one foot shoved between the metal pipe that formed the top of the fence and the barbed wire. Holding the coiled wire with both hands, he swung his other leg over the top. The loose wire shifted as he moved, and he lost his balance.

He fell to the inside of the fence, one leg caught in the loose strands of wire. The barbs dug in, cutting deeply into his calf and the back of his knee. The clatter of the fence when he banged into it provoked a ferocious barking in the yard. July twisted on the fence to look behind him as he remembered the Dobermans. The barking reached a frenzied pitch but came no closer. The two dogs were chained near their doghouses at the side of the building. They'd be let loose at night.

His hands still clenched a strand of wire he'd grabbed as he fell, though most of his weight was supported by the leg caught above his head. He squirmed until he freed his leg and hung by his hands, while his feet sought purchase.

His jeans were torn and bloodied. Muscles burned from the back of his knee to his butt. He climbed down a few more feet and dropped awkwardly to the ground trying to land on his uninjured leg, and limped across the lot to the refrigerator. Either the thumping had stopped or he'd been too distracted to hear it again. He paused before he opened the door, not sure he wanted to look inside.

The door resisted opening and he feared for a moment that it was locked. He yanked at it in panic. Suddenly it came free with a sucking sound. A stench of rot wafted out to the open air. Rust marks where the racks used to hang showed they'd been removed long ago. Alice was tucked in a ball at the bottom. She blinked at the light and lifted her arms weakly, like a child imploring a parent to lift her. Tears stained her face, but she made no sound. July pulled her out and hugged her to him tightly.

Alice sucked air rapidly, hungry for oxygen. After a minute or two, she was able to stand on her own. She must have only recently started running low on air, he thought. July broke a window in the junkyard building, sending the dogs into a wilder frenzy. He climbed inside the building and started rummaging for a key to the gate. He found it in the big metal desk in the office.

All the way home Alice cried as she told him how one of the boys, Billy, had wanted to have sex with her and she'd said no. He would have tried anyway but the others had banged on the trunk and the doors to say they were headed over to Lisa's. They had left and Billy had shoved her into the refrigerator. He'd told her he was going to tell the others that she had run away crying and no one would look for her. Billy had known about her claustrophobia. He might even have known that refrigerators were airtight.

The next day, Zelda was working. Alice hadn't said anything about the junkyard to their step-mom and so July had kept quiet too, though he was looking forward to seeing Billy and Alice's other friends soon. They would never mess with his sister again once he'd finished with them.

Alice had seemed distant since her rescue from the junkyard. When she didn't come down for lunch, July went to her room. He knocked on the door but there was no answer. He opened it. He experienced a moment of incomprehension when he saw her sitting in her open window. Her legs dangled over the edge, down the two-story drop, so all he could see of her was her back.

"What are you doing?" he said stupidly.

Alice didn't answer. She was balanced twenty feet above the concrete patio. He came into the room, headed for the window.

"Stop," Alice said, and he did. There was a command in her voice he'd never heard before. Little girl things had dropped away from his sister overnight. The emerging hormones and fights with Zelda, the schoolyard traumas and struggles for acceptance had sloughed off, leaving someone older than her thirteen years sitting in that window. Someone reflecting on a short life and contemplating an eternity.

July didn't know how to deal with this new Alice; he stood uncertainly in the middle of the room.

The adult July pulled back. Alice's room wavered. No. They couldn't make him watch this again—though he had known all along they would. A battle raged in his head as his consciousness fought to emerge, trying to escape the coming events. His willpower fought back, trying to force himself to push through this final test. He'd come this far, he had to finish it. He had to. The room solidified.

"Alice, what are you doing?" It was the same question he'd just asked and yet it wasn't. He said it seriously this time, slowly. He was not quite seventeen. He didn't have the faintest idea what to do or say, but he knew his next words had to be the right ones.

"Alice, just come inside. Come inside so we can talk." He took a step toward her. She turned her head to face him for the first time. He saw the abyss in her eyes...

"No!" July yelled, suddenly breaking the connection to his past. He scrambled to his feet, fully now in the alternate Utah desert. Those eyes. He'd tried so hard to forget that look in her eyes. His Alice. His sister who had never gotten to have her Wonderland. He couldn't bear to watch her die again. It was too much to ask.

His willpower evaporated like the shimmering heat waves around him. Everything gone except the overwhelming instinct to escape this memory. "No!" he yelled again. He only knew of one sure way to make it stop. He turned a hundred and eighty degrees. He turned east. And he took his first step.

Something hit him with the force of a train. July flew backward and slammed into the ground. His shoulder blades hit rock, grinding into the unyielding surface as Bill's weight landed on top of him.

Bill lay atop him like a lover. His chest pushed against July's chest, and his hip bone ground into July's to prevent July from throwing him. Bill's large hands held July's biceps and one knee was cocked so that both of July's legs were pinned.

July pushed at Bill's arms and he struggled to break free, but it was a feeble thing. Bill outweighed him by at least forty pounds and July had no fight left in him. The memories had drained him. They had emptied him of everything. He had let his sister die. Why shouldn't he die as well? And if he couldn't really die in this place, then even better. His hell could be to relive his past over and over, forever. Perhaps that's what this was all about. Perhaps he *had* died in that car accident in San Diego and he'd been in hell ever since.

Hot tears ran from the corners of July's eyes into his hair. He'd let Mia down by losing two jobs in a row. He hadn't taken care of her as he had promised to do. He hadn't been worth his father's love or time. His mother's drugs and alcohol had meant more to her than he and his sister had and, in the end, he had not only watched her die, he'd helped her die.

He had tried his whole life to be the one who took care of the people around him and he had failed each one. His sister worst of all. She looked up to him, depended on him, yet he was the one who had started her drinking. She had seen him drunk and high and rebellious and she had imitated it. She had needed him at the end, needed him to say the right thing, but he hadn't. He had killed her as surely as if he had pushed her out that window.

"Let me up," July sobbed.

Bill didn't move. July turned his head, met Bill's eyes, deep brown but not crazy, not this time.

"Don't you end up like me," Bill growled. "Every single day I regret running away from my life, when all I had to do was face up to it. They were trying to help me and I screwed it up like I screwed up everything else. You don't have to turn out like me."

July didn't answer. He didn't have the heart to tell Bill he was wrong.

Chapter 23

Valerian heard Steve's front door open, and saw July close it behind him as he left. "Oh shit," she said.

For the past ten minutes Steve had been everything she'd always wanted him to be. He apologized for the things he'd said and done before she left, and he'd even given a halfway believable explanation for his actions. She had earned his undivided attention finally, and the intensity of it emphasized how rarely she'd received it over the past year or two. It was almost uncomfortable to be so much in his focus. He had kissed her in front of July. Then she had kissed him back, on the forehead, a goodbye kiss to that person she had loved when the young Kansas farm girl had first met the red-belt with movie star good looks in her Taekwondo class.

The front door closed and July was gone.

Steve followed her gaze, still holding her against him. "Let him go. Once you spent some time with him, the newness would wear off and you'd find he was as flawed as everybody else. At least we already know each other's shortcomings, and we know we can get past them." He tipped his head to catch her eyes. She was still looking at the door.

He was wrong on at least two counts: they wouldn't work this out and she already knew July's flaws: a childhood that most people wouldn't have survived with their sanity intact, a solitariness that ran so deep he was alone even when he was with other people, a man who carried guilt and regret and resentment like a cross. She had seen his flaws and she cared for him on a level deeper than she had ever felt for Steve.

She had no idea what a year or a lifetime with July might be like. What she did know was that he was one of the most genuinely good-hearted people she had ever met. And he had just walked out the door.

Valerian pushed free of Steve.

"Babe, don't do this," Steve said. "Three years together. Don't throw that away. I love you, Valerian."

She pushed the sliding door open and turned back to him. "I love you too, Steve, but I need to move on." She did love him. She loved him for the things he had taught her and for the times, long ago, that had been good. But they were over now. They had been over for some time. "I'm not Valerian anymore. Go back to Phoenix," she said as gently as she could. "Find someone who's right for you."

She left him standing there on the deck and jogged back to the wide cobbled street in the village center. She looked for July as she ran, but pulled up short when she saw the two police officers just ahead. They were still talking with the man on the restaurant patio, the one who had been on the cell phone when Steve and July fought. They didn't seem to be talking about the fight anymore, just chatting as if they knew him personally.

Val turned around and started back the other way when she heard the man with the phone say, "There. That's the woman that was with them."

"Ma'am," one of the officers said in a loud voice. She debated pretending she hadn't heard, but in the almost empty village it would be ridiculous. She turned back to the officer. It wasn't that she worried about speaking with the police, she was only worried that the delay would cause her to lose track of July entirely.

The officer asked her name and wrote it in a small notepad. He asked for ID and she pulled her wallet from her purse and removed her driver's license. When he double-checked the address she told him truthfully that she had just rented a place in Minturn this morning and didn't remember the address. The officer looked doubtful. She was asked to describe the confrontation that had occurred and explained it as a simple misunderstanding with no hard feelings. Both men were just passing through and, no, she lied, she didn't know their last names.

These weren't like the police in Phoenix, who had gangs and traffic and a high crime rate to worry about. A simple fight that was already over would have been nothing there, not even worth their time. These policemen were more like the four officers in her hometown, who knew everyone by name. She worried that they would pursue this further and suppressed a sigh of relief when they told her to call if she remembered anything else.

As soon as the officers were out of sight, she took off at a run again, headed for the parking garage. She found her way through the labyrinth to the place she was certain July's truck had been. It was gone.

She held her head in both hands and stood that way a long moment wondering what to do next. She didn't have a car, she didn't know the buses, she hadn't written down the phone number for her new rental, and July didn't have a cell phone. She tried to think of it as an equation, but there were too many variables.

The chirrup of a car alarm turning off echoed loudly off the concrete walls. Two off-work waiters in black pants and white shirts walked past her toward the car, chatting.

"Wait," Val called out. The two men turned, looking surprised. "Are you going anywhere near Minturn?" she asked. "My ride took off without me."

The driver said they were going past Minturn, and could drop her off on the way. Val had no idea if July would be at the condo, but she could start by seeing if his stuff was still there. If his things were there and he wasn't, she would wait for him until he returned. If they weren't…well, she'd decide that later.

The waiters both lived in Eagle, but they were good enough to take the turn off to Minturn and drive her all the way into town, a couple of miles out of their way. When they pulled up in front of the condo, she played her next card.

"I'm trying to meet up with my friend. If he isn't here then he might be in Eagle, at a hotel where we stayed last night. Would you mind very much waiting for just a minute while I check?" She got the strange look she deserved, but the driver said they would wait.

Val sprinted to the door, fished the key out of her purse and hurried inside. July's things were gone.

"Shit!" she said again.

He was probably an hour west of here, driving down I-70 and headed for Flagstaff, but she wasn't going to give up without checking every possibility. She ran back to the car, hoping the men were still waiting for her.

"Sorry," she said, "I'm really sorry. The friend I need to find isn't here. If you could just drop me off in Eagle at the hotel by the interstate, I promise I won't ask for anything else."

The passenger looked like he was beginning to regret having agreed to the ride, but the driver was cheerful.

"Sure," he said, "we're headed there anyway."

Fifteen miles down the road they took the exit to Eagle and she pointed to the hotel on the right. She scanned the parking lot for July's truck as they pulled in but didn't see it. If he wasn't here, she resolved, she would hitchhike back to Flagstaff and look for him there. Even if he didn't want her around, she refused to leave things the way they were now.

They dropped her off in the hotel parking lot and Val nearly cried with relief when she saw the old Silverado in the side lot. He'd parked in front of the same room they had shared the night before. Val knocked on the door, but there was no answer. Peering through the curtain she saw his stuff on the bed but didn't see July. Maybe he was in the bathroom or had walked across the street to a restaurant. She took a last look, hands cupped at the sides of her face, nose pressed to the glass of the window. About to turn away, she caught a glimpse of pink on the floor, poking out just past the end of the bed.

She tried the door, even though she knew better, then ran to the front office. The man was at the desk this time, his accent as strong as the woman's. Val asked him for a key card to the room. He looked suspicious.

"I'm not supposed to do that, seeing as he checked in alone this time."

"He called me to say he wasn't feeling well," she lied for

the third time that day. "He had an operation recently. I need to check on him. You can come with me if you want, and see if he's okay."

At least most her story was truthful. If the man wouldn't open the door for her, she could always call 911. She'd get into that room one way or another, but the sooner the better.

Val gave him her most innocent farm girl look. The man finally nodded. He opened a cabinet under the desk and rifled through the key cards hanging there until he found the one he was looking for. Following her outside, they walked around the building to July's room. The man knocked on the door but got no answer. Val was at the window again; she had hoped July would be awake by now, but she could still see his casted arm stretched out on the floor. "I think he's unconscious."

The desk clerk swiped the card through the reader and opened the door. He stopped short with a surprised "Oh," when he saw July's arm poking out past the far side of the bed.

Val ran to July. She stroked his face but he didn't wake or move at her touch. "You'd better call 911," she told the man. The clerk hadn't moved, as if he might see blood or death or something else unfamiliar and uncomfortable if he came any farther into the room.

"Yes. Yes, I'll call." He hurried out the door.

The variety of emotions that flooded Val babbled to her in an incoherent clutter, as if each thought spoke a different foreign language and she had to translate them all into something she could understand. Among the surfeit of feelings, there was relief that July was here where she could help him instead of in some wreck on the interstate, concern that he had fallen unconscious twice in one day, and trepidation for where he was now, knowing how much he feared that other world.

He lay on his stomach, right arm folded beneath him, left arm stretched out toward her. His face was slack, more relaxed than he ever allowed it to be when he was conscious. Even in his sleep he seemed to retain a measure of tension. Val leaned forward and kissed his cheek. She stroked his back and whispered into his ear. "Please come back to me, July. Please."

Chapter 24

Bill lay on top of July. All fight had gone out of July and he sobbed like a small child.

A fist-sized ball of fire appeared near his face. Bill didn't seem to notice the apparition. The flames touched July on his right cheek, like a gentle kiss. The heat from the fire didn't burn. It was soothing. Maybe Val was reaching out to him somehow from his own world. Perhaps she was there now, with his body.

Between Bill's physical restraint, July's surrender, and the strange, fiery reassurance, his self-loathing drained away. He felt like his last lifeline had been cut, the last of his protective instincts that hid him from his memories. His fight and resistance and self-protection had been stripped from him, leaving him bare to the world. He felt deflated and desiccated, like a dead animal, so flattened on the freeway that nothing is left but the pelt.

"Let me up," he said again to Bill. The man narrowed his eyes. "I won't run," July promised.

Bill pushed himself off July and stood, looking ready to tackle July again if he tried anything. July heaved himself to a sitting position, hurting everywhere and not minding the pain. Physical pain was easy compared to what he had left to do.

"I'll finish it," he told Bill. He turned his back on the man and faced the crevice. He felt Bill's solid presence behind him, watching to make sure he stayed put, though July knew Bill couldn't watch him forever. If he really wanted out of this, one step backward would do it. He could outwait Bill, dodge him, club him with a rock long enough to take one step, any of a dozen things given enough time and determination.

He looked over his shoulder at Bill, standing sentry behind him. July nodded once to reassure him, turned back, and let the memories in. The images started immediately, as if the powers that be knew that he teetered as close to the edge of failure as he did to the crevice in front of him.

July stood in the middle of his sister's room, looking into her empty eyes. He didn't know what to say, though he was sure there was one right thing that would make her come away from the window and come back to him. "Alice, your friends are bozos. I know they hurt you, but you've got your whole life to make other friends, better friends."

"It's not just them. It's everything."

July knew what she meant, he even agreed with her, though he would never say so. His motivation to keep going had always been Alice. What did Alice have?

She may not remember their mother, but that trauma was written somewhere on her soul. She'd been through the same parade of stepmothers and girlfriends that July had, the same absentee father, and she was the age now that July had been when he suddenly started acting out and rebelling. It had been a confusing time; a time of hurting himself as much as others had hurt him. But this was never an answer that he'd sought.

July took another step toward her. Alice turned away from him and looked down. July launched at her, so sure she would say one more thing, so sure he could reach her in time.

Alice leaned forward. She slipped off the sill silently. Slowly. Deliberately.

His fingers brushed the back of her shirt. The fabric fluttered toward his hand but he was too slow. A slip of material caught between his first two fingers but the last of her weight leaving the windowsill pulled the cloth through his hand like trying to grasp a handful of water. And then she was gone. He watched his sister fall. Alice rolled forward, falling headfirst, arms wide—like a hawk, reveling in the dive.

July recoiled at the sound of her head impacting with the concrete. Her skull compressed as if made of something softer than bone, and then her neck bent at an angle too extreme. Her small body tumbled to lie supine. July stood in the window and watched the blood pool in a disc-shaped halo around her head. The way the old paintings portrayed saints or the Virgin Mary...

The pictures stopped and July found himself staring at the narrow crevasse. The days and months that followed that event played on in his mind, though the memories weren't the forced images of before: his father arriving home for the funeral and crying for the only time July could ever remember, the self-loathing and second-guessing that July had put himself through, wondering what he should have done or said to change the outcome. July had been the one to call the police. Giving his statement had turned into questioning, and then into defense, as the officers probed for circumstances that didn't exist. Eventually, documentation of his distress at the scene and his lifelong closeness to his sister exonerated him from a potential manslaughter investigation.

July stared dry-eyed at the desert landscape. He knew the tears would come again later, a flood too big for this dry land.

There was a rustle of heavy canvas behind him and July turned to see Bill walking away to the east, wearing his oiled duster once more despite the warmth of the day. He wondered if Bill wore the same shirt, jeans, and jacket every day of his existence here, like a ghost haunting a house, condemned to forever wear the clothes in which it was buried.

He sat by the lip of the crevice, knowing it would stay only a foot wide if he stepped across now. Relived that Pat and none of the others showed up, he stayed there a long time, his mind as silent as the land around him.

Standing finally, he stepped across the small and stable crevasse, and walked west. About a mile later he found Pat waiting for him, sitting in the shade of one of the incongruous cottonwood trees near a dry riverbed. It was the original Pat, black hair braided into cornrows with a bone-white bead at the end of each braid, though he now wore a white sleeveless T-shirt, baggy jeans and tennis shoes. The round face broke into a wide smile at the sight of July, though his dark eyes somehow conveyed both sorrow and joy.

July sat across from him. He felt empty inside, as if someone had shoved a fist down his throat, grabbed onto everything that made him who he was, and ripped it all out of him. He didn't know if he would ever feel like a whole person again.

"It's a rough way to do it, isn't it?" Pat said. "A lifetime of habits challenged all at once."

July just nodded.

"So if you went back again, what would you do differently

to save your sister?"

July shook his head. "I saw the look in her eyes. I don't think anything I could have done or said would've made a damn bit of difference."

"I don't either," Pat said.

"There are other things I'd change. I wouldn't have started her drinking, that's for sure."

"She may have started on her own anyway. You were subjected to the same set of influences and both dealing the best you could," Pat said, reasonably. "You were far from the only person she modeled her behavior after."

"I know."

July pulled his knees up and rested his left forearm across them. He put his chin on his cast and reached down with his other hand, picking up a pinch of sand. He tried to drop the grains one at a time back to the earth, but they were too small and fell from his fingers quickly.

"I know that my mother's addiction wasn't my fault, and that I couldn't have made my dad love me and Alice any more, and that Mia's insecurities weren't something I could cure for her. I've always known those things."

"You have, July, but you've kept that knowledge shut away from you. That's our way of dealing with things. The personality you got from me takes the blame. Tries to cure everyone. Thinks we're strong enough to get through anything. We hide all the bad stuff away so that we can keep going."

July flicked the last grains of sand from his fingers.

Pat leaned back against the tree. "I told you that we all have our flaws. Everybody here has a different set of tools, good and bad. I guess that's what makes your world go around."

"So can you tell me now what this place is?"

"I don't know the grand scheme any more than you know who created your own world, or if your lives are determined by fate or free-will. I don't know who brought you here or why. You met some complicated criteria or maybe your lottery number just came up, or it's all part of some equation we don't know how to solve yet. I do know that the few people who come here have good in their hearts and they haven't lost that no matter what they've been through."

"It still wasn't right what happened to Bill."

"I agree. But maybe your relationship with him was just another part of something that needed to happen. I know you both surprised me in the end."

"He saved my life. Can you tell me what you know about him before I leave?"

Pat gave him a mildly surprised arch of one eyebrow, then shared what he knew, mostly about the trials he'd gone through when he first arrived in this world.

The day was getting late.

"So, am I done here?" July asked. "If I take a fall on a construction site and knock myself out, am I going to wind up back here again?"

Pat smiled his wide, quiet grin. "No. You're done here."

July wondered if he was going to feel lost without Pat's confidence and support—however vague his guidance might have been. "Will I ever see you again?"

"Sure you will. Every time you meet someone based on my pattern." Pat stood and held out a hand to help July up. "You take care of yourself, July. You're going to be just fine."

Still holding his hand, Pat reached forward. They embraced, lightly at first, then in a fierce mutual grip.

"How do I get back?" July asked, when they separated.

"Close your eyes," Pat said.

Epilogue

"Our remedies oft in ourselves do lie..."
Wm. Shakespeare, All's Well That Ends
Well

Chapter 25

July recognized the hospital smell before he opened his eyes.

As soon as he lifted his head a nurse was there telling him he was in the emergency room and asking how he felt.

"Pretty good, actually," he said, and smiled at her.

She gave him a concerned look and went to get the doctor.

July looked around the room, not even a room really, just a curtained-off space. The nurse had left the curtain pulled back slightly, enough that he could see the nurses' desk. Val was nowhere in sight. Maybe he had misinterpreted the little fireball, or maybe it was just some representation of her in his life even if she was already gone.

The doctor came in and checked July over. He said he was tempted to admit him but agreed to July's request to do a repeat CAT scan and see from there. The nurse came back in to take a set of vitals before they took him to radiology. "Your friend Val said to let you know she's in the waiting room."

So she was here.

"Thanks," he said, choking on the emotion in that one word.

The doctor looked over the CT results. He told July what he'd expected to hear, that the tests didn't show any new bleeding. His vital signs were stable and July assured him he was feeling much better. He promised to follow up with a neurologist as soon as he could get an appointment.

"I have some more good news for you," the doctor said. "It looks like you can get that cast off today." He'd ordered x-rays on his wrist and shoulder also, to make certain he hadn't reinjured them in his recent falls.

An aide came in with a cast saw and cut through the thick fiberglass. She used spreaders to break it into two halves and then scissors to cut through the padding and stocking underneath. When she pulled it free, his arm looked like a pale, white fish, all scaly and soft. The limb felt lighter than it ought to, and the skin felt tender and fragile. She held the cast over the wastebasket and looked at him questioningly.

"Kids often want to keep theirs, even though they're pretty gross by the time they come off. Just checking."

She was holding it with Bill's scrawled message facing him. He stared at the words in black magic marker. He shook his head no and she dropped it in the can.

"Good choice," she said.

When they wheeled him out of the ER, Val came running to him. She squeezed his hand but she seemed as much at a loss for words as he felt. She helped him check out and went to get the truck.

There was so much to say between them that neither of them said anything for a long while. They broke the silence to fill it with inconsequential chit-chat. She asked if he had a headache and if the hospital staff were nice while she drove them to the condo. She'd brought his things from the motel and he moved them back into the bedroom for the second time that day. It was only late-afternoon but they lay down on their sleeping bags together. Val cuddled into July's shoulder and he wrapped his arms around her, able to feel her for the first time with both his hands.

She began first. "I know what you think you saw back at Steve's motel, and I'm so sorry." She traced one finger in a small pattern back and forth on his chest. "I have no intention of going back to him. He kissed me, and I'm really sorry you had to see that, and then I was trying to say goodbye to him when you left. Pretty crummy thing for you to have to deal with just a few hours after we'd made love."

"I jumped to conclusions without waiting for you tell me what was going on."

"I was so scared that I'd lost you," she said. "I didn't know how I'd ever find you again."

"Well you didn't lose me, and you'll have a hard time getting rid of me now."

"Did you go back again?" She said it quietly, as if she could say it softly enough that he wouldn't have to hear it if he wasn't ready.

He nodded his chin against her hair, and she tipped her head to see his eyes.

"I have a lot to tell you," he said. And he did. He told her about his father and his stepmothers. He told her about his mother and New Mexico, and he told her about Alice. He told her the things Pat had said and about Patty and Patricia and Bill. He talked the afternoon away and she listened to it all.

The next three weeks passed in comfortable camaraderie. Val scored a couple of fire dancing gigs, but July had been right about the off-season. Even in these little towns that survived on tourist industry, if there were no tourists, there was no industry. Travis came and went, busy with the last of the motocross races for the year and the media events that his sponsors had arranged, but for the most part, July and Val had the condo to themselves.

July healed in more ways than one during those weeks. Tears and sadness and memories came unexpectedly and often, and flitted away again just as quickly. Val's quiet understanding was as helpful to him in those days as her warm presence every night. Three weeks wasn't going to heal a lifetime of hurt, but it was a start.

He called his father for the first time in weeks and enjoyed hearing the jovial voice at the other end. He even smiled at his dad's stories about Louise and the Brick House and the other things that made his father happy. At least, they made Walter happy for a while, though both of them knew it wouldn't last. Next, July called his lawyer.

"I'm glad to hear from you," his lawyer said. "The police ruled the accident no-fault last week, but I had no way to get in touch with you. What this means is that both drivers were essentially found to be at fault, and so there's no need to wait for a court decision on liability. The insurance for the car that hit you is ready to settle, but I never take an initial offer. We'll haggle it out for a bit, but we're getting close to a number I think you're going to like."

"Is it going to pay all the bills? I've been in hospital two or three times since I left San Diego, and I had to have surgery about a week ago."

"The settlement is over and above medical costs. This is the pain and suffering settlement we're negotiating. All medical expenses are paid, no matter the policyholder's personal limits."

He wanted to say that he'd already settled up with his pain and suffering, but he didn't think his lawyer would understand that.

July and Val got to know the area. They also began frequenting the library to use the computers, Val for fire dancing gigs, July for his own research. A week later he found the information he'd been hoping to access. He leaned back to talk to Val around his cubicle and saw that she was in a job search site for mathematicians. His cynicism experienced a brief resurrection. He wondered where in the world her talents might take her, and if she would invite him to come along. That evening, though, it was July who told Val that he was leaving.

"It's just to Denver," he said, after he had explained his reasons, "but I'm not sure how long this is going to take."

"Are you coming back?"

Her uncertainty made him uncertain. "Do you want me to?"

"Yeah, I mean, if you want to," she said cautiously.

"I'd like to very much."

"Sheesh!" she exclaimed. "Quit doing that to me! I keep thinking you're going to just ramble off without me one of these days."

"The rambling I've done hasn't been by choice. I've wanted my whole life to settle down in one place with one woman, and now that I've found the right one, if you want me gone you're going to have to push me out. But speaking of, I have been wondering how well I'll fit into the life of a professor or researcher or whatever it is you plan to do with that PhD of yours."

"Well whatever it ends up being, you fit. So come back to me, okay?"

"Okay." He smiled. "Promise."

Chapter 26

July was in Denver by mid-morning of the following day. At a traffic light, he studied the inset for the city of Denver in his battered atlas. The cover and top pages were torn off and the next few were brittle from being puked on, washed off, and then drying in the Arizona heat. Colorado was in fair shape, though, and he tried to memorize the route to the hospital before the light turned green.

With the full name and criminal history that Pat had supplied and the research July had done at the library, finding what he sought had been easier than he'd expected. He found a parking space at the side of the ancient, state-funded building. By the look of the place, the state hadn't had much funding in a very long time.

He let the truck engine rattle to a stop and took the elevator to the fourth floor. When researching this place on the library computers, July had read that the building had been a tuberculosis hospital back at the turn of the twentieth century.

As he traversed the drab hallways, he thought he could feel the ghosts of the thousands who had died here, their lungs bleeding and convulsing as they lay on cots that must have lined large, cold rooms.

The long-term care ward of the building that was now a rehab ward took up the entire floor. July found his way to the nurses' desk, which was as stark and unadorned as the rest of the hospital. The large, marshmallow-soft woman sitting behind the desk seemed as stupefied as the comatose patients she cared for. Perhaps the hiss and pump of the life-support machines had hypnotized her.

"William Masloch," July repeated. "I'm here to see William Masloch."

The woman levered from the chair. She wore a white sweatshirt and purple sweatpants under a white lab coat, and when she emerged from around the desk July could see a pair of slip-on bedroom slippers on her feet. Her name-tag read "Mary, R.N." Her arms stuck out from her body as she led him down the hall. With her palms turned forward, it gave her a posture of supplication, as if she waited, always hopeful, for some divine gift.

"Are you a relative of Bill's?" she asked, as she walked in front of him.

"No," July said. "Just a friend."

"I was here when they transferred Bill to this hospital nearly twelve years ago. You're the first one I know of to come see him. Family and friends usually come for the first year or so, then family maybe for a bit longer, but even the best of them only hang in there so long. Holding the hand of someone who never talks or moves, you know, they just can't keep it up for long." She turned left into a room with four beds. All four patients were on life-support. "That's him over there."

"Thank you," July said as the woman turned to leave, but his eyes were fixed on the man in the second bed on the left. The patient was emaciated; the thin form under the covers nothing like the strong, stocky man that July had encountered in that other world. A feeding tube was taped securely to one nostril. The near end of the tube rested on Bill's chest and had a bright yellow clamp holding the folded end closed, opened only for the daily feeding of some liquid sustenance that July could only imagine. The far end had been pushed like a drain snake down Bill's throat to terminate somewhere in his stomach. July remembered the unpleasant sensation of having his own tube pulled after the car hit him. He'd only been unconsciousness for two days.

A dozen years of immobility had stripped Bill of more than just muscle; they had taken his choice, his dignity—everything except life itself. The familiar mustache was there, as well as a beard that looked due for trimming. All the patients in the room had mustaches and beards, easier than keeping them clean-shaven July guessed. More tubes ran out from under the covers, draining bodily fluids into the thick plastic bags.

A large corrugated tube from the respirator was inserted into a plastic adaptor that fit into the hole in Bill's throat. The slow hiss and pump of artificial breath made by the four respirators in the room played like a fugue, each one initiating at a slightly different time. July looked around the room for a chair, but there were none. He sat on the edge of Bill's bed and took the withered hand lying limp on top of the covers.

July thought of the coyote that had danced in the doorway of Coit Tower and wagged its tail. He thought of the small globe of flame that had touched him on the cheek like a kiss when

Val had found him on the motel floor. If those two people had been able to reach July while he was in that other world, then July, who had actually been to that world and seen Bill there, should surely be able to reach him.

"Bill, listen to me. You've passed your test, man. You've been there a dozen years, hashing and rehashing what went wrong, thinking about your life." July leaned close and gripped Bill's hand harder, hoping the physical connection would help.

"I don't know everything about your life. No one will ever really know what you went through except you, but I found your police records and I know a little about the people you fell in with: the motorcycle gang, the drug trafficking, the stepfather who started it all by beating you senseless every time he got drunk." July tried to tune out the hiss of the respirators and the thought that the nurse might be listening at the door. He poured every ounce of his energy into trying to reach Bill.

"I've been thinking about it a lot, Bill. By the time you wrecked your bike, it sounds like you had a pretty vicious heroin addiction. Maybe you went to that place where you're at now to save your life, but maybe you couldn't come back until you were clean, so that it didn't just start all over again. I'll tell you what, buddy, twelve years on life-support, you're clean as a whistle."

July studied Bill's face for any flicker of consciousness. He wondered if his hunch was wrong. He had promised Bill he would do everything in his power to get him out of that world, but if this didn't work he had no idea what to try next.

"Maybe you just failed that first time because you weren't ready yet, but maybe if you'd stayed here you would have died. I think you're ready now, Bill. I think that you saving my life proves that you're ready. And I'll challenge God or the devil himself if they say different."

July leaned forward until he and Bill were shoulder to shoulder. July spoke into his ear in a low, urgent whisper. "Try, Bill. You've got to try. You're ready." July squeezed his hand harder. "Start walking Bill. Walk west until you find that obstacle you couldn't pass last time. I'll be right here with you, for as long as it takes."

July sat up, but he continued to hold Bill's hand. He stared at the man's thin face, willing any kind of sign; a twitch of the mouth, a flicker of an eyelid. There was no change but July was nothing if not stubborn.

He tried to remember every detail of desert he had traversed, the obstacles he had encountered, the talks with Pat. If intent was what it took to reach someone there, then July would show more intent than the most competitive marathon runner, more perseverance than a mountain climber on Everest.

Late morning turned to early afternoon and still there was no change. The nurse wandered into the room three times. Once to offer July a chair, once to push a thick, beige liquid through the feeding tubes of the four patients, and once when an alarm sounded, requiring her to suction out the gob of mucous and saliva that clogged another patient's airway. He watched her work and saw her stroke the man's hair as she suctioned, telling him he'd breathe better soon.

July said nothing to her, unwilling to break his focus on Bill for even a moment. The rest of the time, he was alone as she attended to the conscious long-term patients in some of the other rooms—the sufferers of mass infections, chronic infections, or whatever else sentenced someone to this bleak ward. A young aide, as small as the other nurse was large, came in an hour or two after the feeding to give the men a spit-bath. July told her that Bill could skip his today.

July was reluctant to even leave Bill's side long enough to go to the bathroom, but at last his body insisted. He rationalized that Robert Vegas and Val hadn't been in physical contact with him when he was unconscious, and even if Val had been, it hadn't been continuous. Of course, he was also trying to accomplish more than just a fleeting impression on Bill.

Doubt crept in, but July pushed it back out, putting his long habit of not thinking about things he'd rather avoid to good use for once. He sat at Bill's bedside, sometimes talking out loud, and sometimes focusing silently on their mutual goal. July tried to remember how much time had passed in the real world each time he'd gone to the world of the patterns. Pat had told him once that time had no meaning in their world. He believed it, his own unconscious spells had lasted anywhere from moments to days with no relevance to time passed in the alternate world. It did nothing, however, to help him know if his efforts were working or not.

He hadn't eaten since morning and was wondering if anyone could bring him food or if he would have to go downstairs to the cafeteria. Mary, the large nurse, came in the room to let July know she was going off-duty and another nurse was taking over. July thought it might be less a courtesy to him than curiosity to see why he was still there. The woman stared at his and Bill's joined hands.

"Are you going to be here tomorrow?" she asked.

"Most likely," July answered.

"Well, okay then. I guess I'll see you tomorrow." She lingered in the doorway obviously wanting to ask him more questions. July turned back to Bill and heard her do a last check on the other three men in the room then shuffle away, her breathing nearly as loud as the respirators.

The sun had fallen far enough in the sky to shine through the window and onto Bill's bed. July fought not to close his eyes for a few minutes as he listened to the scuff of her slippers receding down the vinyl floor.

A convulsive squeeze compressed his hand.

July jumped, fully awake in an instant. He stared at Bill's face looking for any sign of consciousness. He wondered if it had been nothing more than a muscle spasm. Maybe twitches like this happened routinely in the unconscious.

It happened again.

"Mary!" July called after the nurse. His voice came out loud and alarmed. He let go of Bill's hand and leaned over the man's face.

"Bill. Bill can you hear me? Wake-up, Bill. Come back to your own world."

Bills eyelids fluttered open partway then closed again. July remembered waking up after two days of unconsciousness, how the light had burned his eyes. He wondered what it would be like after twelve years.

Mary returned to the room, looking at July suspiciously. She probably thought him a madman.

"He's waking up," July told her.

Her look said that he was no longer 'probably' mad. She leaned out of the room. "Lucy," she called. The girlish aide had been named Courtney, so Lucy must be the night nurse. Mary hovered in the door waiting for Lucy to arrive, unwilling to come any closer to July without backup apparently. Bill's eyes flickered again. Lucy hovered behind Mary now.

"See?" July said to the nurses, but they hadn't.

"Bill, I'm here. You did it, man. You made it back."

It took some convincing to get the nurses to actually come into the room and observe Bill. When Mary finally witnessed Bill's eyes opening and closing, she stared at July as if he might be a sorcerer, but when Bill's efforts at consciousness became more evident, the nurse in her took over. A considerable hustle and bustle on the part of the two nurses ensued. A doctor was called, family contact was attempted, tubes and vitals were checked. Mary stayed on until well after her shift had ended.

July waited at Bill's side until a doctor arrived from the acute care ward downstairs.

"He's unlikely to gain full consciousness or motor skills right away, if at all," the doctor told July. The nearest specialist for this sort of thing is in Chicago. We'll put a call in to consult with him."

The room was a beehive of activity as Bill showed increasing signs of alertness and July decided it was time to go. He removed a small box from his jacket pocket and placed it with a card on the nightstand in the corner.

"Make sure he gets this when he's fully awake, will you?" July said to Mary as he left the room. She stared at him, an expression of wonder still painting her face. She nodded

Bill needed the gold Krugerrand coin more than July did, and anyway it had been given as a thank you to July for saving Robert Vegas' life. It seemed only fitting for July to pass it on to Bill for doing the same for him.

Out in the parking lot, July started the old Silverado, found his way back to I-70, and pointed the truck toward the mountains. He pulled into Minturn about three hours later. An unfamiliar anticipation built in his chest as he drove down the main street toward the condo.

He saw Val as soon as he turned into the large adobe covered carport that served as a garage for the units. She was practicing with the unlit poi, using the empty parking spaces to swing and twirl the fist-sized balls on their chains. When she heard the truck's loud rumble, she dropped the poi to the garage floor. Stepping aside as he pulled into the parking space, Val gave him a big wave and a radiant smile.

It felt good, coming back to her knowing that Bill was in this world again, and that with time, both he and Bill would heal. The attic of his memories had been opened to the sunlight; his soul was at ease and, best of all, he was thoroughly falling in love. July turned the truck off, truly home for the first time his life—not home in this building or this town, but with Val, wherever the future might take them.

Thank You!

Thank you for reading our book and for supporting stories of fiction in the written form. Please consider leaving a reader review on Amazon and Goodreads, so that others can make an informed reading decision.

Find more exceptional stories, novels, collections, and anthologies on our website at:
digitalfictionpub.com

Join the **Digital Fiction Pub** newsletter for infrequent updates, new release discounts, and more. Subscribe at:
digitalfictionpub.com/blog/newsletter/

See all our exciting fantasy, horror, crime, romance and science fiction books, short stories and anthologies on our **Amazon Author Page** at:
amazon.com/author/digitalfiction

Also from Digital Fiction

Dirk Quigby's Guide to the Afterlife
by E.E. King

About the Author

Due to a varied work background, Liz has harnessed, hitched, and worked draft horses, and worked in medicine, canoe expeditioning, and as a roller-skating waitress. She also knows more about concrete than you might suspect.

Liz is a 2014 winner of the international Writers of the Future contest and has multiple short story publications to her credit spanning a wide range of science fiction and fantasy sub-genres. Her novels written under the name L. D. Colter explore contemporary fantasy and the dark/weird/magic realism that currently dominates her own reading, and ones written as L. Deni Colter venture into the epic fantasy realms she grew up reading and loving.

Her website can be found at: **http://lizcolter.com/**

Sign-up for her newsletter, here: **L. D. Newsletter**

Copyright

A Borrowed Hell
Written by **L. D. Colter**
Executive Editor: Michael A. Wills

CPSIA information can be obtained
at www.ICGtesting.com
Printed in the USA
LVHW02s2145020718
582503LV00004B/1003/P